LEGOLAND

GERARD WOODWARD

LEGOLAND

Short Stories

PICADOR

First published 2016 by Picador
an imprint of Pan Macmillan
20 New Wharf Road, London N1 9RR
Associated companies throughout the world
www.panmacmillan.com

ISBN 978-1-4472-8867-1

Printed and bound by CPI Group (UK) Ltd, Croydon, CR0 4YY

Contents

THE FAMILY WHISTLE

It had been a good day for Florian. She had had some success in the shops, being among the first in the queue when she heard that there was some real coffee for sale in Faber's, and had managed to buy half a kilo of arabica. Then she had found some white silk stockings in Schmidt's, and didn't even have to queue for them. On her way back, she had dropped quickly into her husband's bar on the Promenadeplatz, and had shown him, in a furtive moment while she sat at a table chatting with his craggy manageress Myra, the stockings, and he had given her a quick, appreciative kiss, promising he would bring home something good when they closed that afternoon. But then he always did, even if it was a single sweet pastry left over from the day, or one slice of black ham. By means of such little luxuries they felt richer than they had ever been before the war, even though, by any accepted standards, they were far poorer.

By the time Florian got home to their third-floor apartment on Max-Joseph-Strasse, closing the reassuringly solid oak door behind her, it would be just half an hour or so before Wilhelm returned. She may as well have waited in the cafe so they could go home together, but Wilhelm never liked her doing this, since she always got involved in the clearing up. Florian enjoyed helping, but Wilhelm had always insisted that his own wife should never be an employee, no matter how casual.

Florian went into the dining room and placed her gleanings of the day on the table, laying them out like a little trove. She spent a while arranging them as though she was an artist preparing a still life. The tin of coffee formed the centrepiece. The silk stockings, still folded, shimmered beside it. A packet of eggs. A handful of black cherries. A block of butter. Everything so perfect, beautiful, promising. She really wished she was an artist.

There was a knock at the door. A quiet, rather tentative knock, like the one a nervous child, expecting to be told off, might give. Was Wilhelm back so early – had he forgotten his key? It had happened once or twice before, so Florian went straight to the door and opened it.

There was a man standing outside. Tall but desperately thin. He had vague, hollow eyes and his cheeks were sucked in. He was wearing a nearly new, unbuttoned greatcoat over filthy, tattered clothing. He was the sort of man you saw frequently a few years ago, wandering hopelessly in the city, sometimes being led by the arm by a stern-looking woman, or sometimes by children. The returning soldiers, starved and stunned, sometimes from years in captivity, struggling to recognize the world they had returned to. They were turning up even now, all these years after the war, mostly from

Soviet slave camps. The Russians had hung on to their prisoners with a grim, sulky determination after the war. She presumed this man was one such, and had forgotten where he lived. She wondered if she should give him something – perhaps a piece of cake – before sending him on his way.

'Florian,' came the surprisingly deep, though trembling voice. It was not a voice she recognized, any more than the face it came from, though the shock of hearing her own name spoken, and of seeing the smile forming on that same mouth, revealing grey, broken teeth, made her cling to the door a little tighter. The smile hung on the face like a little pinned memo, expecting the same in return. When it didn't come the smile quickly left the face, and a look of hardened disappointment replaced it. The head cocked itself, the chin turned up a little, bathing the face in light from Florian's hallway, which allowed Florian to examine the man's eyes closely for the first time. Little distant pearls. 'What's wrong, Florian? Don't you recognize your own husband?'

It was a foolish reaction, but without thinking, Florian slammed the heavy door shut, with such force that the dinner gong, which had sat unused on the hall table for fifteen years, found its voice and chimed smugly. The man on the landing had been slow to react, but now he was knocking sharply on the door.

'Don't be idiotic, woman. It's me, Wilhelm. Let me in, why don't you?'

Florian leant with her back against the door. Her

breath was short, her heart unsteady. She could see, down the long tiled hallway and in through the open dining-room door, her still life on the table, and suddenly felt protective of it. The man on the other side of the door went on, 'What is it, Florian. Have you got another man? I'm reasonable, we can talk it through.' He had found the crack in the door, the little hairline fracture that ran vertically a few inches from the hinge. At some points it was just wide enough to act as a peephole, though no one would notice it otherwise. But this man had found it, and had brought his lips right up to it, talking so closely that Florian could see a patch of moisture forming on the plasterwork nearby.

'We can sort it out. A little misunderstanding. It's been a long time after all – no one would blame you. Florian, I've been through hell these past few years. When did you last hear from me, eh? I was in Libya. You know what happened to me? I rowed across the Mediterranean in a little dinghy, no bigger than the ones they have on the boating lake in the Hofgarten. I was the last German out of North Africa. Saw all my comrades killed. Made it all the way to Sicily. Greeted like a hero in Syracuse, they said they would recommend me for the Iron Cross first class. Then the next thing those bastards did? Sent me straight to the Russian Front without even a day's leave. Out of one cauldron, straight into another, though you wouldn't call the Russian front a cauldron, more an icebox. A deadly, deathly icebox. Can you hear me, Florian? Why won't you let me in?'

Slowly, through the crack in the door, the voice was doing its work – monotonous, quiet and, though tremulous, under extreme control. The tremor was masking something more resonant beneath, a profound undertone that Florian was beginning to recognize. The man gave a loud cough, still with his lips to the crack, so that spittle shot through. She caught a tang of his breath, an empty larder smell.

'You would feel sorry for me, Florian, if you saw what I had to go through on those snowy plains. Little boys, my fellow soldiers. Little boys of eighteen years, and some were younger. Some had lied about their age to get into the army, such patriots, you would have been proud of them, Florian. And the Russians were merciless, when we got bogged down. I was lucky to be taken prisoner. They took very few prisoners but slaughtered our little boys like they were vermin, I saw whole schools of young men wiped out by a single flamethrower. That's how it seemed to me, Florian. Those boys, so young. And when we were taken prisoner, we soon learnt we weren't so lucky after all, but were to face an ordeal far worse than death, far, far worse. Marched across icy wastes, half naked, starved. Some people were eating insects and spiders – our only food. It was shame on mankind that they did this to us. And all the while taunting us – you're nothing but a filthy Nazi. And I would call back, always, and you're nothing but a filthy communist. They would laugh at me, Florian. They would laugh at me, then beat me across the face . . .' The voice paused. In the ensuing silence only their breaths spoke. 'I know you are still there, Florian. I can see your shadow under the door. And I can smell you, and I can smell all the smells of our home. Nothing has changed. Why won't you let me in?'

Florian came away from the door and turned round to face it. She cleared her throat, unsure, quite, of what tone of voice she should use. She decided she should try and sound as neutral and as matter-of-fact as possible.

'I am sorry, sir, but I must ask you to go away. If you are claiming to be my husband, then you are very mistaken.'

There was a pause on the outside. A shuffling sound, as though the man was repositioning himself, thinking up a new strategy.

'Florian, you're being stupid. You are shocked, I know. We have all changed. It has been too long. Those evil bastards kept us locked up all those years, I didn't even know if the war was still going on, or if we had lost – all we heard was rumour, and no real news. They only let me out a month ago – and only then did I find the war has been over for four years. Those bastards! And now I come back to find my country in ruins. People looking thin, undernourished, but not the Jews, they look well fed. I passed through the city centre today and wondered who these healthy people were, with their signs saying *Open the Gates of Palestine, Set Us Free*. They were Jews, Florian, Jews staging a demonstration, making demands, and no one was saying anything.'

'No – you mustn't think like that.'

'Oh, I know. Don't worry, I've been told what to think. We're all hanging our heads now, aren't we, saying it was nothing to do with me? I've seen them already on the trains, wringing their hands, making me sick to my stomach, Florian. So I've got to say that I fought on three fronts, lost all my friends and spent six years in a slave-labour camp for nothing? And now my own wife refuses to acknowledge me. For God's sake, Florian,' he thumped the door – Florian imagined he'd hit it with his head, 'open up and let me in.'

'I can't.'

'Why in heaven's name not?'

'You don't understand, whoever you are.' Florian had raised her voice, was almost shouting. 'My husband was returned to me in 1946. Less than a year after the war ended. We have been living happily together for more than three years. Wilhelm saw me through the darkest days of those terrible winters. Now he works, he is supporting us. You, whoever you are, you are not my husband.'

Another long silence.

'What are you talking about, Florian? I am your husband. Your husband is standing here now, locked out of his own home.'

'No. I am sorry, but you have made a mistake.'

'Florian, I know what has happened. The man you think is your husband is nothing but an impostor, a former friend of mine from one of the camps. Of course, we talked a great deal about our lives. We made pacts, like all the men did, that if anything should happen to one of us, the other, if they survived, would inform their friend's loved ones. So in the course of many years I must have told him so much about you and about our life that he could have passed himself off as me. He knows all our secrets. We did look similar – same height and build, we could be taken for brothers – and then you must have been easily led, having not set eyes on me for so many years, and wondering how much I could have changed in all that time, you were ready to make allowances for me not being quite the same, for being different in some indefinable way, isn't that what you felt when you first met this man?'

Florian was thinking back to the day that Wilhelm first appeared. It had been under similar circumstances, a knock at the door, a cautious conversation, but that time she had no reason to doubt the man was who he proclaimed himself to be. By then the war had been over for nearly a year, and the city still seemed empty of men. It was rumoured that there were millions of soldiers still held in the prisoner-of-war camps, hundreds of thousands in Europe, held by the Americans and the French and the British, perhaps millions in Russia. Why were they allowed to hold on to them for so long? Why were they so reluctant to return them? The war was over, Germany was no longer a threat, it no longer even existed. It had been said that their status had changed, the men in the camps were no longer prisoners of war, but had been reclassified as 'disarmed enemy persons', and so were no longer protected by the Geneva Convention. How wonderful, to get around a law or a treaty by simply changing the names of things. Then the population of men gradually increased, but they were shocking people, in tatters, skeletal, ashen. Some died within days of arriving home. She knew of housewives who were terribly upset by the state of their returning menfolk. All the married women of the city lived in dread of what figures might turn up on their doorsteps.

She had been fortunate. Not a single bomb or shell had landed in her street, or within a hundred yards of their building. And when the occupying armies arrived, for some reason they hardly bothered with the upper levels, rarely climbing beyond the second floor. She was troubled only once, when someone tried to batter her door down, but it had stood firmly. The only danger was in leaving the apartment to find food and water.

So she had survived, and when Wilhelm called, things were just beginning to return to something like normal. She was down to her last drop of perfume when he knocked. By chance she had applied it that very morning, in a kind of ritualized, reverential act of self-anointing, knowing it could be a long time before she saw any more. And one of the first things Wilhelm said was, 'Ah, to breathe that scent again, after all these years . . .' It did strike her as odd. She had been given the half-bottle by a friend in 1943, and had never used that brand before then. It should have been a strange smell to Wilhelm.

The man on the other side of the door suddenly burst upon it, in a brief cry of frustration.

'This is nonsense, Florian, you cannot have been so foolish as to have been taken in by that fellow. You know what he is? A nasty little conman. He told me, before the war, he was well known in Berlin. He owned a nightclub in Friedrichshain, until it was closed down by the Nazis. Only it wasn't a nightclub like you or I would think of going to. It was nothing more than a knocking shop. A brothel. You wouldn't believe the stories he told me about his life before the war. They amused me while we were in the camp, but only in the way that men together will be amused by such stories – in the real world they would have disgusted me. And I dread to think how many times he must have got the clap – Florian, if you have been intimate with this man you are at great risk – I'll be frank with you – at great risk of catching something nasty.'

'Stop it,' Florian suddenly called back through the door, 'I won't listen to such talk. How could I believe you are my husband if you stoop so low as to tell such tales on a former friend . . .'

She was annoyed, because she had indeed suffered since taking the new Wilhelm into her bed. A horrible urinary infection that lasted for weeks. The doctor said he had seen it all before in the wives of recently returned soldiers. 'I am afraid even the warriors of the Wehrmacht were guilty of taking things further than is necessary from a military point of view,' he'd said. She wished he'd spoken in less vague terms, but she realized afterwards that he meant Wilhelm had probably ravished some poor Russian women on his way to Stalingrad, just as the Russians had done on their way in the opposite direction. 'It will all come out in the wash,' the doctor had said, giving her rump an encouraging pat as she left his surgery, his customary parting gesture, which she had always thought quite normal, until now.

'A former friend who does this to me – what do you expect? You think I should just let him move in on my own family and not care about it? What would you think of me then? Florian, I'm amazed at you, that you should be so easily fooled. You cannot believe for a moment that I am not your Wilhelm. My memories are your memories. I remember our wedding day in the Church of St Ludwig, Marianplatz, and that excellent reception provided by your father – the old goat, I used to call him, and you told me off, do you remember? You remember where we met, at that strange party held by that official of the union – I can't remember his name but you were somewhat overdressed. How could I ever forget what you looked like to me on that night, in that white dress sewn all over with mother-of-pearl, with that high neck, almost like a ruff. And I was surprised, the first time that I saw your skin, that it shone in just the same way. You remember me saying that you looked like mother-of-pearl? I could stand here for hours recounting the moments of our courtship in every detail. Surely you won't make me do that before you let me in . . .'

It wasn't quite enough for Florian. She sobbed when she heard her beauty described through the door, but she sobbed because she was remembering how the other Wilhelm had said almost exactly the same thing, about the dress, about the wedding, those were the things he remembered as well. Whoever was the impostor among these two, a great deal of reminiscing had been going on in the labour camp.

'You say you told your friend all the details of our past together. How do I know you aren't that friend, and are now trying to pass yourself off as my husband?'

The man laughed for the first time. 'Think about it logically, Florian. If I was the friend, and had been released three years after the true husband, why would I come here pretending to be him, when I would know that he was already here, that he would have settled himself back into his old family, made love to his wife in such a way that she remembered every touch and every scented breath? It would be a waste of my time. If you have two men claiming to be your husband, it is clear that it would be the first one to return home who would be the impostor.'

Yes, Florian could not help but appreciate the logic of this argument. And Wilhelm was such a logical, methodical person, always cutting through her wayward, woolly ideas with the sharp instrument of his reasoning.

'And where is this other Wilhelm? I would very much like to meet him. Is he cowering now in the back bedroom, or has he already hopped out of the window and down the fire escape?'

'No, he is out at work.'

'Work. Well, I expect there is a lot of work for a joiner now, with all these houses being rebuilt. He must be doing very well.'

Florian was silent. She knew that Wilhelm's failure to take up his old trade would count against him in this man's eyes. Wilhelm said that he couldn't carry on in the joinery trade because of eye problems, and instead he managed to get bar work in one of the few bars that were still open in those days. Then, as the city slowly rebuilt itself, he worked very hard indeed, and then, just recently, went into a partnership with a rough, tough Berliner to open their own cafe on the Promenadeplatz. A respectable bar serving the clerks and office personnel of the business district, not the shady, seedy gin palace or knocking shop that this other man imagined.

'So is he a good joiner, this Wilhelm of yours? I've heard he is one of the best.'

A drop of moisture had formed around the crack in the door and was running in parallel down it.

'If you don't go away, I will have to call the police,' said Florian, her one last attempt at resolve. How she loved the Wilhelm that had returned to her. She had never known anyone so kind, so loving, far more loving than he'd been in the days before the war, when, almost the day after their marriage, his romantic streak seemed to evaporate. The new Wilhelm loved his children all the more, greeted them just like you'd imagine someone who hadn't seen them for six years would, he wasn't afraid of them, he seemed to treasure them. And they, though much older and with few memories of their father before the war, responded. They felt treasured in ways that few people can. Anxious at first about having this stranger come to live with them, they soon adored him and, strangely, began to talk about their childhood for the first time, as though it was something that happened in the distant past. They realized that their lives were beginning to make a story.

The man outside spat on the floor – Florian couldn't be sure, but that's what it sounded like. She heard the click of spittle on the stone slabs of the landing. A dirty habit that her true husband would never practise, unless it was something that he'd picked up in his years in the army and in the prison camps.

'So when will he be home, this husband of yours?'

'Soon . . .'

She regretted saying it. If this man was determined to stake his claim, it was an incentive for him to hang around and challenge her Wilhelm when he came up the stairs – perhaps it would get violent. She should have just said nothing, and he would have gone away. After a while he would have given up; he couldn't stand on the landing for ever.

She heard his voice, further away this time. He was

talking to someone else – someone must have come out
of one of the other apartments – one of her neighbours.
He was probably trying out his claimed identity on them
– but there were few people left who would know her
Wilhelm, or would have a clear memory – so many had
fled the city in 1945, and they didn't seem to have
returned. Older ones (and many had been older people)
had died since. She could only make out a few words.
The man who claimed to be Wilhelm was sounding
agitated, almost bullying in the way he was talking to
the person whose way down the stairs he must have
blocked – 'You must remember me – look at my face –
look at it . . .' she heard the man saying. Of the
interrogated one's replies she could hear only a faint,
apologetic murmur. Then a dismissive cry, 'To hell with
you then,' and the footsteps returning to the door. Then
a soft thump against the woodwork, a diffuse, distributed
noise that was not a knock demanding entry, but something else. Then a sliding, shifting, rubbing noise, as
though someone was nervously polishing her door.
Wilhelm must have been leaning his back against it. She
could picture him, his back against the door, one leg
raised and the knee bent so the sole of his boot rested
against the lower panels. A cough. A shuffling sound.
Was he actually scratching his back against the door –
massaging himself? She thought she heard a little moan
and sigh of pleasure come from the man to confirm this.
It was as though, denied entry, he was making use of a
surface that was in closest proximity to what he desired,

as though the old woodwork was the extreme outer layer of her self, a sort of skin.

There was the sound of metal tapping and clicking, for a moment a busy, industrious sound, things being unwrapped and unscrewed. Was he going to have lunch out there? Then a horribly close sound that seemed, for a moment, to rip the door open as though it was made of cardboard – the sound of a match being struck against it. He'd been rolling a cigarette, and the smell of tobacco quickly arrived in the apartment. It was not a brand she recognized, certainly not the Ecksteins Wilhelm used to smoke, but some horrible coarse Russian tobacco from the Crimea or somewhere.

Where would this end? She tiptoed up the passage to the dining room to glance at the clock on the mantel-piece. Twenty past two. The cafe would have closed for the afternoon. Wilhelm might be home in ten minutes. She glanced again at the goods on the table. The cherries, the coffee, the stockings. How she wished this man would go away and allow her to use these things. Why was she tiptoeing? She didn't want the man outside to be aware of her position. But he seemed to sense it anyway. While she was at the far end of the passage he suddenly called out.

'Hey, are you still there?'

'I think you should go now,' said Florian, suddenly realizing her furtiveness had no purpose, and walking noisily back to the front door as she spoke. 'This is a pointless exercise. I know you are not my husband, you know it, that person on the landing you just spoke to knew it, so I want you to go now, this minute, or I will call the police.'

'You have a telephone that works?'

Florian didn't answer.

'But I have just thought of a way of proving my identity to you once and for all. You'll find it is the joiner who is the impostor when I ask you if you remember the family whistle.'

Florian could tell by the volume of his voice that he was still talking with his back to the door as he said this. Now, it was amplified as he came off the door and turned around to speak directly through the crack again, a puff of that rank tobacco preceding his voice. 'You remember, we never used it much but in those days it was important we had a way of identifying each other, children included. You remember? It went back to my father's days in the trenches, the signal he gave. You could whistle it to me now, couldn't you. And you know that your husband would never, ever, ever teach anyone else the family whistle, no matter how close a friend, no matter how trusted a comrade in arms. The whistle would be like a key that would unlock everything. I'll tell you what, that first Wilhelm of yours, that fake joiner who comes home to you every night with his hand punctured like a sieve with his bad nailing and sawing, I bet you a thousand American dollars he has never whistled our family whistle. He can't do it.'

'And can you?'

Florian knew the end was now close. She had never asked the first Wilhelm for the whistle – she had never thought of it, she had forgotten all about it, but that was because the first Wilhelm didn't need to prove anything, he wasn't in contention with another man claiming to be Wilhelm. She realized the new Wilhelm's reply was going to be the whistle itself. She heard him reposition himself, so that his mouth was right up to the crack, she heard him wet his lips, she heard the inrush of breath as he prepared, and when the whistle came, it was moist, breathy, and beautiful. She remembered it from the days of her courtship, when he would whistle it through the door of her uncle's vacant basement flat, where their early secret liaisons occurred, she remembered when he taught it to the children, so that they would always know who to let in and who not. She wondered how she had ever forgotten it, this haunting tune, that began with those two repeated notes (how like the call of a cuckoo, Florian thought), then a trill, a quick flourish and it was gone. Where had it come from – perhaps it was a tiny portion of a Mozart symphony, or a refrain from some long-forgotten music-hall lament. Florian never knew, but she realized that it meant that the person on the other side of the door was her true Wilhelm. The song came a second time. And no words were spoken by either husband or wife, as Florian delicately turned the lock, lowered the handle, and slowly pulled the door towards her.

Then suddenly the door was in her face, and knocking

her back against the wall. All the quietness and gentleness that had silted the conversation through the door in the long minutes of its duration were swept aside by its opening. There was less than a half-inch of gap before Wilhelm took his chance, making sure that it wouldn't close again. In a moment of cold, silent energy he was in the apartment and the door was closed behind him. He grabbed hold of the shrinking Florian, took her by the shoulders, examined her in a momentary frenzy of looking, then stuck his face right into hers and kissed it, forcing his tongue into her mouth in a way that suggested an interest in taste rather than affection or passion, as if he was confirming her identity, taking a big lick of the inside of her mouth. For her part she caught the strong flavour of bitter tobacco with nothing but emptiness beneath it.

Then he took her head in his hands – rough dry fingers teemed about her scalp and chin, worked her mouth open, moving the jaws as though on a piece of broken gadgetry. Then he did the most extraordinary thing – he blew into her mouth, she felt the puff of cold air. Then what was he doing? Looking in her mouth – what for – checking her teeth? Then pain. A sharp jab. He'd gone in there and given her tongue a rough bite. Not hard enough to do any damage, but enough to bring a stream of tears from her eyes. Wilhelm stepped back, wiping his mouth. Now he had her hair in his hands. He pulled her up by it so they were face to face.

'You rotten little whore,' he said, 'I would be within my rights to thrash you to death for this. So just say a prayer of thanks to the Almighty that I'm not a man given to jealousy, and I'll spare you your life.'

He pushed her roughly along the hall towards the dining room. She begged for a moment to go to the bathroom so she could deal with her mouth, because she thought it was bleeding. She dried her face in there, and tried to compose herself. Wilhelm, her first Wilhelm, was due back any moment. She could lock herself in the bathroom and wait for him to return, let the two of them sort it out, perhaps the first one would win. But it was no use thinking like that. The second Wilhelm, having successfully invaded, was not going to give up his new territory.

As she came out of the bathroom she found him waiting for her outside. He had taken off his greatcoat and she was shocked by the thinness of the body beneath. He looked as though he could have blown away in a breeze. His strength was all in his anger; there was no muscle in his body at all.

'You will give me something to eat first, then I will wash, then we will see to other business.'

There was a sound of a key in the lock of the front door. Both heads turned to watch. But the new Wilhelm had put the bolt on.

He took hold of Florian again, whispered urgently in her ear.

'If you still want proof – just ask that man for the

family whistle. I will give you both that one chance. Ask him for the family whistle, see what he does.'

The struggling with the key in the lock came to an end, and there was a call.

'Florian, are you in there?' That voice, so mellifluous and musical – how could she have ever thought it belonged to her husband? 'I can't get in. Florian.'

Florian and the new Wilhelm both approached the door quietly. There was more knocking.

'Florian – can you come to the door? It's stuck.'

'Wilhelm,' Florian called.

A pause.

'What's wrong, Florian? Is there something wrong?'

'Wilhelm. Listen to me . . .' Florian looked at the man beside her, who nodded insistently. 'I want you to give me the family whistle.'

'What?'

'Through the door, give me the family whistle.'

There was silence. Such a long silence. Florian stood two feet from the big dark oblong of the door, believing, just for a moment, that she might hear the whistle, that same melancholy tune far more sweetly sung. But what she heard instead was footsteps departing. They moved slowly away from the door (backwards, she imagined), then paused at the top of the stairs. Then she heard them descending, quickly, lightly, down the first flight, and the second. Then they were gone.

She turned. Wilhelm was already in the dining room. She could see him through the open door. He was examining the things on the table. He opened the tin of coffee, stuck his nose in and sniffed, closing his eyes with pleasure. Then he gestured with a big, sweeping arm for her to join him.

UNION STATION

I was looking forward to seeing Union Station again. It had been two weeks since my arrival and, although I could happily have stayed two weeks more, deep down I knew it was time to leave. On the morning I was to put everything behind me, Neil said he would give me a lift to the station in his pickup truck. I was hoping he would. His place was on the edge of town and a taxi was ten dollars.

Neil is my cousin, though he is nearly twenty years older than me. We hadn't really met before, not until I took up the long-standing offer, issued regularly to family members far and wide, to come and sample the mountain air at his guest house and cafe at the foot of the Rockies, the intriguingly named Prospector Inn. Suddenly finding myself with a little bit of money, and some time on my hands, and a hankering to visit the United States, I'd taken up the offer, flying to the nearest big city and taking a train from there.

The place was all I'd dreamt it would be – log cabins, creeks with sweet torrents of water winding through them, teetering crags of red rock, lonesome pines, elk wandering nervously through the yards. You'd never have guessed Neil was an Englishman; in his baseball cap and check shirt he looked and sounded every bit the big-hearted Midwesterner. He took me into the woods with his Ruger to shoot cougars and blacktails, he took me down to the river to hook bass and catfish. We drank Coors from the bottle and had pancakes for breakfast. One night, both drunk, he summed up his life for me by pointing to a pokerwork plaque that hung in pride of place over the bar. It read 'A fisherman lives here with the catch of his life!' We touched knuckles and drank to the future, giggling.

The catch of his life was Lou, a true girl of the mountains, though now a hard-bitten, weatherworn working woman, who did most of the waitressing in the cafe, constantly ferrying food to and from the tables. Her sharp jaw, black-rimmed eyes and brassy hair concealed a tender and warm personality. When I was feeling delicate she offered to make me green ginger tea. When I was feeling giddy she gave me a little packet of Dead Sea salt. She said my electrolytes needed topping up. What made salt from the Dead Sea so special, I asked her. It's just special, she said.

She was there to see me off that morning as I climbed into the truck, having slung my rucksack in the back. It was the only time I'd ever seen Neil's pickup carry any sort of cargo.

'It's been really special having you,' said Lou, hugging me one last time. 'We're really going to miss you.'

Then she handed me something.

'Here, you nearly forgot this.' It was the little plastic pouch of Dead Sea salt. 'Remember to take it, whenever you start feeling light-headed . . .'

'Any other salt will do the same thing,' said Neil as we set off down Canyon Boulevard through the creek and into town, 'I don't know what's so special about the Dead Sea.'

We were silent for the rest of the journey. For a moment I wondered if there was something wrong. Neil was never silent, and this morning his driving was tetchy. He swung the truck violently a couple of times. I heard my rucksack rolling around in the back. Then suddenly we were there.

'I'm not a man for goodbyes,' he said, 'it's best if you just jump out now and have done with it.'

'It's best that way,' I agreed as I climbed out.

'We'll see you again for sure,' Neil called as I slammed the door. I hauled my rucksack out of the back, feeling for a moment as though I was showing off my manliness for one last time, in managing the awkward lift with a single sunburnt arm. But Neil wasn't looking, and he didn't even glance back as he drove off, leaving me alone on the sidewalk.

It was too late to do anything about the fact that Neil had dropped me off at the wrong place. It took me a minute or so to realize I was nowhere near the railway station. Neil had dropped me at the bus station instead. The Transit Center, as it was called. There was a long-bearded beggar nearby, the sort you see at many of the intersections in the town, holding a scrap of cardboard which briefly summed up his plight. 'Looking for Work. Will try anything.' Elsewhere some tired-looking local buses got ready to pull away. Others arrived with few passengers to unload.

I went up to an empty bus where the driver was sitting in his seat, reading a free newspaper.

'Can you tell me where the station is?' I asked through the open door.

'Station?'

'Yeah, railway station – railroad,' I corrected myself.

'Railroad station?' As though I had asked a ridiculous question.

'Yes, railroad station.'

His reply was full of a kind of tense patience, as though he wasn't sure if this was all some sort of joke.

'There's no railroad station in this town. Nearest railroad is seventy miles away.'

'No,' I said, thinking the man probably wasn't local and must be mistaken, 'there is. I arrived here on a train two weeks ago. The station's called Union Station, it's a huge old building, Victorian – nineteenth century, it's right here, somewhere in the middle of town.'

'Well, that's great,' said the bus driver with the same air of tired patience, 'but there's no station in this town, never has been and never will. I've lived here all my life, son, and one thing we don't have is a station. Probably one of the biggest towns around here without a station

. . . Where do you want to go? The only way out of this town is by bus.'

He spread his hands, as though offering me personal use of his vehicle.

'No, look,' I said, reaching into my jeans pocket, 'I've got the return ticket right here. How do you explain that, if there's no railroad station . . .'

I handed him the ticket. He looked at it sceptically and for not very long, before handing it back.

'Never seen one of those before,' he said, 'doesn't have the word railroad anywhere on it, this could be a ticket to a bowling alley for all I know.'

I gave up with the bus driver and went in search of someone else to ask. There were some black women sitting on a bench in one of the bays.

'Hi, I'm looking for the railroad station.'

I was dismayed to find they responded just as the bus driver had, with cautious disbelief (was I mad, they were thinking, or just stupid?). After a while one of the women piped up loudly, as though speaking for all of them,

'There's no railroad here, mister. You want to go anywhere you got to get a bus, or rent a car, or stick your thumb out.'

I resisted the urge to go through the same argument I'd gone through with the driver, to tell them about how I'd arrived in the town by train, that the station was an imposing, unmistakable, nineteenth-century structure with the words Union Station in great big red letters curving over its central arch, that there was a big plaza in front of it, full of taxis and buses and people milling around.

I asked several other people. I asked the waitress behind the counter of a coffee shop, I asked one of the street-corner beggars, and I asked a contortionist who was performing in the pedestrianized mall on 16th Street, and who had just unknotted himself before an audience of three or four. They all gave the same bleak answer, that there was no railroad station in the town, and that if I wanted to go anywhere, I would have to get a bus.

My faith in my station was beginning to fade. I was finally convinced of its non-existence when I came across a large tourist map of the town on display, not far from where the contortionist had been performing. There was no railroad station marked on the map, whose detail was so close that almost every other building in the town was depicted and named.

Yet my memories of the station were as clear and as vivid as any I had of the whole holiday. It had been a three-hour ride on the train, across vast plains with hardly a building or tree to interrupt the view. I had been thrilled to be travelling by train across America, or a part of it at least, on a historic railway. Union Station was palatial, a high steel and glass arch over the platforms, a vast ticket hall almost big enough to have its own weather system. It seemed the embodiment of the grandeur, glamour and verve of American railways. I read an information display that had said how Union Station was one of the oldest and most significant stations in the country, on the historic transcontinental railroad, the first to span the continent from coast to coast. There was a modern statue, in bronze, of an ordinary couple, a man and woman in 1920s clothes, embracing. It was a beautiful object, the embrace so tenderly caught, one of those moments of passion a railway station sees a hundred times a day, captured for ever.

Surely I couldn't have made all that up, imagined it all. I had been in no other towns in America; I couldn't be confusing it with anywhere else. I remembered it so clearly. And what's more, I could hear the railroad, hear it at night from my room at Neil and Lou's, that moaning freight-train sound, the long wail of those deep, discordant horns. I heard it the night Lou came to my room, in her towelling night robe, stealing in silently through the door, appearing at the end of my bed, making me sit up urgently.

— What are you doing here?

— I came to see if you were OK.

— But it's the middle of the night.

— I've brought you something.

She held up a little plastic pouch with a vacuum fastener.

— It's the salt I told you about. From the Dead Sea.

— You didn't have to bring it right now, in the middle of the night.

— But you need it now, in case you get dehydrated. Your electrolytes need topping up.

She was beautiful in the moonlight, which seemed to edit out all her imperfections. Her skin was blue and smooth, her hair silver, her eyes soft and dark.

Just a few grains, she said, taking my glass of water from the bedside table, and sprinkling them in. She stirred the potion with her little finger, then offered it to me. I drank. I could hardly taste any salt. Then Lou drank from the same glass. Our lips touched. I didn't think about Neil, about the family, about the rivers full of fish. I didn't think about anything but the convergence, halfway across a continent, of myself and Louise. And in those precious moments I heard the freight train wail, and I now realized that whatever that sound was, it must have opened up a railroad station in my mind, a big steel-arched one, with a statue of lovers embracing, and shafts of sunlight falling sideways through an almost infinite ticket hall, so heartfelt, so real. I believed I had arrived in Lou's world though its magnificent doors, and that I would leave it the same way. And it stayed there, a moment of love rendered in imagined architecture, a part of me. If I thought back to its granite walls, and how they sparkled, surely that was sea salt in amongst the quartz, making the stone shine.

No one ever knew about us. It was only for one night. No harm was done to anyone. But now, in the centre of town, it was heartbreaking to realize that no station existed. That the trains never came here. If I wanted to leave, I'd have to get a bus, rent a car or stick out my thumb. Well, I didn't want to do any of those. But what choice did I have? Maybe I'll just have to sit here, on 16th Street, and wait until they build a railroad station.

A Night Crossing

The ferry sailed in the late afternoon. Arnold stood by
the rails on the top deck, close to the funnels which
spewed their dark fumes, as though there was a whole
factory somewhere down in the bottom of the ship. As
always, they gave the sense of tremendous effort for very
little reward. All that power being created, enough to set
the colossal structure shaking from top to bottom, and
yet a slow and ponderous rate of progress, so that the
boxy, commercial, shorefront regions of the city seemed
to drift past him for hours.

The ship was full to capacity, and Arnold was alone
on it. He had not travelled abroad by himself before, and
was interested to know what it would feel like. As they
began to enter the wider waters of the Channel and the
messy, industrial stretch of English coast began to recede,
he felt a great sense of excitement, a relish for travel that
he hadn't felt for years.

It was an overnight voyage and he hadn't booked a
cabin.

He enjoyed exploring the ship, remembering how he
loved the arrangement of decks, the narrow, steep and

sudden staircases, the public areas where one could wander or linger, the bars and lounges. Everything seemed stacked and precariously balanced, like a card house. There were many families in full holiday mode, wearing shorts and sandals in anticipation of the hot weather to come. The children were excited, though some of them seemed scared, and sensed they were in a place governed by strict rules, so that they hesitated at every doorway, wondering if they were allowed through. Sometimes the adults were as nervous. Arnold chuckled inwardly at the ungainliness of the English abroad, and mentally set himself apart from them.

Suddenly hungry, he made for the cafeteria, which was crowded and chaotic. It seemed that, with the excitements of embarkation over, everyone was feeling hungry. Big sweaty families were gathered around tables eating ravenously. Arnold was a little shocked at how disgusted he felt. He watched one family in particular. The father was eating an all-day breakfast. He rolled a piece of bacon up as though it were a sock, and tucked the whole thing in his mouth as one. Then, cheeks still bulging from the bacon, he pushed more food in, talking all the while. The children seemed to find knives and forks a novelty. One had stabbed a sausage and was eating it like a lollipop. A girl grabbed chips by the handful, as though they were dead grass. The family kept up a constant push and pull stream of conversation, where the children, fidgety in their chairs, sitting on their knees and leaning far forward across the tables, had to be continually brought back from the brink of bad behaviour by scolding delivered so routinely it was ignored.

By contrast, at another table, an older couple, probably in their seventies, conducted themselves with impeccable elegance and decorum, using their cutlery like delicate instruments of dissection, working their way through their food as though painting a watercolour. They seemed to belong to a different culture entirely, relics of the age of straight-backed manners and deference. They had even dressed properly for dinner, the woman in pearls, her hair gracefully drawn back, the man with a triangle of silk handkerchief poking from his breast pocket. They radiated a sense of old European gentility of the sort Arnold imagined still lingered on in forgotten corners of the great Continental cities, somehow untouched by revolution or war. He felt, almost, that he wanted to shield this graceful couple's eyes from the barbarities of bad taste and vulgarity that were emanating from the English family. But then he suddenly caught a phrase coming from the messy table – the thick-necked, sunburnt father; was he really talking French? Had they taken the trouble to learn? And the children – suddenly he caught a snatch of the girl's speech, eating chips with her fingers, saying, 'Tu connais Valerie? Non? Tu connais Nicola?' They weren't just speaking French, they *were* French. At the same time the elegant couple suddenly revealed their national identity, when the man lifted up a copy of the *Daily Mail* to read, as much as if he'd just waved a Union Jack.

Arnold was astonished to find himself in conversation. He had hoped for it, but not expected it. While he had been observing, he himself had been observed. In all his years of people-watching, he had never felt his curiosity returned, but this time he had not only been observed, but singled out and approached. The man who did this was someone he remembered from the train for his extraordinary dress sense. He was wearing denim dungarees over a yellow shirt. A wine-red velvet jacket and a scarlet neckerchief. His fine, dark features were topped by a flat black cap, which he never took off. He spoke with a strong French accent, so strong that for a moment Arnold wondered if he was an Englishman performing a parody, and his first instinct was to reply in kind, to crank up the joke. Luckily he held back just in time. The man spoke in a low, confidential tone.

'My good friend, might I interrupt you? Whenever I see a person reading a book, I have to find out what it is.'

Arnold had, as ever, employed the solitary person's *do not disturb* sign – the book to read. This time it was a badly scuffed Penguin Modern Classics edition of André Gide's *The Counterfeiters*. The man lifted the paperback as it sat in Arnold's hands, raising the top of the spine with finger and thumb as though sexing a kitten. Arnold felt trepidation. Suddenly the book was representing his life, like the passport he hadn't had to show at check-in. It had become the basis for the stranger's assessment of his character. He saw how he was taking moments to comprehend it, to get his bearing with the title and the author. Perhaps the stranger was intimidated. In fact Arnold had not been enjoying the novel, and had lost the thread.

'Why don't you read it in French?' the man finally said. It seemed a form of half-approval.

'I would if I could.'

'I have read Sir Arthur Conan Doyle in English, and I am a fool. You can surely read Gide in French. I can see you are a smart guy.'

Arnold laughed. 'No. I can hardly understand it in English.' And he laughed again, pleased with his joke. But the Frenchman didn't get it, and even seemed disappointed, as though he believed that Arnold had admitted to a cognitive impediment.

The man took a seat facing Arnold, but offset himself so that he was turned towards the windows and their oblongs of smooth grey sea. He seemed to relish holding the initiative in the conversation. It was his turn to speak, and he was taking his time.

'I think we are going to a better place, you and I.' Arnold wondered if the man had intended the morbid reference. He thought not. 'England is finished.'

'Is it?'

The man turned to him, nodding sadly with his eyes closed. 'It is a Third World country now.' He said this as if it was a fact so well established he was tired of repeating it. 'A Third World country.'

Arnold wondered if this was some sort of bait he was being offered. He was not offended, just astonished that the man should speak so freely in denigration of another's country. He wondered how the man would react if he returned the criticism.

'What about France?' he said, speculatively.

'France? I'm not from France. I am a Breton.' The man said this in a half-amused tone, his face suddenly animated and jokey. He then made dismissive hand gestures, and wrinkled his nose. 'France, England. They're both finished.'

He said his name was Eric. He said that he was a musician, and that he had a girlfriend who lived in London. Neither wanted to leave their country and live with the other, so their relationship was conducted across hundreds of miles, each taking turns to visit once a month, sometimes more. He didn't think the relationship could last much longer, not unless one of them moved. 'She thinks I should move to London, because I'm a musician, and so I can work anywhere, while she has a job in a bank. She couldn't work in a bank in France. She can't even speak French. But I can play music anywhere. That's what she says. But I play traditional French folk music. The music of Brittany. I have regular work there, a hungry audience. In London no one would understand my music and they would not want to listen to it.'

'Really?' said Arnold. 'Are you sure about that?'

'I know it for a fact.'

'I'm sure I would like it.'

'Then you would be an exception. Oh, I could probably play two or three times a year. In Brittany I am
playing two or three times a week.'

'Difficult,' said Arnold.

'And I don't like English cities.'

'They're not all bad.' Arnold already felt he understood Eric quite well. His remarks about English culture
were not designed to offend. Rather, he was one of those
people who can't help saying what they think, and who
say whatever is in their heads.

'I prefer it here,' said Eric, turning to face the window
again, 'the open sea. Nothing out there. The waves, the
seagulls. I wanted to be a sailor when I was a child. Or
rather, my mother wanted me to be a sailor. My father
was a fisherman. But I hate fish. I didn't want to follow
him to sea, and he had to sell his boat when he retired.
They had both been hoping I would take it over, right up
to the end, as if I would suddenly change my mind. But
now I wish I had. I would love to be at sea for weeks on
end, with my nets, and my crates of ice . . .'

He talked like this for a little while. Arnold was
charmed by him. There was something innately comical
about Eric, both in his appearance and his manner, yet
the comicality was unintentional. He amused Arnold,
and relaxed him because he sensed that he required nothing, or very little, in return. Eric might tell him everything

about his difficult girlfriend, or his fisherman father, but he didn't expect Arnold to expand on his own love life, or childhood, and in fact seemed that he could not have cared less about them, and Arnold was thankful for that.

Suddenly, with a little nod and wave of the hand, Eric stood up and left, adjusting the black cap on his head, taking a glance out of the window, as if checking for signs of land in the grey expanse of sea, then wandered off slowly, aimlessly. Arnold watched his departing figure recede into the further reaches of the ship, noticing, as he passed beyond the final row of tables before leaving the cafeteria, how he seemed to wave at someone casually. Could he really be such a regular traveller on the ferry, for the sake of his English girlfriend, that he knew other passengers?

The sun was setting over the Channel. Arnold hadn't really put much thought into the fact that this was an overnight sailing, and that before long it would be dark, and he had nowhere to sleep. He had assumed, somehow, that with the rush of adrenaline and the excitement of being at sea he would be awake all night, and wouldn't need to sleep. Or if he did, there would be lots of comfortable benches or chairs to spread out on. Or that he would fall into friendship with a group of backpacking students and be up all night playing cards. He had brought a pack with him.

After a little while Arnold also left the cafeteria and went out onto the open deck. The last time he had stood out there he was watching the retreat of the English coastline, but now there was no sign of land in any direction, and for a moment it felt as though a trick had been played – that while he had been inside, mysterious agencies had been hard at work dismantling everything.

He went back inside and toured the decks again. The cafeteria had emptied, but the lounge areas were full. The comfortable armchairs on which he'd earlier hoped he might be able to spend the night were all occupied. Eric, who hadn't booked a cabin either, had earlier said that by night time these chairs would become empty, as those passengers with berths returned to their cabins to sleep. Arnold didn't feel so sure. A lot of the people in the chairs looked settled in for the night. Some had even started to sleep, had stretched themselves out across two or more chairs and had draped themselves with coats for blankets.

He searched all the decks. There were several lounge and seating areas, but they were all fully occupied. Only the cafeteria had vacant seats, but these were hard upright chairs in wood veneer with chrome armrests, impossible to sleep on. Suddenly he felt like a homeless person in a floating suburb, looking for a scrap of shelter, something to lie beneath. He wondered if the floors would be too uncomfortable, too hard, or if he had anything in his luggage that would serve as a mattress and pillow. He hadn't slept like that since his own backpacking days, and the prospect made him feel awkward and nervous.

At the front of the ship, on Deck B, there was a bar.

It was as crowded as all the other parts of the ship. There were twenty or more small round tables with padded stools, no proper chairs. Further along, the bar seemed to merge into a large seating area where soft leather loungers were arranged in rows as in a theatre, before a tall gallery of windows that gave on to a forward view of the open sea, now quite invisible in the blackness. The clientele in the bar were the same sort of odd mix of classes and ages you would get in a motorway service station, where everyone, no matter what their background, had to go, through lack of choice. There were middle-class families with well-behaved children; there were young couples on romantic breaks; rowdy parties of young men. There was one group, a stag party, who had marked themselves out with a uniform. They were wearing purple football shirts with their nicknames on their backs – El Gordo, King Colesy, Taff, Chaz, Power, Dalster, among others. Their shirts also displayed their itinerary, as though they were on a tour, like a rock group. When he got a chance to get close enough Arnold could read 'Mario's Stag Tour 95 – St Malo, Rennes, Nantes, Bordeaux, Toulouse'. What happened, he wondered, when they got to Toulouse – a plane back? Or had they not thought that far? He became fascinated by this group and observed them carefully. They seemed to exemplify a form of friendship that was new, or at least that hadn't seemed to exist when Arnold was younger – the large group that is closely bonded, carefully ranked, and in which each member serves as a particular 'character' and has a role that formed early, in school, and which has survived the potential fractures caused by work or college. The only thing that can divide it is marriage, which he supposes is why stag celebrations have become such elaborate rituals in recent years.

Arnold bought himself a drink and settled down on one of the few available chairs, and took out *The Counterfeiters* again. He had forgotten to mark his place when he'd been interrupted by Eric, and spent his time dipping into different pages, trying to pick up the thread of the novel again. As he tried to read, the rowdiness of the bar increased. The families with young children had begun returning to their cabins, leaving the area to the youthful and the heavy drinkers. A pianist who had been tinkling at an upright piano, almost unheard by anyone in the bar, came to the end of his contracted hours, and left the instrument to the applause of two or three people who happened to be seated nearby.

Arnold had found where he'd left off in the novel, though he couldn't quite connect it to what had gone before, even if he could remember what that was. He looked up from his book to notice an extraordinarily attractive young woman on the next table, curled round on the back of her chair to look at him.

'You can read with all this?' She was French but recognized that he was English. Arnold wondered how. She couldn't possibly see, from her vantage point, that he was reading an English text. And the noise around them had become so great that he had to ask her to repeat her question.

'No,' he replied, 'I am only pretending to read.'

He thought it was rather a witty answer, and was pleased with himself, but only for as long as it took him to realize she had taken his answer seriously.

'Why do you pretend to read?' She looked puzzled.

'To give myself a cover,' he said, but he had taken his joke too far, and the girl's English couldn't make sense of it. She asked him to repeat what he had said, and Arnold then felt the only way out was to abandon the conversation altogether. He shook his head and tried to dismiss everything he had said as a poor joke, in the hope that they could start again. But the girl shrugged and returned to watching the antics of the stag party, turning the beautiful back of her head towards him.

Arnold tried to work over what had just happened, and whether he had blown the best chance of sex he was likely to have on the entire trip. He was the sort of person who couldn't help but believe that any young woman who spoke to him for any non-practical reason was making a pass at him. And this young woman's beauty was so exceptional it did make it seem unlikely that she was making a pass, but nevertheless he kept pondering (instead of reading) the correct course the conversation should have taken if they were to eventually make love – either here on the ship or later, in France. And he wondered if there was any possible way he could re-open the dialogue.

With the paid pianist gone, the piano became an object of interest. El Gordo from the stag party took up his place at the keyboard, played chopsticks and some other simple tunes, urged on by his friends. He quickly came to the end of his repertoire, so went through it again. He could see that a third round would be too much, and so just sat there, looking at the keyboard, and saying, 'That's all I know,' in a voice that seemed more apologetic than necessary. Arnold presumed he had previously boasted of far greater abilities at the keyboard. Now he was reduced to prodding the instrument tentatively, as if to rouse it into a state where it could play itself. Defeated, he left the instrument and started banging a rhythm on an empty table, as if to announce that his real musical skills lay in drumming. He was getting loud ribbing from his friends for not being able to play more on the piano, and they were now all around the keyboard, King Colesy, Power, Dalster, Chaz, each wondering who among them had the hidden talent to make music with the thing. King Colesy suddenly sat on the stool and spread his hands, poised as if to embark on something impressive. Than his hands seemed to wither before him and his whole body slumped, as though his pianistic memory had been instantly wiped. More jeering. They lingered around the instrument, fingering and poking at the keys. Some of them made general appeals to the bar – 'Does anyone know how to play this thing?' It seemed that the piano, to them, had suddenly become a treasure chest of delights that must remain locked unless the key could be found. How rare the skill of piano-playing seemed. It was a skill that Arnold possessed in a limited form. He had enough to produce something that would impress the stag party – a few jazz numbers he'd learnt, and which sounded far more difficult than they were. And he could extemporize endlessly at the keyboard if he wanted to. 'Come on! Someone must be able to play the piano. What? No one on the entire ship?' King Colesy shouted this, in a strong south London accent. Arnold wondered if he should present himself.

He saw the girl at the next table look around her to see if anyone was volunteering. She had been following the progress of the stag team with amusement, as had many in the bar – they had become an alternative form of entertainment, though most enjoyed the spectacle while pretending not to notice it. Arnold was one of these. He saw the beautiful girl's hair swing back and forth as she again took in a sweep of the bar, then looked directly at Arnold.

'You can play!' she suddenly cried out, beaming.

The stag party looked over to him. One of them whistled, another gave a thumbs up. 'Over here,' one of them called chirpily, as though asking for a football to be kicked in their direction, then pointed at the keyboard. Two of the team spread their arms in an offering gesture, presenting the vacant keyboard for Arnold's exclusive use.

How did she know – that he was English, that he played the piano? But Arnold couldn't trust himself to take the moment. He had never played in public before, and though no one would have cared how well he played, as long as he played something, he was aware that he might make a terrible fool of himself in the beautiful girl's eyes, if she was using this as some sort of test, some sort of appraisal. To pass, perhaps he only had to participate, perhaps that was all that was required. To be game. To be up for it. To be one of the boys, to be cheered on by El Gordo, Power, King Colesy, to be slapped on the shoulder by Dalster, perhaps they would hoist him aloft, the game Englishman who wouldn't let music die in the late-night bar of the cross-Channel ferry. A hero. They would have danced around him. He would have been the star of the evening. And what would the beautiful French girl have made of it? What could have happened?

The moment when Arnold could have taken his place at the keyboard passed very quickly, and too late he realized it would never return. He had thought that El Gordo and his friends would have been more persuasive, would have spent more time trying to cajole him up to the piano, but when he didn't respond immediately, they gave up. And without their cajoling, without their beckonings and thumbs ups, there was no access to the keyboard. To have gone up there after the moment had passed would be to go up there as a stranger, not as the friend he had, for just a few seconds, been. The reality of this loss, of his missing of the tide, settled coldly on him. The girl had lost all interest in him, indeed had disappeared altogether. The piano became a distant thing at the far end of an enormous, empty room. King Colesy's boys had left it stranded and isolated, uncared for, abandoned, and had moved on to another part of the bar, exhausted with the effort of being uproarious.

Arnold cursed himself, kicked himself, for not being quicker off the mark. He felt suddenly drained, just as El Gordo must have felt at the keyboard – inert, helpless, talentless, stupid.

He decided to leave the bar for one last tour of the ship.

People were falling asleep in their chairs, if they were lucky enough to have chairs big enough to fall asleep in. Where before he'd seen activity and excitement, now he saw a desolate sort of stillness; people slumped, propped up on rucksacks, apparently oblivious and in deep sleep, but in bright light and noise.

In the restaurant he saw one group of people, all teenagers, sitting around a table asleep, their bodies crashed forwards and resting on the table. It was as though someone had cast a spell. As he walked further towards the stern of the ship, on different levels, he felt more and more like the only person awake in an enchanted kingdom. The resourcefulness of the sleepers was surprising, how they had managed to carve a niche of sleepfulness out of the most hard and unlikely material, but Arnold couldn't imagine joining them, even if he could have found a space. He could sit somewhere, even lie down, but he could never imagine himself falling asleep.

Eventually he returned to the bar, unable to suppress a feeling of defeat. The bar was less crowded, and there was a more subdued atmosphere. The counter area itself was closed and the grille had been lowered. Arnold was disappointed, he could have done with a drink. People were drinking from bottles and cans of beer they had brought on board with them, or had purchased from the shop for just this eventuality. There seemed to be resolve among some of the passengers that the only way to survive this voyage was to drink the night through from end to end.

Arnold saw someone signalling to him. Eric, still in his black cap and red neckerchief, was standing in a far corner of the bar with two others. One was a rather rough-looking man he didn't recognize, with long lank hair, and the other person was the beautiful girl he'd spoken to earlier. To Arnold's intense delight, Eric remembered his name, and called to him.

'This is my English friend,' he said, 'come and join us.'

The lank-haired man seemed amused, and reached out to shake hands, saying something in French far too quickly for Arnold to make out, but which caused the other two to laugh.

'Did you finish your book?' said the girl, pleasing Arnold by signalling so clearly that she remembered him from such a brief conversation. He looked at the others to see if they were impressed that he had had previous contact with the girl, but they gave no sense of being so impressed.

'No,' said Arnold, 'tonight is not a night for reading.'

Each of the three had a bottle of beer. Eric offered his own to Arnold, and Arnold gratefully took a little swig. Eric insisted, through facial gestures, that he should have some more. So Arnold drank again, and began to feel far too indebted.

'What is it a night for, then?' said the girl.

Arnold, emboldened by fatigue, and a mouthful of alcohol, said, 'It can be for anything you want.'

The girl looked blankly at him, and he wondered if he'd said something that didn't make sense to a French speaker.

'It is not much of a night for sleeping, either,' said Eric. 'I have never seen the boat so crowded. There are no seats anywhere.'

'What will you do?' said Arnold, but his question didn't seem to have been heard.

It seemed that the man with lank hair spoke no English, and every now and then the conversation would slip into French, sometimes for long exchanges, which Arnold would attend to as much as he could, and laugh punctually with the others when the moment seemed right, but otherwise he was adrift in his linguistic ignorance, and he longed always for the conversation to come back into English, which it did when the others realized he needed to be brought back into the flow of talk.

Arnold did his best to read the beautiful young girl, trying to gauge her level of interest in him, which veered from none at all to mild amusement. The more he observed her, the more beautiful she became. She seemed to have just stepped out of a French film of the sixties, so much so that, when he thought about her later, he saw her in black and white. She had a way of laughing that indicated something throwaway and insolent in her outlook on things. He dared to wonder if anything could possibly happen between them; he was only ten years her senior, he estimated. She seemed unattached, adventurous. He began to wonder, stupidly, if he was in competition with the other two males for her attention. He began assessing himself against Eric – with his dungarees and neckerchief he looked, to Arnold, ridiculous, – but perhaps in the eyes of a young French woman he was the apogee of manhood. As for the lank-haired man, in many ways he seemed Eric's opposite – portly, dirty, unkempt, nothing remotely sophisticated about him. But if Arnold was in competition with these two, he lacked the most crucial asset – language. The conversation swept past him and supplied the young woman effortlessly with entertainment. When it slipped into English the conversation became retarded, clumsy, laden with misunderstandings. Arnold felt the disadvantage acutely, like the little brother whose siblings have to wait for him to catch up.

Eric encouraged Arnold to have another swig from his bottle (an elbow nudge and a quick thumb-flick towards the ledge behind them where the bottle resided). As Arnold was swigging, something odd seemed to happen during a French stretch of the conversation. The lank-haired man, it transpired, was a member of the crew, and it seemed that he was suggesting that they go down to his cabin, where he had a bottle of brandy. He was a man full of gestures and mimicry. When Arnold finally understood his role (after much heavy-handed explaining of maritime French), the man did an elaborate mime pretending to blow down a message pipe to the engine room, and to stamp on the floor and to shout down through it the only English words he had spoken all evening, 'Full Steam Ahead!!' Everyone laughed.

'Et mon ami?' Eric said, gesturing with his head towards Arnold. The crew member, who was called Leon, hesitated, as though he too had trouble with French (though Arnold secretly adored the use of the word 'ami' no matter how sincerely meant). Leon gave Arnold a long, half-amused stare, as though assessing him for a specific role. All through this voyage Arnold had felt he was being assessed in one way or another. Leon then stepped over to Arnold and made a mime of shaving Arnold's face, making a rasping sound as he produced each stroke of an invisible razor. Arnold felt the pressure of the man's hand on his shoulder, and the scrape of his fingers across his cheeks, the roughness of his stumpy fingers. The others laughed again. Arnold once more felt left out of the joke. There was nothing

unusual about his own unshavenness, indeed Leon himself had a thicker growth of stubble.

There were hurried discussions in French that Arnold
couldn't follow. Glances were thrown in his direction.
It seemed they were weighing the decision to invite him
down or not. Arnold wondered if he should try and
advertise himself in some way, promote himself as a good
companion for the night – but what was going to happen
down there? For a moment a sordid pornographic fan-
tasy entered his mind, that these three were going down
into the depths of the ship, to the secret quarters forbid-
den to passengers, to Leon's cabin with its soft lighting
and brandy bottles, and they were going to play strip
poker or some other game of seduction and end up in a
sexual threesome, the beautiful girl stripped and compli-
ant, the men sweaty and slack-jawed with lust as they
were received willingly into her body.

The image was impossible to conjure fully, but even
as he struggled with the idea, it was too late. Heads were
nodded, hands were shaken, the trio moved away from
the wall where they'd been standing with no indication
that Arnold should either follow or stay put, and in the
absence of any such cue, he was left stranded in the bar,
watching his three companions shuffle off.

The bar itself was nearly empty. The stag party was trying
to keep up a strain of lively banter, but even that was
beginning to die down. They had set up their own sleeping area with blankets and cushions, an encampment in a

wilderness that didn't exist. Some of them seemeded to have fallen asleep, but an equal number seem determined to stay awake for as long as possible. Others had done the same, and the bar was now transformed into something like a refugee camp, with sleeping bags spread out, and a sense of collective endeavour, the spirit of the air-raid shelter, of something to be got through together. There was nowhere for Arnold to go.

Impulsively he began following Eric and his two friends, though they were now out of sight. He tried to pick up their trail, leaving the bar, then down one of the wide aisles to the side of the ship – he thought he could just glimpse them at the far end turning through a doorway. He rushed after them, but by the time he arrived where they'd been, there was no sign. He descended a stairway. On the lower deck things were even quieter. A sleeping kingdom. He nearly tripped over an unconscious body spread out on the floor. Thinking that Leon's cabin must be in the lower reaches of the ship towards the stern, he descended again, looking for an entrance to the staff quarters. He passed through a doorway that led to a narrow corridor from which doorways led to the passenger cabins. A woman in a nightie with a toothbrush in her mouth suddenly appeared, but took no notice of him. Occasionally he passed a cabin where there was the muffled noise of a small party going on, with the transgressive air of a children's midnight feast. Soon he was in a labyrinth of corridors and doorways. He descended again, and came across a door that must have led to the car deck, because there was a notice prohibiting passenger access to vehicles during the voyage. Nearby he found a door marked *staff only*, and passed through. Then countless doors, most of them shut. He listened. He suddenly felt trapped and in the wrong. The area beyond the 'staff only' notice had become distinctly different in quality. There was a roughness to everything, a shabbiness. There were doors that were open, that led through to what looked like workshops, or boiler rooms, or laundries. The smell was rank, rubbery, like a mechanic's garage. The noise of the engines was far greater here, the rhythmic booming seemed to pass directly into his body, up from the floor. He felt he was standing right over the engines with only thin metal between them.

He had now lost all hope of finding his friends. He stepped through an open portal and suddenly found himself in an enormous space, so vast after the cramped corridors he'd just passed through it took him a moment to understand it. Cars, vans, minibuses and coaches parked nose to tail in tight-packed rows almost as far as he could see. To his left the great door that was raised like a drawbridge, and beyond it the open sea. He could hear the water churning behind it. For a moment he imagined there might be some lever he could pull that would open the door to the ocean, and all the empty cars would roll out silently into the water.

The place seemed desolate, unsupervised. It was as though he had come across the plundered booty of the modern world stored in a cave. The cars twinkled and sparkled in the riveted gloom of the deck, cars held prisoner, or hostage. He drifted out from the doorway and walked among them, fascinated. They bore traces of their owners to such an extent he felt he could match them with the people he'd seen on the decks above, spotting here and there a car that held, like a vitrine, the matching sun hat of some blouse he'd noticed. And there, on the back seat of another, was the lost toy a child above had wailed about.

The thought suddenly occurred to him that here was the perfect solution to his lack of somewhere to sleep. These cars were guaranteed to be unvisited for the night. If he could find one that was unlocked he could creep in, spread out on the back seat, and get a few hours of warm and comfortable kip before the night was out. It seemed too audacious to be possible, and as he walked as innocently as he could amid the rows of parked cars he tested a door handle to find it was firmly locked. But even so, among all the hundreds, there must be one . . .

And then he came across a larger vehicle, not a people carrier but a minibus, that loomed above the estate cars, dark blue, and a little dusty. He walked up and peered in. Purple football shirts, a road atlas spread out on one seat, stacks of six packs on the floor at the back, a dangling Garfield. El Gordo, King Colesy, this was their vehicle, there was no mistake. And when Arnold tried the handle, it opened. Of course it did, for what did they care, that gang of friends, for their privacy or security? They had each other. They had always had each other, and their friendship already reached into the future, like a forward wake, stretching to the horizon. Even if they found him, they wouldn't care. They would laugh. Here's the man who never played the piano. Here's the man who lost the girl. They might jab him in the ribs, kick him in the arse. What else? They might let him tag along. They might make him an honorary member, if he told them he had nowhere else to go.

And so Arnold slunk into the stinking minibus, and burrowed down into the spare football shirts. He wrapped himself in them, for warmth. What name would they put on his, he wondered. What name?

The Dogs

The house was unusually full and all the chairs were used up. Sharon, Callum's second wife, insisted he use the last of the dining-room wheelbacks, saying she was quite happy to sit on the floor, and so the new family placed itself at the centre of the older one, Callum awkwardly positioned in front of the television, his wife and stepson on the oatmeal carpet next to him, blocking the tiny, but real, Christmas tree. The older family (Callum's mother, siblings and their partners and children), surrounded them on three sides, but did their best to make it seem as if they weren't trapped.

Callum himself didn't appear trapped at all. He was relaxed and chatty, a little sunburnt from a brief winter holiday just before Christmas, grateful for the upright-ness of his chair, which everyone understood was granted him on account of his weak back. Sharon, on the floor, must know about his weak back, they all thought, how could she not? But Sharon didn't look comfortable where she was, although the shape she made was a neat and elegant Z, propped up on one thin wrist. When, occasionally, she lifted this wrist, to part her hair or stroke her son, it was as though she was momentarily floating, and you wondered how she stayed up, but all the time she was on the carpet, the lowest of all of them, apart from the dogs, but they were shut in the kitchen.

Callum's mother kept up a tired strain of conversation. She'd been ill, and wanted people to know about her suffering. Afraid of seeming self-pitying, she spoke instead as if her illness had been something they'd all experienced – 'You know how it is in hospital, they try their hardest but in the end you're just a number to them – you're filling a bed and their main task is to empty that bed and let the next poor soul in . . . It's always the same with pain, isn't it? When it's there you can't imagine life without it . . .' By this means her suffering was shared equally among all the guests in the room.

Presents for the children, including Sharon's son Jordan, were given out, and were received with a certain amount of weary uninterest. The children realized they'd already had the best of their presents, and knew not to expect too much from this second round of gift-giving. After a flurry of unwrapping, the gifts themselves were examined with puzzlement, then put aside. The conversation resumed its gappy awkwardness.

'Christmas is for children,' said Callum's mother, as if to explain why there was nothing for the adults, and beamed a horrible smile all around her. 'It's not nice growing old.' She directed this remark, still with the same smile (as if to get the best value out of it), at one of her prettiest and quietest little nieces.

Someone broke into a long and detailed story about their car, how it had a life-threatening fault that three garages had failed to spot. He produced photographic evidence, flash photographs of the underneath of his car, which would mean nothing to anyone but a mechanic. Nevertheless they were passed around, and discussed, as if they were holiday snaps. During this story it could be seen how Sharon was grateful that the attention of the room was focused so clearly on a single thing, far removed from herself. Out of the spotlight it could be seen how her attention had wandered. She was able to discreetly rest her tired eyes. The stepson (and step-grandson, Callum's mother had mused, wondering if such a term existed), continued to look around him in a sense of frightened wonder, but then found an opportunity to talk about a little adventure he'd had, and then look shocked and delighted by how successfully he'd managed to hold the whole room's attention. He had brought laughter from everyone at all the right moments, he had recycled some overheard, mature-sounding phrases. Reassured that her son now seemed more at ease in the room, his mother thought that this would be a good time to go outside for a cigarette.

'You'll have to go out the front,' said Callum's mother, 'is that all right? You can't go out the back because the dogs are in the kitchen.'

The dogs had been a scratchy but invisible presence throughout the afternoon. They had just been walked around the estate and their paws were muddy. That's why they were locked in the kitchen. From the kitchen door there came the occasional urgent sniff, and desperate scraping of claws.

Sharon lifted herself gracefully from the floor and, holding her smoking paraphernalia in one hand, picked her way carefully across the room towards the door. This meant passing closely beside Callum's mother, who hadn't stirred from her electric armchair. She grabbed the young woman and pulled her down so that she could whisper loudly at her, 'I can't trust them yet, not with strangers,' she said. Sharon nodded, understandingly, as if her life was one long journey through a landscape of vicious dogs. Callum's mother went on, 'Give them a few more visits, they'll get used to the smell of you, even if they can't see you, and then they'll be less surprised when they meet you face to face. They'll be prepared, and so will you be.'

No one else could quite hear this conversation. Callum's mother had chosen her moment well, because there was a sudden surge in the ambient noise. Another anecdote had reached a triumphant conclusion. Released, Sharon left the room and went out of the front door, closing it behind her. Callum's mother laughed, knowing there was no way back in. She would have to ring the bell and draw the whole gathering's attention to herself once more. How little she would like that. Callum's mother had never seen anyone so uncomfortable.

Now she turned her attention to the step-grandson, alone on the floor. Suddenly an idea struck her.

'Jordan, would you like to try out my chair?'

Jordan evidently thought the offer rather baffling, because he looked at the old woman with a face slack with puzzlement. To explain herself, Callum's mother brandished the handset that controlled the chair. Seeing that he still didn't understand, she gave a demonstration, pressed a button on the control and, to Jordan's slowly dawning amazement, rose gently into the air.

For a moment it seemed an impossible event, some sort of elaborate trickery arranged purely for his entertainment. This strange and difficult old woman levitating, with that fierce grin on her face. He soon realized what was happening, that it was one of those chairs he had vaguely heard about that old people have when their knees or their hips or their ankles have gone. But he did wonder how far the chair would propel her. He could see now that the movement wasn't just upwards but forwards. Callum's mother was being levered by near-silent electricity into a standing position, and shortly managed the entire transition, from seated to standing, without having moved at all. As she became entirely vertical, and took her first steps away from the chair, Jordan felt as though she had been delivered to him in a tipper truck, like a heap of tarmac. The chair looked the same, thrust violently out of alignment from its former, normal position. It looked like a chair that had gone mad, that someone had thrown but which had frozen in mid-flight. It was as though time had stopped still.

'Don't worry,' Callum's mother called to Callum,

who was still in the resolutely static dining-room chair. He had paid no attention to the spectacle of his mother's chair in full flight. 'It's quite safe. Callum! I said no need to worry, it's quite safe!'

'What?' Callum said, having at last heard a little story to its conclusion. He seemed to treat the gathering as a more realistic form of telly. 'Oh. Good.'

He didn't know what she was talking about, and his mother knew it. She merely wanted to remind the entire room of those stories that were in the papers a few years ago, of little children who had died playing with these special chairs. They had trapped themselves in the mechanism underneath, and had been crushed, unable to switch off the chairs as they lowered. The idea had haunted Callum's mother for a long time, unable to stop herself imagining what those chairs had actually done to the children. When she realized she would need one herself, she had to fight through a series of horrifying visions of what could have happened to her own grandchildren if this had been a few years earlier.

'They have a failsafe fitted,' she said, 'a cut-off . . .' She baulked a little at the expression. The children who'd died under the chairs must have been very tiny. The metal struts underneath were just like scissor blades; powerful, relentless jaws. 'If there's any obstruction it immediately switches into reverse . . .' She thought back to the many times she had allowed her real grandchildren to play with the paraphernalia of her disability, watching them race merrily around the garden in her electric wheelchair.

They'd almost flattened her battery with a whole after-noon of circuits round the carp pond. How oblivious they had seemed to the nature of the vehicle they were riding. They had no notion that it represented, for their grandmother, a horrible harbinger of old age, a slow grey chariot that would take her to her grave. She thought that seeing it used as a plaything might help domesticate the machine, but instead it had just seemed macabre, as if they had been playing with crutches or artificial limbs. But what must they think? When the children arrived at their own old age, in that impossible-to-imagine distant future, and have their own wheelchairs, would they greet them like recovered toys from a half-forgotten past? Well, who knew what the world would be like then? Someone on the radio the other day was saying today's children had a good chance of living to two hundred or more. Eternal life, in all but name. Wheelchairs and Zimmer frames will only ever be playthings to them. And they will take it all in their complacent stride, never knowing any different. Living for ever will be just some-thing they shrug about, like everything else, not thinking about all those poor souls down the millennia who'd had barely a chance to live before their number came up.

Callum's mother wished she could live for ever, not because she didn't want to die, but because she wanted to see the faces on those two-hundred-year-olds when they realized what a mess their longevity had caused. Unimaginable horrors awaited them when the following generations came along to claim their dues. Compulsory euthanasia would become inevitable.

Callum's mother held out the control fob to Jordan.

'Would you like to try it out? Come on.'

She sensed that no child can resist the lure of a control panel, no matter what it operated. How they loved pressing buttons, she thought. And sure enough Jordan was up off his knees in a moment, and reaching for the switch.

'You climb in and I'll lower you, then you can have a go yourself. This button is for lowering the back, this is for raising the footrest . . .'

Jordan climbed into the chair.

It had amused no one (apart from the grandmother) when they had referred to it as an electric chair. 'You've got to see Grandma's new electric chair,' Callum had said when she'd first bought it. Did he even know what an electric chair was? Even the flashy bits of history were passing into oblivion.

'Up to go up, down to go down.'

Jordan pressed the required button and began descending in his grandmother's electric chair. He was uncertain about whether or not he should feel amused by the experience, because he was at the very edge of childhood. One more growth spurt would see him permanently out of its realm, until then he still had a vestige of childish innocence. But it was not enough to make him play in the chair. Once it had touched down he decided he'd had enough. He had been enjoying the attention of the adults in the room and he was not going to let it go now.

'Thanks, Grandma.'

'Don't you want to go up? Going up's more fun than going down.'

She couldn't understand why Jordan tittered at this, but then neither, she suspected, did he.

The front doorbell rang. Callum's mother was surprised by how this instantly brought the room to a hush, which only proved how light and fragile the conversation really was. Or maybe it was the reaction of the dogs, still cooped up in the kitchen, who met the doorbell with a volley of barks and growling, and more scraping of claws at the kitchen door.

'It'll be Sharon,' said Callum's mother, pleased at how Sharon's retreat into a smoker's moment apart had back-fired and made her the centre of attention. 'She must have let the front door click shut and locked herself out. Don't worry, I'll go, I'm standing up after all.' A couple of men who'd begun to lift themselves from their chairs returned to them when they saw the logic of the argument. Callum's mother was already at the living-room door and through to the hall, taking small, tired steps in her too-tight-seeming slippers.

Even through the warped and frosted glass of the front door, Sharon's silhouette looked sheepishly guilty. She opened the door and noted Sharon's look of startled surprise that it was she who'd had to manage to journey down the hall to let her in after her doorstep indulgence.

'Trying to give them up,' she said as she stepped in, waving away any last wisps of carbon, 'they're just too much hassle these days . . .'

'Everything's too much hassle when you get to my age,' replied Callum's mother through another broad smile.

'You didn't have to come to the door. Callum should have come.'

'Callum didn't even know you'd gone, dear.'

Sharon stopped halfway along the hall and turned to the older woman.

'Have we done anything to upset you, Maeve?'

'Of course not,' said Maeve, with real feeling, suddenly realizing she had gone too far and had become unsubtle.

'But we did mean to come on Christmas Day itself . . .'

'Don't even mention it. I had a lovely day with Brian and his family. Don't even talk about it. You know how much I love both of you . . .'

Suddenly she had Sharon between her arms and was hugging her tightly. The little thing was trying not to squirm, clutched to Maeve's broad and heavily shored bosom. All Maeve could see was her ponytail, hanging limp and golden. She stank of nicotine.

'Thanks,' said Sharon, released. Maeve was annoyed to see there wasn't a trace of moisture in her eyes. The dogs were still scraping at the kitchen door as they passed it into the living room.

'Jordan had a good turn in the electric chair,' she said,

as Sharon returned to her spot on the floor next to her son. But no one seemed to hear her.

Nothing was turning out as Maeve had imagined. The cigarette seemed to have actually done Sharon a lot of good, she seemed relaxed and happy down there on the carpet. If that's what fags can do for you, perhaps I should have taken up the habit myself, she thought. She'd never smoked because there had been no one to introduce her to the practice, and smoking, it seemed to her, was not something one ever chose to do. Everyone who smoked had to have a smoking mentor, someone who encouraged them and guided them through the ordeal of their first cigarette. No one would ever go through that out of choice. For most of her life she'd felt as though she'd had a lucky escape – but now it seemed the smokers were having long, happy lives.

She lowered herself into her chair, tired and defeated. She looked all around her, at the people in the chairs and on the floor, the tinsel sparkling on the tiny tree, the garish, scrolled origami of the stars that hung from the ceiling, and couldn't help but admire the determination of everyone in the room to be seasonably sociable. The laughter, the gaiety. There was nothing for it, she would have to set the dogs on them.

It was not that she wished to harm anyone, least of all her step-grandson or his mother, she just wanted to shake them up a little, remind them that life was not something to be taken for granted, to be sailed through without a thought for those who'd suffered in the past, and who continue to suffer, to make the journey so smooth. She would manage, by some contrivance or other, to get one of the party to go to the kitchen for her, an action that would inevitably lead to the release of the dogs. She really intended no harm upon anyone, least of all those on the floor, who would be on the same level as the dogs, whose silence was somehow more ominous now.

Maeve had seen a child attacked by a dog once. She must have been in her early twenties, the days when she could take walking for granted, with perhaps only the slightest twinge in her knees and ankles, so slight she could usually ignore it. She had been walking in the park when she had seen a commotion going on at the far end of an enormous lawn, a beige mastiff was throwing a doll into the air repeatedly, then shaking it, throwing it, shaking it. The screams of delight turned out to be the screams of a mother who was watching her infant child being savaged. It had all been too far away for Maeve to become involved. There was soon a large crowd about them, someone had separated the child from the dog, and was giving the dog a terrible hiding. Maeve walked on, barely breaking her pace, only glancing now and then at the terrible scene in the distance – a child near death, a mother in agony, a dog being whipped and kicked, its yelps of pain and fear sounding almost human. The experience had forced a series of nightmares upon her that had shaped her view of life more than she realized.

She made a straining and exaggerated effort to get out

of her chair, seemingly to have forgotten about the electric lift. Someone noticed her and asked if she needed help.

'I was just going to make a cup of tea,' she said to the helpful wife of someone. As planned, the helpful wife offered to do this for her, and took orders for drinks from everyone in the room – teas – coffees – white – black – with sugar – without – she made a little masque out of the whole thing with polished theatricality, playing the role of a flustered waitress, and then running off to the kitchen. A charming girl, thought Maeve, as the kitchen door opened, and she heard the yelp from the helpful wife as the dogs made their escape.

The dogs, it seemed, had lost all their energy, and came out of the kitchen at a sedate walking pace. They had also lost their size, or so it seemed to Maeve. During their confinement she had lost all sense of their proportion, and had thought of them, somehow, as giant hounds baying at their gate. This made their smallness quite shocking, as though a man had returned from the kitchen as a child. More puzzling was the effect they had on the room, bringing cries of delight and cooed greetings from all corners. The dogs wagged their silly stumpy tails, lifted their ears and did everything short of smiling. They approached the human part of the room, and by a strange metamorphic process, made it more human. They kissed the feet and knees of those on the floor, and arched their necks when hands were put to their woolly scalps. It was Sharon they were drawn to more than anyone else, as though sensing the traces of countless other dogs on her hands. They put out their mauve tongues as though savouring something wonderful on her skin. Sharon was now undeniably the centre of the room, along with Jordan. Maeve sat back in her electric chair and tried to understand the spectacle. Mother and child being made love to by her own dogs. It was as though some trick of perspective had rearranged the room, so that everything converged on them.

THE FACE

Everyone had their turn wearing the mask, though it hadn't been planned that way. At first it seemed there was a deep inhibition against wearing it at all, and no one was keen to be the first. Instead it was, once unwrapped, passed around, held at arm's length like something shockingly risqué or putrid, giggled at, shied away from. It was unfolded, held up, waved like a flag, stretched, examined, its eyes located and stared into. At last some-one was brave enough to put a hand inside to test the feel of its interior, to probe the volume within. None of the family had encountered an over-the-head, rubberoid mask of this sort before. It seemed too extravagant to be a mere novelty toy but must surely be something theat-rical, something rare and specialized, something they were rather lucky, privileged even, to have.

In the constant round of passing the mask, it became forgotten by most whose gift it was, or from whom. The younger children were urged to try it on first, and they proved to be surprisingly unwilling, seeming instinct-ively to resist the idea of enveloping their heads in something so quiveringly synthetic, and instead they

71

passed it from one to the other as though it was a time bomb, and this became, for a while, a game in itself.

The very youngest was the first to succumb, and he was almost too young for the mask to make any sense, for once he'd drawn it over his little blond head, it seemed not to belong to the body on which it was perched. But at least it could now be seen in all its three dimensions, and the mother couldn't help but draw a breath of shock at the chilling ugliness of the thing, even though she couldn't be sure what kind of animal it was meant to be. There was something crudely simian about it, though its prominent muzzle could also have been that of a bear, or some indeterminate hybrid, with a blend of sinisterly human qualities as well – it looked at times like a bad-tempered granddad, while its green pallor suggested something more other worldly, or mythical.

It was the oldest son who decided it was a gorilla. He had ambitions to study zoology at university, and so his declaration had some authority behind it, and the family were relieved that both his reputation as someone knowledgeable about animals and the identity of the mask were at once affirmed. It was a silverback of the Javanese mountains, he said, with a ridiculous specificity that no one challenged. The mother thought he could be right. There was something in the shape of the mask's head, its bulging crown and its thickening outwards towards the neck, that suggested the designer's intention to represent a particular species. But surely there was exaggeration there as well.

The children laughed at their littlest brother once he had donned the mask. Everyone laughed. The laughter gave the child/gorilla a new kind of life, and power, which he seized immediately in order to generate more laughter, rocking and turning and wagging his head. Seeing this power, the other children suddenly became eager for a turn in the mask, and were nearly pulling it off each other's heads in their hurry to be the next to wear it. The two girls were the first to begin acting out the role the mask gave them, making chimp noises, scratching their armpits, bouncing with both feet on the couch. Their mother had to tell them to behave, but already she was feeling a loosening of her control over her family, and a certain helplessness in the presence of the mask.

As the mask was passed up the family according to their age, it was noticeable how it changed character with the wearer, or rather its power over the wearer took different forms. As the wearers became older, the mask became less funny and more sinister, perhaps even frightening. When it came to the older brother's turn, he was the most inhibited. The mask didn't release him from himself, as it had the other children. When it was his turn, it seemed to freeze him. He stood up but remained still, or would just turn his head slowly from side to side. The younger children cowered on their couch, and the longer their older brother remained still, the more terrified they became, until the mother had to break the spell of her older son's ape-transformation, and demand her turn in the mask. The younger children were so surprised by their mother's decision to wear the mask that they gasped and clutched each other with excitement, as though a treat far beyond their expectations had been promised. And when, with some reluctance, her older son pulled the mask from his head (how red, shiny and dishevelled the mask had made him, as if he had been lightly simmered), there was an atmosphere of hushed awe as the mother pulled the now moist mask onto her head. The children pushed each other out of the way to get a better view, fascinated to see what the mask would do to their mother. Perhaps it was because she was wearing the pleated red dress at the time, and the long red shoes, and her thin gold necklaces, but the gorilla mask looked elegant and majestic. It was as though evolution had leapt forward a million years, and apes had gained dignity and wisdom in a single generation. It was not funny seeing their mother in a mask like that, it gave them more a sense of wonder, as though a new species had appeared in their midst.

Then, when the mask was passed on to the grandmother, another treat beyond the children's expectations, the mask became funny again. To see the glossy, assertive head balanced on the thin, weakly curved body of the elderly lady was irresistibly comic, especially when the wearing of the mask seemed to have no effect upon her, and she continued talking and using her old, reliable gestures just as if she was unmasked. She made it seem as if wearing a gorilla mask was a perfectly normal thing to do. She even made it seem as though being a half-human, half-gorilla was a normal thing.

The father was the only one not to try on the mask, even though the children went to great lengths to entreat him; he declined, and the sternness of his refusal suggested to everyone that he had a more visceral distaste for the process of mask-wearing. He had, it was well known, a fear of small, restricted spaces, and there was hardly a smaller, more restricted space than the mask.

It seemed that in the days and weeks after its arrival in the household, people wore the gorilla mask at first as a kind of performance for the other members of the family, then later in a more individual and casual way. The family might be sitting around in the living room and someone would notice the gorilla mask lying empty and half-folded on the coffee table, and then, almost without thinking, put it on and wear it for a little while. Then someone else in the room might look up from reading the newspaper and notice the mask, and start with a jump, and then laugh. And then that might prompt a session of mask-wearing among the children, as they tried to revive the novelty of the time when it first appeared, and had been so shocking. They were beginning to grow used to the mask, though if they tried hard enough they could still find it unnerving.

The eldest son was the first to try smoking with the mask on. This delighted the younger children, delighted them and horrified them at the same time, because as their eldest brother put the cigarette to his gorilla lips, they could see his tongue protrude, glistening pink through the opening of the mouth, to receive the cigarette. And the eldest daughter felt that the tongue couldn't be regarded as human, because in the zoo she had seen a real gorilla, and when it put its tongue out it seemed that a human being was inside the gorilla, poking its tongue out through the gorilla's mouth. Now, in the living room, she suddenly felt the reverse fear, that there was a gorilla inside the gorilla mask, poking its gorilla-tongue through the slit. She had to run from the room, and couldn't say why.

The experience of seeing the gorilla blow smoke through its rubber lips was a startling and strangely joyous one, giving the mask an even greater semblance of life, but it was a difficult operation to perform, and at his first attempt, the eldest son had to pull the mask from his head very quickly. Smoke had become trapped between the mask and his face, and had stung his eyes. To the observers, who saw smoke coming from the eyeholes as well as the mouth, it seemed as though their brother's head was on fire – more so when he pulled the mask off and released a general cloud of blue smoke. Now it seemed he had been more than simmered – he had been grilled.

There was a certain technique to smoking with the mask on, and the grandmother was the first to acquire it. It seemed to come quite naturally to her, and the children delighted in seeing her in her armchair, with her long cotton dress, her white stockings and slippers, with the ebony head of a gorilla, and more than that, a gorilla with a Player's No. 6 in its mouth. She would draw extra-heavily on the cigarette so that its tip would glow furiously, like something smithied in a forge, and the paper burn faster than the tobacco, so that long curls of paper-ash would fall off. And then she would release the quick mouthfuls of smoke which would pour from every orifice – her eyes seemed immune to the fumes – and it seemed as though the mask was boiling with rage, or about to explode.

Once, the mother sat at the upright piano and played an old swing number while wearing the gorilla mask. It was a difficult feat, because she couldn't play properly unless she could see her hands, and this was difficult through the small eyeholes – she had to lean forward and bend her head down so that she was looking directly down on her fingers a few inches away, which made her seem like an obsessively attentive animal musician, an over-cautious gorilla frightened of playing a wrong note.

When the eldest daughter began learning the violin, she couldn't resist attempting the same trick, and to her surprise found that her ugly, novice-scraping and screech-ing at the instrument became instantly more mellow and smoother when she wore the mask. It was because it made her more reliant on touch, her mother said.

The use of the gorilla mask ran its course. It began to lose its power to surprise and shock. By an unconscious process it was slowly moved through the house to areas less frequently visited. From its earlier positions of prominence on the kitchen dresser or living-room coffee table, it began to reside among the unloved things – the junk mail and bills in the hall, or the piles of free newspapers that accumulated on the worktop. Layers accumulated above it until it was swept up with a tide of other material and placed somewhere else, in a cupboard, or sorted out, chucked in a box, put under the stairs, waiting to be rediscovered, for something to be done with it.

And then someone might suddenly remember it, when there was a party or a family gathering in the garden during the summer – you must see this, one of the children got it for Christmas, have you seen them? They go right over the head, strangely realistic.

It became a family ritual that the mask was retrieved at Christmas and that someone would wear it during Christmas dinner, managing to get a paper crown to settle on the big blunt head, and even managing the feat of eating with the mask on, a more difficult task than smoking and, as the mother pointed out, a less hygienic one. Once when he began dribbling gravy and dropping stuffing, she implored her eldest son to take the mask off, her reason being that he was making a terrible mess, but in truth she was more horrified than she had thought she could be at the sight of the clumsy gorilla at the table, at his paralysed, helpless face, his greasy, stained chin –

could it really be her son inside, and not some gentle, mumbling brute of a stranger?

At a certain point during the summer holidays, when the weather was hot enough for everyone to be outside and the kitchen chairs were dragged out to the parched lawn, the paddling pool was patched and pumped up, and the children were splashing and playing with hosepipes, and the adults were sitting under the trees or reading in deckchairs or tending the roses, the gorilla mask would be brought out, and worn, in turn, as it had been last at Christmas, when they had played Monopoly around the big table. In their light summer clothes the children looked less disturbing and the mask was more obviously a mask, because it didn't match the reddening skin on the exposed arms and legs. There could be no doubt that these were human children cavorting with a rubberoid mask on their heads. The mask lost some of its powers because of this. It became harmless and helpless, a severed head that could do nothing but wobble and topple from body to body of the human family. Sometimes the children didn't even wear it, but treated it like a football, or Frisbee. Someone dipped it in the paddling pool and filled it with water, carried it, silver streaming from its eyeholes, to throw at someone else. It ended the afternoon draped on the top of the washing-line pole, like the head of a traitor.

——

The mother wondered when it was, exactly, that she began to dread the mask's reappearance after these seasonal absences. Perhaps three, perhaps four years after its arrival. She couldn't be sure. But now she found the laughter was being forced from her by a belligerent, demanding bully – the mask. When she was coaxed into wearing it, she did so grudgingly, and noticed that the children, although they demanded that she wear it, did not laugh at her when she did her usual fooling around. Instead they seemed merely satisfied that a ritual duty had been fulfilled, an obligation met, a sacrifice made. Apart from the father, there was no one in the family who did not take part in the mask-wearing sessions, from the youngest of the four children, up to the grandmother. One season they even put the mask on the cat. Though the mask was big enough to swallow the cat's entire body, it gave the mask a new kind of verve, revivified and reborn as it walked across the room, for only a few paces before the cat shook it off. To see the head march across the carpet with only the grey paws of the cat supporting it was a disjunction so great it seemed miraculous.

When the grandmother died, no one gave a thought to the mask. Her death was not a surprise because her health had been declining for many years, but her sudden absence from the community of the family created a different type of shock, one that was spatial and physically disruptive. It meant a room had to be emptied and

rearranged. The father and elder son disposed of the
room's single bed, carrying the stained divan down the
stairs with a certain clumsiness that seemed wilfully
disrespectful, to the mother at least. The chair she had
occupied in the kitchen was revealed, in her absence,
to be structurally defective beyond repair – it couldn't
have supported anyone but the grandmother's depleted
frame – and so that too was disposed of. It seemed, to
the mother, that her own mother's death had introduced
a bullying spectre into the household, who shifted and
pulled things about, who threw things against walls,
and knocked them against door frames. But in fact she
had very few thoughts – they had been replaced by a
river of feelings that allowed for no moments of reflection, or reasoning. The only way to temper these feelings
was through the shedding of tears. The youngest son, in
these grief-stricken weeks, found the mask, and put it on
so that his mother might be cheered up. She saw him and
was transfixed by his little presence, and by how vast
and complicated seemed the artificial head he wore. She
stared at him without thinking, taking in the spectacle of
the gorilla mask, and wondering about it. When he saw
that his mother was not going to laugh, or show any sign
of response to the mask, he took it off and offered it to
her to wear. She took the mask, which, having held its
form, now collapsed in her hands. Still without thinking,
she put it on. The interior of the mask was still warm
from her son, and damp with his breath. She could smell
her mother in there as well, and that made more tears

come. But she didn't take the mask off, because she didn't want her youngest son to see her crying, so she cried inside the mask, silently, until she had finished, and then she took the mask off.

The mask was worn very rarely after that. There was nothing new that could be done with it – smoking and eating through the mask were old tricks that no one cared to perform any more. Playing musical instruments, cooking, dancing, they had all been done before and had faded through repetition. The older brother did manage one last flourish with the mask, by turning it inside out and wearing it like that, with the gorilla facing inwards, and the inside surface of the mask facing outwards. The inner surface was shiny green, the folds and textures that gave form to the gorilla face here seeming like strange scars or the mottlings of a disease. It looked like no creature on Earth. Indeed the most frequent comment was that it looked like a Martian. For a little while this new incarnation of the mask inhabited the house, but it soon went the way of the others, and eventually the mask was completely forgotten about.

The family fell apart. The eldest daughter married, and the marriage turned bad. The father died of a heart attack at fifty-five. The eldest son killed himself by jumping from a cross-Channel ferry, only a week after graduating in zoology. The other children grew up and moved away, and eventually the mother was left on her own. Her health became poor. At seventy, she had to walk with a stick, and rarely left the house.

The tragedies that had fallen on her family were separated by many years, and had very different causes. It was as though something clumsy and uncontrollable had entered their lives, and had dispensed bad fortune indiscriminately and thoughtlessly. The weakness of her husband's heart had been a cold, black surprise to them all. The transformation of her daughter's husband from keen but untalented artist to violent alcoholic had been another. And then her son. Her son. Why did he do it? She never knew, nor could even think why. His had been the first tragedy, and the darkest, and the deepest.

Many, many years apart. But now, to the mother looking back, it seemed that they had happened all at once. From her perspective, decades compressed into days. And in this new light, it seemed to her that all these sorrows arrived in the wake of the gorilla mask. She thought this when she took out her daughter's wedding photograph, which she hadn't looked at for twenty years or more. Black and white, even though colour was well established by then. An array of faces, tiered and grinning. The bride and groom at the centre, unconventionally dressed in dark velvet, a look on their faces of defiance, as if to say they were getting married in spite of something. And around them, their family and friends, the groom's far outnumbering the bride's. She had never noticed it before, but then she did. If she looked closely,

she could see that someone in that crowd was wearing
the gorilla mask. He was half-obscured by the wild hair
of the person standing next to him, but the face was
unmistakable. Slack, frowning, indifferent. It made her
heart drain. She nearly fell to the floor. Was it her eldest
son? He was nowhere else in the picture. But not everyone in the family had gone. She couldn't remember now
who had gone and who hadn't. But someone had taken
the mask to the wedding, hid it in their pocket, and
taken it out and slipped it over their head just as the
photographer was bending down to take his shot.

She had all but forgotten about the gorilla mask until
this moment. Not for twenty or more years had she
given it a thought. But now its presence in her mind
was re-established, and she thought that it must still be
in the house somewhere. She had let things accumulate
since those times. Wherever the mask was, there would
be many layers of things on top of it by now. She was
suddenly panicked by this thought, and decided that
she must find it, and remove it. But she couldn't think
where to start. Her house was thick with matter. Things
were stacked on the floor, cupboards were overspilling.
She hadn't the strength to go through it all. She wondered if there was someone she could phone, but would
have felt ridiculous asking anyone to help her. She felt
the aftershock of discovering the presence of an intruder,
but one who had been there all along. Some bully, or
belligerent usurper, someone who took everything and
gave nothing back, some joker who thought the world

owed him everything. Someone like that was hiding somewhere in the house.

She had no alternative but to sit in her favourite chair, and wait for him to show his face.

THE FALL OF MR AND MRS NICHOLSON

On the twenty-sixth of January, at two o'clock in the afternoon, two men arrived at my house, with orders to take me to Mr and Mrs Nicholson. I had been working late the night before and had only just risen. I was still in my dressing gown and holding a tub of fish food in my hand when I opened the door. The men didn't show any sign of disapproval or even surprise. It seemed to be what they expected.

They were casually dressed. I guessed they were in their late forties. They had unshaven, baggy faces, and were both a little overweight. They were wearing sweat-shirts, jeans, mushroom-grey bomber jackets, filthy trainers. I told them they would have to wait until I got dressed, and they came in, without my invitation, as if to make sure I did get dressed.

'Do I have time for a shower?' I asked. The men shook their heads. I went to my bedroom and pulled fresh clothes over my sweaty skin. I felt very uncomfortable. When I returned to my living room I found the men examining my tropical fish tank. One of them was bending down to peer at the fish through the glass, the other was playfully dipping his finger into the water and swirling it around.

'Carmen might bite,' I said, half-jokingly. Carmen could bite, but with her soft little teeth she couldn't do much damage. The man withdrew his finger more sharply than he had intended, then tried to cover the embarrassment by using the same wet finger to beckon me towards the door. 'Do I need to take anything with me?' I asked. The men shook their heads. 'They have everything you need,' the shorter one said.

I had only met Mr and Mrs Nicholson once, and that was about ten years previously. They had been present-ing the prizes at an awards gala and I had been awarded the Nicholson Star for Short Stories. As was usual at these occasions, it was Mrs Nicholson who did the presenting, while Mr Nicholson made the speeches and read out the nominations. It was widely believed that Mr Nicholson read very little fiction, while Mrs Nichol-son was a keen reader of detective stories and symbolist poetry. At that particular ceremony she had clasped my hand and held my gaze with her blue eyes and smiled warmly as she handed me my certificate, speaking to me so quietly I could hardly hear her above the applause that filled the hall. 'Very well done,' she said, and repeated the phrase two or three times, until she had made sure I had heard it. She held on to my hand with such a firm grip I had to pull myself away from her. At one point her face was so close I could smell her breath. It smelt sweet and sugary, as though she had been eating a cake with lots of icing.

I didn't ask why Mr and Mrs Nicholson had sent for me. I knew that it would be pointless troubling the men who collected me with questions like that. They wouldn't even know, anyway. So I obediently followed them down the path to the street where their car was waiting, and where another man was at the wheel.

For most of the journey across the city there was little sign of unrest. Passing through the familiar districts we could see mothers and children playing in parks, people shopping, visiting the library, or using the swimming pool. At one of the police stations we passed there was a protest taking place, but the crowd was very small in number. None of us passed any comment on the spectacle, even though the sight was an unusual one.

Mr and Mrs Nicholson lived in a building known as the People's Palace, which had once been the city's main hospital, and overlooked the central square. A much larger hospital had been built in the Kleverdam District to replace it, and so no one minded about the change of use to which the old hospital had been put. In fact the people were rather proud of the new palace, and the term People's Palace was the informal name adopted by the general public. Its official designation was simply 1 Kleverdam Square.

Today the square itself was inaccessible due to the large crowds that had gathered there. I was quite taken by surprise by the number of people assembled, kept in

place by a thick cordon of police who maintained a
throughway for traffic to move between the square and
the parliament building. Nevertheless, it was not possible, for safety reasons, to use the palace's main entrance,
and instead we entered by one of the many back gates,
which had been heavily fortified.

There had been very little information about the
protest. There was nothing about it on the television or
in the newspapers. And as I had been out of the house
very rarely over the previous few weeks, I had heard very
little by way of gossip. So much so that at first I couldn't
be sure that the crowd gathered in the square was there
for reasons of celebration or protest. I wondered if I
had forgotten that it was Mr or Mrs Nicholson's birthday, or if there was some other important anniversary
to be celebrated. But a closer look at the crowds, as much
as I could see them from the darkened windows of our
vehicle, showed unhappy faces, and banners bearing
slogans of an anti-government flavour.

I had never been inside the People's Palace before, and
I was struck by the lavishness of the interior decoration,
and how this contrasted with the squared bleakness of
the outside. There were chandeliers of cascading crystal,
towering golden statues of working men and women,
mosaics of common folk as Titans and Olympians. There
were swirling carpets, exquisite tapestries filling walls as
big as tennis courts. The lifts were like jewelled caskets,
the floors were deep with soft woollen carpets. What had
been wards were now long rooms full of opulence, but

entirely empty of any sign of people or activity. One was described as the state reception room, and contained a single enormous table, but no chairs. Another was to house the Nicholsons' art collection, but so far the walls were empty. I was shocked at the general emptiness of the place, the wide unfurnished spaces, the tall empty vestibules over which Tiffany domes hung, casting their multi-coloured shadows on nothing. I had expected the bustle of ministers and civil servants conducting the business of state. I had expected a sense of urgency and energy. Instead it was as though the power had drained from the great machine of state, to leave the glamorous shell empty and devoid of function.

I was shown into a room before whose doors stood four armed guards. It was of a more plain design than the rest of the palace, being not much bigger than a respectable suburban living room, with a large desk, two sofas, a television, bookcases and conventionally patterned wallpaper.

There were several people in the room, including a military figure in full dress uniform, with a breastful of medals. There were some men in typical politician's suits, and a small group of media people, one with a small camera, another with a microphone. A large camera on a fixed stand was pointing towards the empty desk, behind which hung the national flag and a rather spindly araucaria. In the centre of all this was Mr Nicholson, wearing his overcoat, scarf and woolly hat, as though he had been out for a long walk in the cold. It was because,

I later learned, that he had just come in from the balcony, where he had been speaking for an hour and a half to the crowd in the square. That crowd could be heard through the tall curtained windows that gave on to the balcony, but which had been firmly closed since Mr Nicholson came in. He was sitting on a stiff-backed chair, one elbow resting on the back of the sofa against which he was positioned, and talking with one of the men in suits. The man in the suit was by far the more animated of the two, not to say agitated; he talked in a fast, pleading voice, bending down so that he could talk directly into Mr Nicholson's face. One got the impression he would have liked to have taken hold of Mr Nicholson by the shoulders and shaken him. Mr Nicholson, on the other hand, talked with a quiet but firm voice, as though explaining the uselessness of the other's point.

The two men who'd accompanied me drifted off into different parts of the room without giving me any indication of what I was supposed to do. People carried on with their business without taking any notice of me. One of the men sauntered over to the tall curtains and tentatively parted them, to peep out into the square. Even this tiny movement was spotted by the crowds, and a cry went up, then a chant whose words were impossible to make out. The other man went up to a bookcase and casually leafed through a leather-tooled volume. There was no sign of Mrs Nicholson. I decided to sit on one of the sofas, clearing a space for myself among the heap of newspapers that were spread out on it.

Eventually the conversation between Mr Nicholson and the man in the suit came to an end, and at that point the man at the bookcase indicated my presence to the old man with a jerk of the head. Mr Nicholson turned to me and gave me a long stare, but his expression was of a sort of tired indifference, as though I was just another thing he had to deal with. He gestured with a turn of the wrist that I should come over to him. He gave the impression of a man who was too tired to even stand up. So I went over to him and sat on another stiff-backed chair that one of the men put in position.

'You are the writer?' he said.

'Yes.'

'Good. I need you to write me something.'

'OK.'

'You are one of my wife's favourite writers. She advised me to call you in. She will be here in a minute.'

'What do you want me to write?'

Mr Nicholson looked puzzled. 'A speech.'

'I see.'

'What did you think you were going to write? A detective story? No, I need a speech. A good one. The best one I have ever made. I will be speaking from that balcony in one hour. The crowd outside are hostile. Ridiculous. I would call them barbarians but they are gaining influence. I have to do something to appease them. Just half an hour ago I made a speech promising a wage rise of twenty per cent. Across the board! They laughed at me. They jeered and booed. Barbarians. These are people who laugh at a wage rise. You see, then, what I need is a speech that will get to their hearts more than money can. You understand? And I need another speech for the television broadcast I will make one hour later.'

'Mr Nicholson, I have never written a political speech before.'

'So? My previous speechwriters have written hundreds, and they were still no good. You write stories to move people. That is what I need. What's the difference?'

I couldn't answer at first.

'It's a difference of genre, I suppose.'

'That sounds like prevarication. If you are a writer, you can write anything. All that matters is that you are good with words. Don't worry, I will give you a few facts I want you to include. My wife will be here in a minute. She will be better at explaining. She is a big admirer of your tales.'

I wondered if I had the option of refusing the commission. Mr Nicholson seemed to read my mind, because he said, 'You needn't think you have any choice in this matter. Now that you are here you are trapped, along with the rest of us. The only way out of here is by cutting a path through that crowd out there, and I would much rather do that with words than bullets. To put it quite simply, the future of our great country rests on the words you can produce in the next sixty minutes.'

'Fifty-five,' said the military man, who had shuffled over and was listening to our conversation. 'And the crowd is still growing. There are coaches arriving from every corner of the country. They are bringing people in on the backs of vegetable lorries.'

'Then the city must be sealed off. How many times have I told you?'

'We have road blocks on all the main roads. But what can they do if a lorry doesn't stop?'

'They can shoot the driver.'

'I confess some of the troops are reluctant to kill their own people in cold blood.'

'Then let them kill in hot blood. It is your job to produce fighting men.'

Just then Mrs Nicholson entered the room, and the atmosphere changed abruptly. She issued a long string of oaths, the colour and tone of which I had never heard coming from the lips of a woman before, nor the volume and pitch, which was attenuated and loud. She immediately began issuing commands and commentary, at such speed I was unable to follow what was happening. She beat her fists upon the decorated breast of the military man, and sent him from the room with orders to talk some sense into the army he was, supposedly, in charge of. Having voiced her anger and frustration, she then stalked about the room muttering and drawing her stole, a fine check-patterned piece of fabric, carefully about her. I felt as though I had intruded upon a private marital dispute, because she continually hurled comments and criticisms at Mr Nicholson, as though she was complaining about him not pulling his weight in the housework. Had he had a shed to retire to, I feel he would have done so at that moment, but husband and wife were trapped in the room, along with the rest of us.

It was some time before Mrs Nicholson noticed me. By then I had moved away from the part of the room occupied by her husband, and was standing by the desk near the window. Her demeanour seemed to change immediately, a warm smile bloomed on her face and she held out both arms as she came towards me. She took me by the shoulder and delivered her face to my lips to be lightly kissed, once on each cheek, and then once more on the left cheek. Three kisses was a sign of great affection and affinity.

'I am so glad you were able to come,' she said, as I blinked away the strong smell of eau de Cologne, 'we are in such desperate need of a good wordsmith. My husband has sacked all his speechwriters, and his advisers as well. Do you mind me using the term "wordsmith"?' I had hardly time to shake my head before she went on, 'I think it is a very dignified and noble term, for someone who fashions artefacts out of words, just as a blacksmith does with iron. You may take that analogy to heart. We need words as strong as iron to come from your pen. We want words that will rain down on the ears of the great public like bullets, like hammers.'

I began to wonder if either Mr or Mrs Nicholson were familiar with my work at all. What she demanded seemed the very opposite of my usual writing practice. I had never thought of words as hammers or bullets. I thought back to my quiet little stories, with their gentle metaphors and subtle (so I liked to believe) observations, and tried to imagine their words raining down from the sky like missiles. It was impossible. Mrs Nicholson seemed to detect my doubts. 'Is something the matter?'

'I was just wondering why you chose me, among the very many excellent writers who live in this city.'

This produced a look of charming imprecision on Mrs Nicholson's face, of the type that one never sees on leaders of any nations. I felt a sudden thrill of connectedness with the woman, an entwining intimacy so unexpected that I could hardly breathe for a few seconds. It was as though a painting in an art gallery had reached out and touched me.

'But your writing is of a very different order from that of anyone else. You have a very special power – to move people, to stir their passions, to persuade them of the truth of something. In your stories the worlds you have invented come to life with such persuasiveness, you can only feel, as a reader, that you have been there.'

I was distracted, momentarily, by what sounded like a burst of rifle fire outside, but which was quickly identified and dismissed as firecrackers.

'I think there are many writers who are like that. It is a basic requisite of the job.'

'No. You are very wrong. Some writers are full of wonderful ideas, but lack the skills to bring them to life in a believable way. But you – you can bring people and places to life as much as if they really existed. And that is what is lacking in the kinds of speeches that my poor husband had to deliver to the general public earlier today and yesterday. Long strings of facts and figures, but with nothing to persuade the audience of their truth. There was not even the slightest metaphorical tinge to them. They didn't even speak of the nation as their mother. Even the most basic political thinker should understand that the nation is their mother. Then they will realize – those people outside – that in directing their impatience towards the leadership of their country they are slapping their own mother in the face.'

I thought back to the stories I had written, and in particular the one for which I had been awarded the Nicholson Star. If Mrs Nicholson had read any of my stories, that would most likely be the one. 'The Button'. It was about a city that was terrorized by a giant button. Whenever there was some calamity in the city – whenever there was a fire or a street accident or a power failure or a riot or disturbance of any kind, a giant button could be seen running away from the scene, glimpsed down a side street, or on a bridge, or scampering along a concrete walkway, or disappearing into a pedestrian underpass. The button was a typical button, an archetypical button, you might say – round, brown, four-holed, the sort you see on a sturdy overcoat. The button had a pair of legs – so people reported – but descriptions of the legs differed from eyewitness to eyewitness – some said the legs were in trousers, some that they were in tights, some that they were bare. The city was driven mad over speculation as to who the button might be. There were suggestions that he was a rogue advertising mascot for a button or clothing manufacturer, who'd stolen his costume and gone out of control. But no such manufacturer could be found to account for the rogue button. Meanwhile there was speculation about what the button could mean, that it was the insignia of a revolutionary group, or an underground movement of some sort. In the newspapers there were long editorials on the symbolism of buttons – how they represented a coming together, the joining, the fastening of two halves. How did that work politically? Could it be a symbol of fascism, or communism, or anarchism?

'The Button'. It ends badly, that story, for the city. Struck by a plague of paranoia, both for what the button portends and for speculation as to its identity, the populace eventually consume themselves in a tide of slaughter and burning, until there is nothing left but ashes and blood. And a button, watching from the mountaintop overlooking the city.

As a story it was very unlike anything I had ever written before, or have since.

'There you are,' said Mrs Nicholson, pointing to the table, 'we have everything you need. You will write a speech for my husband at this table. Or if you prefer, you can sit on one of the couches. Or on the floor. I don't know how writers work. Would you like to use the colonel's laptop? I don't think he'll be needing it. Or do you like to work on paper?'

It seemed that I had forgotten how to write, or what

I needed in order to think of stories. Did I work on paper normally, at home? Or did I use a computer? Suddenly I thought of the fish. How long would I be here? Would I be back in time to give them their food? How long can a fish live without food? I once left them for a whole day without any food, and I have to say, they didn't look well.

I decided that I worked with pen and paper. A pad of paper was provided, but it was wide ruled, which I hate. And no margin. The pen was a good old-fashioned fountain pen which Mrs Nicholson fished out of Mr Nicholson's inner breast pocket, without Mr Nicholson seeming to notice.

'Astonishing isn't it, really? A pad of paper and a pen, and with that you can change the course of history. I suppose that is why you like being a writer really, isn't it? The power?'

I laughed inwardly again. Mrs Nicholson accusing me of having a hunger for power? This was a woman who had desired nothing else all of her adult life, and for a good part of that life she had wielded near-total power. No one knows how much influence she exerted over Mr Nicholson, although from what I could see in the room at this moment I felt the rumours to be confirmed, that she was the real power behind the throne, and that Mr Nicholson was nothing more than a cardboard president. She continued to work the room like a hostess at a cocktail party, though instead of idle chitchat she was dictating the orders of state and planning the future of our country, which would be determined in the next few hours. She moved from minister to minister discussing and planning, commanding and berating. I could see that everyone in the room was in awe of her, was even frightened of her. Of Mr Nicholson, there was nothing to note. He continued to sit in his chair with a glum look on his face. He rested his elbow on the chair back, just as if he was in the back room of a coffee shop discussing the racing form, having just lost a few pounds on a frisky nag. But he was passive. He had given up. He was letting everyone else do the work and the worrying, and he was going to do nothing but wait until someone had come up with a plan.

The blank paper stretched before me like a cement path. Rarely had a pen felt so heavy in my hand, or as blunt. Unused to my grip, its nib scratched and scored the paper, spluttered, juddered, nearly split. Blobs of ink fell and formed black abscesses on what few words I'd managed to write. I thought back to my story about the button and realized that I had written it without once attempting to understand or answer the questions it put into so many of my readers' minds. Who was the button? That simplest of questions. My readers thought there must have been clues as to who it was, and they searched everywhere for them. They wondered if the button was someone famous in the real world – some dared even suggest he was Mr Nicholson himself, or (given details about the slenderness of the button's legs) that he was Mrs Nicholson. Others that he was a figure from history, that he was Trotsky, or Christ, or Socrates, or Dante. Many candidates for the identity of the button were suggested, though I had never even given the matter any thought. I had not considered the question, because the identity of the button was as much a mystery to me as it was to the citizens of the little city in which he appears. And therein lay my problem with Mr Nicholson's speech. How was I, a writer of fiction, expected to bring forth facts into the world in such a way they could be believed, when my natural inclination is to pose questions?

I glanced over from my desk towards Mr and Mrs Nicholson, at the other end of the room. To my surprise they were drinking tea from delicate white china cups while perusing some documents. Mrs Nicholson noticed me and came over with a sheet of paper.

'How are you getting on?' Her face went stony when she saw the page I'd been working on, empty but for a few words and ink blots. 'Is this all you've done? Where's the rest of it? Do you realize if we don't have a speech in the next thirty minutes we will have no alternative but to order the army into the square? Here, perhaps this will help you.' She handed me a sheet on which there were lists of numbers, figures that showed how inflation had been brought down in a steady curve for the length of the Nicholsons' presidency; they showed also the figures for crime, which were as low. All the other measures – unemployment, obesity, divorce rates, all these had fallen steadily. The only things to have risen were longevity and incomes. And the projected figures were even healthier. Prosperity was rising steadily. Prices were coming down. Homes were being built all over the country. Very impressive figures. But of course they were rubbish. Had I not seen it for myself, I would never have believed it. The figures were simply plucked out of the air by Mr and Mrs Nicholson. I had seen them in the act, making up the numbers, jotting down whatever looked like a reasonable and believable number for whatever economic sector they were considering. It contradicted the evidence of one's eyes in the most striking way. I had seen the dole queues and the bread queues. I had seen the homeless people on the streets and I had seen how heartlessly they were dealt with by the authorities (high-pressure water hoses). I had seen the people driven out of their homes, which were then cleared away for some grandiose structure or other – the great stadia in which no sports are played, the empty-walled palaces of culture curated only by rats and small bears, libraries of empty shelves. And now I was being asked to write as though I had seen none of these things. I was not one to be disloyal to the Nicholsons, but I began to quaver at the thought of incorporating these spurious 'facts' into my speech.

'Can these figures be backed up?' I asked Mrs Nicholson.

'Of course they can. Why do you ask such a ridiculous question?'

'I just want to make sure.'

'But you are a writer of fiction. Why should you care?'

'I didn't think you wanted me to write a work of fiction. You wanted me to write a speech that had the power of fiction.'

'If you don't write something in the next twenty minutes you will lose the power to live, I can tell you that. Now just incorporate these facts without making the speech boring, and I think you will now need to work very fast, we want an hour's worth of words from you. Would you like an incentive?'

She glared at me in such a way that I felt my heart withdraw into a shell. When she left me I began writing, but I wrote as if I was writing the first draft of a piece of fiction – spontaneously and with little thought about what I was writing or where it was going. I free-ranged across what areas of my imagination had not been locked down with fright. At last the pages began to fill. The words came so quickly I was tripping over my own handwriting. My imagination was freed up by the fact that I began to sense that the speech I was writing would never be delivered. The crowd outside was now reaching a new pitch of volatility. The barricades between the square and the palace were beginning to crumble. The protesters spilled out beyond the square to fill the streets as far as could be seen. The whole city, it seemed, was becoming a site of protest. Mr Nicholson did nothing but sit with his head in his hands. The feeling was that it would be too dangerous for him to make a personal appearance on the balcony. Mrs Nicholson, who had been absent from the room for a few minutes, appeared with blood sprinkled across her face.

'On learning that the army is no longer taking orders from him, I have just personally executed the commander-in-chief of our armed forces.'

At this, Mr Nicholson lifted his head from his hands, but only in order that he could look at the ceiling in despair. Mrs Nicholson took a tissue out of her handbag and, using the glass over an eighteenth-century portrait that hung on one of the walls, dabbed at the blood on her face, having dampened the tissue with spit. From then on what little control I had over my life receded beyond reach. I was at the mercy of Mr and Mrs Nicholson and the small world that was left to them. Did they mean to utilize some sort of evacuation plan, and if so, would I be part of it? Or would I be left in the palace when the mob finally broke through – and what must I do then, hide in a cupboard, or pretend to be an innocent orderly, a cleaner or janitor or odd-job man? I was at the mercy of this late-middle-aged, childless, married couple. And it was against all reason that I felt a certain affection for them, even as Mrs Nicholson wiped the blood from her cheek. I realized I was watching a rare moment in history, the evaporation of the aura of power from a couple who had possessed it for most of their lives. The panic and despair and depression that the couple were exhibiting only served to render them more human. I heard Mr Nicholson suddenly blurt out – 'Forty per cent. If we cut defence, foreign aid, bureaucracy, sack the civil service except for the vital functions, we could make wage rises across the board of forty per cent. Tell your writer friend to tell them that.'

'You're dreaming,' Mrs Nicholson said. 'They don't care about their wages any more. They have been fed so many lies by our enemies they no longer believe anything we say to them. You, you – ' she pointed to the two men who had brought me – 'get everything ready, we need to go now.' The men looked troubled, doubtful, unsure of procedure. 'Well? Are you just going to stand there?'

The people in the room began getting ready. The film crew had begun filming the events as they were happening. Having removed the camera from its tripod where it had been carefully set up to film the broadcast that would now never be made, they pointed it at whoever was talking, and no one in the room seemed to mind, or notice. Gradually we began moving towards the main doors, shuffling together without any clear sense of purpose or where we were going. Once out of the doors and into the large concourse that led back towards the dome, two of the men in politician's suits suddenly began to run off in the opposite direction, without a word. 'Let them go,' said Mrs Nicholson, not that anyone was trying to stop them. Mr Nicholson didn't even seem to notice. 'And you,' she pointed to the camera crew, 'you can follow them. We don't want you.' The camera crew were slow to respond, and just pointed their camera at

Mrs Nicholson. She signalled to the bodyguards and they immediately pounced on the film crew, taking their camera and knocking the people to the ground, and giving them a severe beating. One of the men fiddled with the innards of the camera, and pulled its memory out, which he then bent in his teeth. Mrs Nicholson laughed. The crew were semi-conscious on the floor, their faces rapidly swelling with bruises, and coagulating blood. My bowels were chilled, as I wondered if I would be next in line for such treatment, but to my surprise I was ushered along with the dwindling party, along a narrow corridor to a service lift.

Then up several levels, the five of us, and out through cluttered corridors, up a narrow staircase and through some heavy doors, suddenly we were out in the open, among the house-sized air-conditioning vents and lift-shaft winding houses. Rounding a block we saw the helicopter, its rotors spinning at a steady rhythm. It looked pitifully small, hardly bigger than a model, I thought at first. The pilot was wearing headphones and reading a map. His face seemed to drop as he saw us approach. He shook his head and held up a hand, fingers spread, meaning there were too many of us. In the noise and the light breeze of the rotor blades I could not hear anything that was being said, but I got the gist of the conversation. The pilot was saying he didn't have enough fuel to take us very far, and that the fewer passengers he had to carry, the further the fuel would take them. The bodyguards suddenly ran off, and the pilot took off his headphones, as if he was about to join them, but Mr and Mrs Nicholson were already climbing into the helicopter. Mrs Nicholson physically restrained the pilot, by placing a firm hand on his shoulder. The pilot continued to shrug and shake his head. He was now saying that the flight would be too dangerous. If the Nicholsons had lost control of the army, it was likely the helicopter would get shot down by surface-to-air missiles. I don't know how it happened but suddenly I was in the helicopter as well. Mrs Nicholson had urged me in to join them, when I had had half a mind to join the bodyguards and take my chances with the crowds. But an unaccountable loyalty had sprung up in my feelings, and I felt duty-bound to stick with the Nicholsons, and see them safely out of the city. And perhaps it was my writer's curiosity that persuaded me to stay with them, to see where they had it in mind to go, to find out what sanctuary awaited them, to see what power looked like when it had lost all the instruments for the exercise of that power.

We lifted off, toppling sideways almost instantly, then lunging forward, clear of the rooftop. Suddenly the ground filled our forward vision, the streets which seemed like gorges cut through cement plains, flowing with rivers of people. It was true, a fact, that the whole city centre was now awash with protestors, the grievances of the people had become a viscous fluid filling every cranny of the capital, had not my heart already fallen through my body thanks to the clumsy aerobatics of our pilot I felt sure it would have lifted to see such a pure expression of popular will. The people had become an architectural phenomenon, filling the space between buildings. I glanced at Mrs Nicholson, who was sitting squashed up against me, and once the helicopter had achieved a more level flight position, I could see, reflected in the window (for she was turned away from me), a look of horror on her face – or was it wonder, awe, terror, as she contemplated the new physical form the city was taking. Mr Nicholson was sitting in the front seat, along-side the pilot, and I could not see any reflection of his face, though I could see his head shake despairingly from side to side, just as it had done for most of the afternoon. Otherwise he was frequently in close conversation with the pilot, who had repeatedly to shout things in his ear to be heard. He claimed, so I could only just make out, to be taking such a swinging, erratic course in order to dodge any possible strikes from the ground. We swooped low, then swung left and right. We felt almost as if he was trying to throw us out of the vehicle. Now Mrs Nichol-son was shouting at him. There were arguments over the flight plan and our final destination. Mrs Nicholson had found a map and was pointing out to the pilot where we should be going, and that we needed to swing round in a different direction. By now we were clear of the city and below us were ploughed fields and quadrilaterals of pine forest. So far the whole journey had been at less than a thousand feet and, most of the time, much lower. Our speed was slowing as well. Mrs Nicholson continually berated the pilot but he kept pointing to his fuel gauge, saying he was running low. They would not be able to get to the destination over the border into our neighbouring state.

In the end the helicopter was brought to land in a field of potatoes, about twenty miles from the city. By now Mrs Nicholson was screaming at the pilot, slapping him on the back of his head, while the pilot protested that it was not his fault that the helicopter didn't have enough fuel. 'I'll get you a car,' he said, 'I just need to get to the phone box. There's one in that layby. That's why I landed here, if you'll just let me.'

'We don't have time to stand in a potato field waiting for a driver, you fool. The army has been following us on the ground. They'll be upon us in five minutes. We have to commandeer a vehicle.'

By now all four of us were out of the helicopter and stumbling through the potatoes towards the nearby road, on which there was little traffic. While the pilot went over to the phone, one of those emergency phones for people whose vehicles have broken down, Mrs Nicholson stepped out into the road to flag down the solitary car that was heading towards us. She stood there, still in her well-to-do housewife's coat with her handbag dangling from her elbow, waving both arms frantically at the approaching car, an expensive-looking sedan, which, for a moment, seemed about to swerve around Mrs Nicholson, but screeched to a halt when she stepped sideways to counter the move. She signalled to us to follow her out into the road, for one of us to take her place while she talked to the driver. The driver, I could see, was a respectable, professional-looking man in his late fifties or sixties, in casual clothes. He looked severely panicked as we climbed into the car. I figured that he had had just been listening to the radio, and had heard about the helicopter on the roof of the palace, and now couldn't quite believe that this outlandish narration had come to life before his eyes. He had probably seen the helicopter itself as it came down.

'I am very sorry,' he said, 'but I cannot drive you anywhere.' His tone was deeply sincere. He may even have once been an ardent supporter of the Nicholsons. But now that they had been ousted, anyone seen to be helping them could find themselves in serious trouble. I too was beginning to realize this, and was spending all my time wondering when would be the right moment to make my escape.

We began moving, the driver, who turned out to be a doctor, hunched and petrified at the wheel, because Mrs Nicholson had produced, from her dainty white hand-bag, a dirty great revolver, and was pointing it shakily at the back of the doctor's head.

The helicopter pilot was nowhere to be seen when we drove off, so it was just me and the country doctor who formed the Nicholsons' entourage. Once we were going steadily Mrs Nicholson put down the gun and began consulting a road atlas that was on the parcel shelf. We were about a hundred and fifty miles from the sanctuary that had been set up for the Nicholsons, and we were all taking turns to try and read the map and figure out where we were and which way to go, when the doctor saw his chance, slammed the brakes on and fled from the car and into a wood by the side of the road. We were too thrown and confused by the sudden halt to make any attempt to chase the terrified doctor, whose departing cry was, 'I have a family! I have a family!' He had left the keys in the car. Mrs Nicholson turned to me and said, 'You drive.'

I wondered what would happen if I refused. Would Mrs Nicholson take her place at the wheel? Perhaps she couldn't drive. As for Mr Nicholson, he looked in no fit state to drive anything. She didn't point the gun at me when she asked me to drive, and I took a certain pride in that fact. I had won the Nicholsons' trust. They had no one else in the world. Everyone had abandoned them. This made them both heartbreakingly vulnerable and frighteningly dangerous. They could not be left alone, for they seemed to be people with no practical skills. They had been driven everywhere for most of their adult lives. They had lived like well-attended monarchs with every need met by their retinues. The only thing they possessed was the authority of command, the ability to compel and instil obedience, but now this was lost on everyone in the nation but me. As such, I felt an enormous responsibility to remain obedient, even though I would far sooner be among the revolutionaries who were presumably, at this very moment, dismantling the vestiges of the Nicholsons' regime, room by room. And so without a moment's hesitation I stepped around the car and took my place in the driver's seat. The doctor had left the keys in the ignition, though I could see there was very little fuel left. To avoid the military vehicles and road blocks we turned off onto country lanes that led into the mountains. We thought there might be a way of using very small roads to reach the border, avoiding the main centres of population and the freeways altogether – but the problem was the lack of fuel. After an hour or so in the mountains, we realized we would have to risk turning back towards the main road to find a petrol station.

And it was at such a petrol station that my journey with the Nicholsons ended. We had taken the precautions of concealment as we re-joined the freeway. Mrs Nicholson lay down on the back seat and covered herself with a blanket while Mr Nicholson decided to seclude himself in the boot, while I pulled into a garage and began to fill up. I don't know how it was that the military vehicles were so quickly upon us. Perhaps the doctor had got word to the army that his car had been taken by the Nicholsons, or perhaps the garage owner had thought there was something odd about the car, but while I was in the shop paying for my fuel the forecourt was suddenly alive with the roar of military engines, and an armoured car, a truck and two jeeps pulled in, soldiers in full armour poured out, and the car was surrounded. I watched from inside the shop as all this was happening. Mrs Nicholson was pulled from the car as if she was a hold-all, and thrown to the ground. She screamed with indignation. Mr Nicholson was quickly found in the boot, and likewise pulled out without any thought to his dignity or comfort. The two were then lifted to their feet and marched around the side of the petrol station, where there was a car wash. I cautiously began to leave the shop, anxious to see what would be done to the Nicholsons. I could not believe that they would be dealt with summarily, without trial or right of appeal, but I heard the shots even before I left the shop, a volley of bullets from several automatic weapons. I was frozen with fear and halted by the flower stand, just next to the night-service window. An acrid fog wafted from behind the building, and I made the corner just in time to see what had been done. Mr and Mrs Nicholson's bodies were lying on the cement at the entrance to the car wash. Mrs Nicholson was lying on her front, her arms spread, her handbag still round her forearm, and her coat spread open like a cape. Mr Nicholson was in an odd position, having first fallen to his knees, and then backwards, so that his lower legs were tucked beneath his body, and his abdomen was pushed up higher than his head. I could see his face had the same fed-up expression it had had all day, though the eyes were firmly closed. Both bodies were oozing little red rivulets. I heard a soldier making a joke about how they should put the bodies through the car wash. Another was carefully recording the scene on a video camera. There was debate about what to do with the bodies. Eventually they were lifted by their arms and legs, two soldiers at each end, and put in the back of a truck. Then the whole squad of vehicles roared into angry life, and with a multiple spewing of blue exhaust, was gone.

The soldiers had taken no interest in the car they had found the Nicholsons in, or who had been driving it. Perhaps they were just so thrilled at having found the pair that they had forgotten about it, or perhaps they thought it was irrelevant. I was no one to be bothered with. Who was I, after all? A writer of whimsical tales that had happened to attract the attention of the first lady of our great country. That had been awarded the Nicholson Star for the short story 'The Button'. I had thought about asking Mrs Nicholson why she had liked that story so much, but I had never got the opportunity. I had wondered if she had any thoughts on who the button was, or what he represented. And now I had lost that chance. One critic had thought the button represented a fascist organization, that it stood for the binding together of the people, just as the bundles of sticks had to the original fascisti. But now I believed that the button represented anarchy, chaos, undirected, unrestrained energy. How can a button, a thing that fastens and contains, represent such an idea? Well, because a button can be undone. A button can liberate as easily as it constrains. It can keep the world in check, or it can release the world to run unchecked.

Odd, how the same thing can be seen so differently. I took myself back to the car, after a little contemplation, in silence, of the bloodstains by the car wash. Perhaps it would be good to drive on to wherever the Nicholsons had been heading, over the border into the sanctuary of our neighbouring state. I could claim asylum, if need be.

And then I thought of the fish, unfed for a whole day, and I drove back to the city.

A Birthday Cockatrice

Carla and Daniel had cooked a cockatrice for their daughter Jodie's seventh birthday. Having divorced three years before (neither of them finding a new partner), they had decided to come together for this one purpose, although they had made it plain to their little girl that Mummy and Daddy would be together for one day only. When the party was over and all the children had gone home, Mummy and Jodie would be going back to their own house. Jodie, however, didn't seem convinced.

'No,' she said, quite matter-of-factly, 'we'll be staying with Daddy.'

Carla and Daniel exchanged baffled glances over the top of their daughter's golden head. Was it a mistake, after all, to cooperate like this, they wondered? Were they giving their child false hope?

The cockatrice had been Carla's mother's idea. Somehow she had managed to convince her daughter that a cockatrice was an indispensable part of any children's party.

'Don't you remember?' she'd said over the phone.

'Your face would light up, and all the other children's as well, when the cockatrice was brought to the table.'

Carla didn't remember, but as if under a spell she made the cockatrice, with Daniel's help, and on the phone almost constantly to her mother for instruction.

'You need to find a good butcher,' her mother had said, 'one who'll sell you a decent capon with the feet still attached.' Luckily there was such a butcher in the town. He also sold them a rabbit, and the capon's still-feathered wings.

At home, with the phone against one ear, Carla performed some difficult surgery. The rabbit had to be decapitated, then eviscerated, then halved, and the lower half of the body, its ribs cut and splayed, forced into the bowels of the capon, the ribs knitting together, the legs of the capon skewered and folded back, the hind legs of the rabbit broken and laid out flat, facing forwards.

The idea was to create the illusion of a four-legged animal with wings. The stitched-together hybrid was then simmered in an enormous pot for four hours (they had to buy the pot specially), and then was left to cool overnight in its own stock. Then it was roasted in the oven until evenly browned, cooled a second time, then glazed with gelatine, beef stock and vinegar.

'This had better be worth it,' Daniel said several times.

Carla made a head for the creature from a ping-pong ball and a toilet-roll tube. She phoned all the butchers to ask if they had coxcombs. They hadn't. She cut out a piece of scarlet leather from an old handbag instead.

An eagle-like beak was made from some gold foil from the neck of one of Daniel's beer bottles. Gold paint was found and the claws of the creature were gilded. The final touch, shortly before the party began, was to decorate the beast with strings of pearls and other jewellery, to affix the feathered wings, spread dramatically, and to place between its front feet a large golden egg.

'I can't help thinking the kiddies will find it a bit scary,' said Daniel, 'are you sure you used to have one at your parties?'

'Yes,' Carla lied, and not looking her ex-husband in the eye, 'we used to love them.'

Daniel looked at her doubtfully. He could tell she was lying. Recognizing her lying intonations had opened the first crack in the ramparts of their marriage, after all. Still, he had to admit they'd made something extraordinary with that cockatrice. It really did look like a four-legged winged creature, something that might have flown straight out of the Babylonian deserts to land in the middle of a twenty-first-century children's birthday party.

They stowed the cockatrice carefully in the unlit oven as the first children arrived.

Parents were soothingly reassured and sent on their way, leaving behind their slightly puzzled offspring. The children greeted the birthday girl as though they had never met before. Out of school, it seemed, and away from their familiar backdrops, they didn't quite know who they were.

Daniel imagined the house would instantly be filled with screaming and mayhem, but instead there was respectful silence, nervous pauses. He mustered them into the balloon-heavy living room for a game of pin-the-tail-on-the-donkey. They began to loosen up a little, though everything, at first, had to be carefully explained. They were behaving as though they were in school, putting their hands up, waiting for permission before doing anything.

'It's like they've never been to a party before,' said Carla, puzzled.

'Perhaps they should eat something, perhaps that will liven things up. Get some sugar inside them.'

It was hard work, but the children did begin behaving more like children eventually. Blind man's buff followed pin-the-tail-on-the-donkey, and then musical chairs, which proved very popular. At last the house was filled with laughter, and Daniel and Carla were relieved to feel that the party was turning into a success.

'Musical statues,' Carla announced to the puffing children, 'and then we can have some food.'

A small cheer went up. Carla watched as Daniel conducted the game of musical statues, hovering with his remote, waiting to surprise the children with silence, and then she went to the kitchen to set out the food. She removed foil and clingfilm from bowls of snacks, set up pots of breadsticks and colourful dips, all the while listening to the music in the other room stopping and starting, stopping and starting, little bursts of childish excitement punctuated by spells of rigid silence. It was so funny, and so sweet, to hear the sound of children having fun, especially when her own daughter was at the centre of it all. It only worried her a little that she really would think that having Mummy and Daddy working so seamlessly together meant that they were all going to get back together. How was she going to do it, at the end of the party, drag little Jodie away from the environs of all her happiness?

Carla tried to put such thoughts to the back of her mind as she removed the cockatrice from the cold oven where it had been kept. She wondered if she should ask for Daniel's help, but as he was busy with musical statues, she thought she should try on her own, lifting the heavy, garlanded tray with its decorated beast onto the centre of the table. Looking at the animal with its feathered wings and its coxcomb, its golden claws and its slightly menacing stare, she felt terribly pleased that they had taken the trouble to make the cockatrice, and could hardly wait to see the delight and wonder on the faces of the children as they came into the kitchen.

Carla noticed that the silence from the next room had gone on for longer than usual. Perhaps they had come to the end of their game of musical statues – but then why the continued silence? Surely there should be cheering, or laughter, or the stampeding of little feet. But there was nothing. She was just about to investigate when Daniel appeared, a troubled expression on his face.

'Something rather odd has happened,' he said.

Unable to explain what exactly, he asked Carla to follow him into the living room. The space here was so emphatically silent she was expecting to find it empty, and so was horrified to discover that it was full of children. They were spread out across the floor, frozen in the midst of dancing, just as they should be for a game of musical statues, yet she could tell instantly that they were not just standing as still as they could – they were actually motionless; not the slightest wobble or tremble or shaking from their young bodies. Not only that, but their clothes were still as well – a frock on one of the little girls, for instance, its hem billowing as the girl twirled, was frozen in mid-billow.

'What have you done to them, Daniel?' was Carla's first horrified utterance, as she walked among the frozen children, some smiling, some grimacing, some halfway through blinking, all captured as if in a photograph.

'Me? I haven't done anything. We were just playing musical statues when . . .'

'When what?'

'Well . . . I thought they were mucking around at first – but touch them . . .'

Cautiously Carla put a fingertip to a little girl's cheek. It was as cold and as hard as a piece of marble.

'They've turned into statues,' Daniel finished. 'They've actually turned into statues.'

It did seem that they were made of stone, coloured stone, perfectly matching the colours of real life, and finely chiselled, so that even individual hair strands were rendered. But when Carla tried to pick up one of the grinning little girls, she nearly broke her back. She was as heavy as an anvil.

'This isn't possible,' she said, 'it just isn't possible.'

'What'll we do?'

They considered all the possibilities – calling the police, calling an ambulance. What could doctors do with a bunch of statues – how do you treat stone?

'The mums and dads will be coming soon,' said Daniel desperately, 'how are we going to explain this little lot? *Yes, your daughter's ready to go home – do you have a wheelbarrow?*'

'They're so beautiful,' said Carla, looking into her own daughter's laughing face, 'they're even more beautiful than when they were real. If nothing else mattered, I would almost like to keep them like this.'

'Don't talk so stupidly. We've got to think of what to do.'

'Are they alive, or are they dead?' said Carla.

'I don't know. I don't know.'

'Movement is one of the definitions of life.'

'But why has it happened?'

As if experiencing a sudden revelation, Carla suddenly blurted out—

'The cockatrice!'

'What?'

'The cockatrice. It happened just as I was taking it out of the oven – they all went quiet the moment I took the cockatrice out of the oven.'

Thinking it ridiculous, but not being able to think of anything better, Daniel rushed next door to look at the cockatrice, which was still sitting resplendently on its platter in the centre of the table. He then rushed to his study and turned on the computer. Within a minute of searching he had come up with his answer.

'Oh my God, what have we made?' He read from the screen. 'According to Pliny's *Natural History* the cockatrice is a monster thought to be born of a cock's egg incubated by a snake. It has the ability to turn people to stone . . .'

'The ideal guest at a children's party. I'll kill my mother.'

'It can be killed by forcing it to look at its own reflection.'

'Kill it? It's not even alive. We spent all day boiling and roasting the bloody thing.'

It was Carla's own inkling that the only possible way of breaking the spell that the cockatrice had cast was to eat it, and Daniel agreed. They sat down at the table facing each other across the cockatrice, and they ate. Cautiously at first, because the creature with its dark glaze and glowering eyes didn't look very palatable, but it yielded, under the knife, surprisingly succulent slices of rich, dark meat. Daniel and Carla ate this meat with no accompaniment, not talking, and deafened by the silence of a dozen statues of dancing children in the next room. They ate slowly and seriously at first, holding their cutlery correctly. Soon they were eating more quickly, stabbing and hacking at the body of the cockatrice, and not using their plates at all. Then they abandoned their knives and forks altogether and began tearing the flesh off the bones, poking it into their mouths. Their cheeks bulged, their mouths overspilled, their chins became shiny with grease and saliva. There was a lot of meat, yet they couldn't stop eating. They couldn't afford to. When Carla showed signs of becoming full, Daniel helped her, feeding her with his own fingers, like a mother bird to her chick. They had to eat every last morsel, he told her, with a muffled voice. 'I can't do it, I can't do it,' cried Carla, spraying chewed cockatrice as she spoke. 'You can, darling,' Daniel replied, picking up the chewed meat and feeding it back to her. They were arm in arm now, feeding each other. And when the cockatrice was nothing but a pile of stripped bones, and Carla and Simon were fingering the last scraps of food into each other's mouths, there came from next door a tremendous crash, like a brick wall falling, which was followed immediately by shrieking, screaming laughter. The children came thundering into the kitchen. Still hot from dancing, they climbed onto chairs and they climbed onto Carla and Daniel, showering them with hugs and kisses.

'Thank you for such a wonderful party,' one of them said, 'we've had the best time ever.'

'I want to stay,' said a little girl, 'do we have to go home?'

'I don't want to go home,' said a little boy, 'I want to stay here for ever. For ever and ever and ever.'

The Unloved

It surprised everyone, not least her husband, when Williamina went to live in a house of her own. Gavin claimed not to know that she'd even bought a property, or had the money to buy one. In fact she'd been saving steadily for years, putting a little aside each month from her part-time job – she was an administrator at the university where her husband was a professor (though in a different department) – not with the intention of ever leaving her husband and setting up on her own, but because she was, as an intelligent, educated woman, concerned that she had no financial reserves of her own, and had been trained since an early age by her accountant father to be aware of the liberating power of money. Now, after nearly fifteen years, she had saved enough to put down a deposit on a small one-bedroomed terraced cottage on the edge of the town, with a view from the upstairs windows of open countryside.

Gavin seemed completely baffled by her departure. He arrived home one afternoon to find a small removal van filling the gravel drive. He had to park in the street and walk, squeezing between the van and the laurels.

Briefcase in one hand and jacket slung over his shoulder (his characteristic pose), he walked slowly around to the open back of the van, as though expecting the vehicle to explain itself, when Williamina emerged from the house with a typed sheet of paper, and a young, rather weedy-looking man in a baseball cap carrying a box.

'Oh, Gavin. You're home early.'

'What the hell's going on?'

'I'm moving out. I told you.'

'Told me? When did you tell me?'

'It doesn't matter. You weren't listening. And don't try and stop me.'

'Where are you going?'

'I'm moving out into a place of my own. I'm leaving you, Gavin. I'm sorry, but I've made up my mind.'

Gavin was embarrassed by the presence of the young removal man who, having dumped his box in the van, had returned and was lingering nearby, awaiting instructions. For this reason Gavin spoke quietly through clenched teeth. Williamina could hardly make out the words. 'What do you mean you've made up your mind? You can't just walk out.'

'I can, Gavin. I can do what I want.' She said this as she walked towards the removal man, and the pair of them suddenly looked busy and preoccupied. She was showing the young man an inventory, and checking off things in the van. Gavin peered in at the stacked contents. Not much stuff, but nevertheless, enough to start a new life with, he supposed. He noticed some paintings in their frames, their backs turned outwards. The mahogany tallboy that had been her grandmother's.

'Bill!' he suddenly called. 'Stop being stupid and talk to me.' He climbed up onto the ramp and crossed it, and grabbed his wife by the arm. 'Come on,' he said, 'stop this nonsense and tell me what's going on.'

'I've told you what's going on. And let go of me.'

'Why are you behaving like this? You're being childish. You need to explain yourself.'

'I've bought a house.'

'Bought a house? Don't be ridiculous.'

'I have. I told you.'

'You told me you were looking for a house.' So he admitted to having the recollection.

'And so I was. And now I've found one, and I've bought it.'

'But what for? I don't understand.'

'I've told you many times how I need somewhere of my own.'

She had, but he hadn't listened.

They talked in this way for a little while. He demanded to know her reason for leaving. She said if he needed to ask, then that was part of the problem. This infuriated him and he told her she was being unfair. But it was true that she had tried to explain her feelings many times. He no longer took any interest in things she said. Often he was so wrapped up in his research that when he came down from his study for dinner it was with a book in hand, reading as he walked. He would sit eating his dinner, the open book beside his plate. If she demanded his attention he placed a finger on the text to mark his place so that he could go back to it as soon as the interruption was over. If she remembered correctly, this is what happened when she first told him she was planning to move out. The finger on the text, though this time the slightly prolonged look of incomprehension, then the brief laugh through the nose before returning to his book. A laugh of disbelief. The professorial laugh. The sort of laugh one gives to a very poor joke. But she had done her duty in announcing her plans. If he didn't believe her, or didn't think she was serious, that was not her problem.

Now, with the physical apparatus of her departure filling the driveway and obstructing his passage into the house, he had to do more than give that brief, dismissive laugh. 'So you were just going to sneak off, disappear without a word?'

'Like I said, I told you I was moving out.'

'You didn't say it was today.'

'Because I didn't want any fuss.'

Gavin became angry in his usual quiet way, but the anger seemed to stem more from his sense of humiliation at being confronted with a scene beyond his control than with the imminent loss of his wife of thirty years. In the end he became sullen, sulky and indifferent. He walked into the house with a shrug, as if to say – *Go on then, leave me. See if I care.*

She wrote down her address and phone number on a piece of paper and left.

Once she had moved out there was no contact for a week, and then he phoned. He asked her if she had thought about the children. She said yes, she had discussed it with them, and they mostly agreed that she had done the right thing. This was not true, they had all thought she was mad, but she had, during many long telephone conversations, persuaded them that she was doing something that was necessary. She regretted how successfully she had put on a good front for the children all these years, acting out the part of the happy, contented wife and mother. Gavin said she had a responsibility towards them. She replied that all those sorts of responsibilities had ended now that they'd grown up and left home. She had stayed married and had maintained a happy demeanour solely for their benefit. Now that she had discharged her duties, she could think about herself. She could be selfish, she had earned that right. Her husband had never been good at talking about personal matters, now he was rendered as dumbly stupid as a baby. He could do nothing but make a sort of bubbling noise down the phone, interspersed with the one- or two-word beginnings of sentences that never got any further. 'I can't . . . You don't . . .'

The second phone call was more reasoned. He had had a chance to collect his thoughts and present an argument. He gave a speech, or rather a lecture. His position was that she still had a responsibility to the children, even if they had grown up and left home. They still needed to know that their mother was available, at home. She also had a responsibility to him, her husband. She couldn't just abandon him without good reason. Since she had adamantly stated there was no other man involved, and since she had also stated that she didn't think he, her husband, was having an affair, nor had done anything warranting such desertion – he had not physically abused her in any way – he could see no reason for her to leave him. If it was her own space she wanted, they had a five-bedroomed house. She could seal off part of it, convert it into a separate apartment, if she wanted. They could build a bungalow in the back garden if that was what she desired. She told him no, that was not what she desired.

Other phone calls came, each one trying a different tactic, presenting her with a different position. When those failed he fell back on pure emotion, pleading with her, begging her to come home. He couldn't cope. He had never cooked a meal in his life, now he was living on Chinese takeaways, Indian takeaways, fish and chips. He was putting on weight, getting unhealthy. He was drinking. He was arguing with people. He had had a dispute with their next-door neighbour, newly moved-in, about an overhanging tree. What right had he to come and complain about a tree that's been there for fifty years? He nearly punched the man.

He said it was unfair of her not to give him an explanation for her departure. She couldn't just leave him without saying why. It gave him no chance to make amends. How could he put things right if he didn't know what needed fixing? Her answer was always the same – if he didn't know why, then that was the problem.

'Oh, so it's all a puzzle, is it? It's a riddle I have to find the answer to?'

Then she heard he had been arrested. He had bought a chainsaw and had climbed over the garden fence and had started cutting down his neighbour's trees. He said it was in retaliation for the damage they'd done to his own tree, the overhanging one they'd complained about. He tried explaining on the phone. He'd been charged with criminal damage, had had to spend a night in the cells. He was fifty-two years old and had never been in trouble with the police in his life, not even a speeding ticket. Now, two months after his wife leaves him, he's up before the magistrates. Did she think there was a connection? I am going to pieces, woman. I can't function without you. It was true. Without her tempering presence, without the consolations of her body and without her skills of soothing and diplomacy, he had reverted to the behaviour of the caveman.

He had no skills at negotiating his way in the world, other than by shows of brute strength. Several times he had turned up unannounced at her new house, sometimes late at night. The primary reason, she assumed, was to catch her in the presence of the lover he so strongly believed she had. One night he had parked the car at the end of her road and sat there all night, waiting to spot this mysterious lover. She knew nothing about it, but a neighbour raised the alarm, unnerved by the man slumped asleep in his car. For a while she worried that this would become part of a pattern, that her husband would turn into a stalker, but gradually he seemed to accept that there was no one else involved in the relationship. He was then back to the problem of understanding why she had left at all. A five-bedroomed house with a quarter-acre of garden, and she had given it up for an old weaver's cottage on the outskirts of town. 'You must tell me,' he said, 'I have a right to know. Why have you done this to me? What grounds do you have for treating me so badly? Have I ever hit you? Have I ever had an affair? What is it?'

'Do I really have to spell it out to you, Gavin?'

'Yes, you do.'

She had given him long enough to find the answer, and he was never going to get it.

'I can sum it up in a single word,' she said to him, over the phone. He was silent, waiting for the word to arrive. She delivered it as plainly as she could. 'Neglect.'

She liked the usefulness of that word, the way it summed up everything that was wrong with her marriage in seven letters. She was not hated, or bullied, or physically abused. She was just neglected. She was not attended to. Listened to. Seen. She estimated that he had paid her no attention for at least twenty years. It was a fate she understood to be suffered by many faculty wives. When she met any, the conversation quickly turned into a kind of competition to see who was the most ignored by their husband. Horror story trumped horror story – the affairs with students, the missed anniversaries, the solitary birthdays – yet each retained a stubborn pride in their spouse's academic standing, able to recite their long lists of honours by heart. Williamina was the same, and could name every paper Gavin had published, every conference he'd been invited to, every award, grant and fellowship. In a way she felt entitled to a share of his honours, since she had devoted so much of her life to ensuring he attained them.

She had become invisible to her husband in all circumstances except sex. It astonished her that he had retained the same bullish lust for her that had been there since their teenage courtship days. In thirty years of marriage his appetite had only slightly diminished, and while she didn't exactly share the same appetite, and wouldn't miss it if her sex life suddenly ended (which it now had, of course), she had been an obliging, dutiful participant in all those years. The frequency had slowed down a little recently. They no longer had sex more than once in a day, and rarely on consecutive days. It was always initiated by him, and he never once seemed bothered by that fact. It always followed the same four-part routine (hand, oral, her on top, him on top). She would always begin the session wishing she could carry on reading her book, and end it in a state of surprised arousal, usually reaching orgasm. She would lie there for half an hour afterwards, with a feeling that she had become luminous. Her husband, within minutes of ejaculation, would be back in his study, his mind flushed and cleared by the exertions, and she might not hear from him again for several hours. Slowly her luminosity would decrease and the feeling of invisibility return.

He, on the other hand, had taken their successful and frequent lovemaking to be evidence of a solid marriage.

'Neglect? Are you serious?'

This time she was silent. Then he suddenly blurted out, 'After all the . . .' but checked himself just in time. He had been about to recite a list of expensive things he'd bought her, expensive places he'd taken her for dinner, the exotic holidays. The white mink coat he'd purchased for her in Rome. The anniversary dinner at the Manoir aux Quat'Saisons. But even he could see that she meant something other than the provision of material things. 'What would you have wanted me to do?' he said, after a long, thoughtful pause. She was ready for this, and came out with something she'd rehearsed in her mind.

'In the thirty years of our marriage, every single thing we have done, every holiday we've taken, every place we've visited, every restaurant we've gone to, every film we've seen, every TV programme we've watched, every house we've lived in, every car we've driven, every dog we've owned, every walk we've done, every topic we've discussed has been chosen by you. I have not chosen any of those things. If I ever suggest anything, it is ignored. It is only since I have moved out that you have shown the slightest interest in what I am thinking.'

'That's just not true, Bill.'

'It is. You have taken my meek acceptance of everything as agreement. My primary purpose in meekly accepting was to make you happy, and also because I knew that not accepting would have led to unbearable behaviour on your part, as I discovered from the two or three times I tried it.'

'But you loved our holidays. Are you saying you were putting it on, pretending to be happy?'

'I am not saying I was unhappy on those holidays, I'm just saying my wishes and desires have been ignored all through our marriage. I have never done anything I wanted to do.'

'But you never said . . . You never complained. How can I be blamed for something when it's never been pointed out to me that anything was wrong, and in fact the opposite was the case, that you went out of your way to pretend that everything was fine. You have never given me the chance of being any better than I am.'

'I have given you many chances, Gavin. So many, and you missed them all.'

He was silent for a long time before blurting, 'How can you have not liked our holidays? You loved the flowers. You always said you loved the flowers. Has it not occurred to you that I was collecting those flowers for you?'

She put the phone down.

Their holidays were decided and planned by him, and were tailored to meet his scientific interests. As one of the country's leading botanists, his plan was to document all the known species of alpine plants and to discover more. They had walked through some of the most beautiful landscapes in the world, first alone, then with young children on their backs, then in tow. The holidays were really extended research trips, the family following in the footsteps of the father.

They had ventured further and further each time, to the east and the Himalayas, to South America and the Andes. Their holidays became serious expeditions – camping on glaciers, walking narrow paths at the tops of ravines, driving jeeps through bandit country. She never questioned the reason for combining holidays with her husband's research needs, but when the children had grown up, she found herself without a real role on these expeditions. Before, her task had been to shepherd the children, keep them amused while her husband went into the inaccessible crannies of a mountain to look for a little plant. Then, without the children, she had taken to staying in the car, or the tent, and reading a book while her husband gathered his specimens. Later she developed an interest in painting, and would sometimes spend the time trying to capture the landscape in watercolour. He never showed any interest in those, and the one time she pressed him to make some sort of comment he said, 'You know, I've never understood the point of painting. Why create a smaller, less perfect version of what is already there?' And it was then that she realized she no longer had any sort of meaningful relationship with her husband.

There was a period of about two months when there was no contact between them at all. Each, it seemed, was testing the other's resolve to be apart. Gavin was wounded after exposing his feelings for her, to so little effect. She could have predicted that this would have resulted in a long silence. It ended finally when he called on her, in person, knocking on her front door.

It was the first time she had seen him in nearly four months and she was shocked. He had put on weight, and at the same time his skin had become baggier, more wrinkled. His beard, usually carefully trimmed, had become wild, and greyer, it seemed.

'What do you want?' she said.

'Just to see you,' he replied.

After a moment's thought, Williamina decided it would be OK to let him in. She stepped back and let him pass through into the living room. There was no hallway. Gavin stood in the centre of the little room, turning slowly to take everything in. He seemed pleased about something. Williamina realized what it was. He was pleased by the smallness of the house. When together they'd lived in a five-bedroomed suburban villa with a quarter-acre of garden, on her own all she could afford was this – one reception room four paces wide. A little yard out the back.

'This is ridiculous,' he said.

'If you're going to be insulting about my house you can leave straight away.'

She could see that he still couldn't understand it. He was wondering why she had gone to such lengths to create a personalized space when she could have done the same thing in any of the spare rooms they had now that the children had left home. She could also sense – even though he tried hard to conceal it – that he was moved by being within that personalized space. The things of her life on the walls and shelves, the books she owned looking very different in colour and shape from his books, which were thick, heavy scientific textbooks – the pictures, some of her old holiday paintings, and others she'd done since. For the first time ever, he showed interest in them. He perused the framed watercolours, trying his very hardest to show appreciation, which amounted to some nodding and humming. He was most attracted, of course, to some of the flower paintings she had done. He had never seen them before, she hadn't wanted to show him. She painted them when he was away from home, and hid them when he returned. He didn't own all the flowers of the world, after all. She would have painted flowers whether he was her husband or not.

'This painting is interesting,' he said, peering closely at one of her favourite close-up flower studies.

'You think so?'

'You appear to have painted *Lilium recursus*, which has six stamens. You've only done five.'

She asked him to leave and he did so.

}{

It was all women on her terrace, or so it seemed. There were just six houses in the row, and her immediate neighbours on either side were elderly women living alone. She had thought this a good thing at first, and foresaw no problems with elderly neighbours. But next door on the left, the old lady had a stairlift which was fixed to the party wall and sent a juddering bolt of grinding electrical noise through the house whenever she used it. And she seemed to use it nearly all the time. Williamina made a visit and took a gift with her, a bowl of plums from the espaliered tree that grew down the south-facing wall of her yard. A gift from one house to another, from one garden to another. Williamina, after having had very little contact with the elderly woman, was sure this gift would be the perfect overture of neighbourly friendship. But the elderly woman was not so easily won. She answered the door with the conveyed sense that it had been a towering effort of will to accomplish the task, peering cautiously out, bent double, and propped on a stick.

'Yes?' she said, in the brisk, impatient tone that is not

heard anywhere anymore except among ancient women of her type.

'I'm from next door,' said Williamina, suddenly feeling as though she was twelve years old.

'Yes, I know you are.'

'I've brought you these – from my garden.'

'What are they?'

'Plums.'

'I don't need plums, thank you. I've got plums of my own. I can have plums any time I like, I don't need your plums.'

And she shut the door.

She thought about trying the neighbour on the other side with the plums, but feared similar treatment. She tried to forgive the old woman because she was frail, confused, frightened, though in fact she believed she was none of these things, but that she was simply an unkind, small-minded woman who had taken a dislike to her, primarily because she was living on her own. Of course, the two elderly neighbours were living on their own as well, but their solitude was forced on them by widowhood. They had both outlived their husbands after long, solid marriages. Whereas she – she must have done something scandalous to move into a house on her own, at her age, who should still be in the full flow of her marriage. Such presumption – how did they know she wasn't also a widow? Well, it was the only thing she lacked, kindly neighbours, and she giggled at the wickedness of her thoughts that they would not be there for long.

No matter how mean and unfriendly they were to her, she had the advantage of years, and would outlive them by a long, long way. They would most likely be replaced by families with young children, and she looked forward to the background music of childish laughter and glee, some time in the future.

The widows were not unaware of the comings and goings of her husband, of their occasional raised voices, of his long car vigils outside her cottage – but there were other men as well, who provided fuel for their belief in her profound immorality. An old friend of her husband's had started calling – Ralph, another botanist, but one with a rather broader view of the world. She had always liked him – he was literary, cultured, aware of the arts in a way her husband was adamantly not. One day he telephoned her out of the blue.

'Ralph? How did you get this number?'

'You sent it to me. When you moved, you sent a little card with your new address and phone number on it.'

'Oh yes, I did do that. I remember now.'

'Do you mind me calling you?'

'No, not at all. What can I do for you?'

'Well, I just wondered if . . . You see, I've just bought a new car, and I'm driving around and around in it and I've got nowhere really to go. I just need to drive around and around in it so that I get used to it. And I found myself driving close to your new house . . .'

'Are you driving now, while you're talking to me?'

'Yes.'

'Do you realize you're breaking the law?'

Ralph laughed. 'In that case, all the better if I can stop and have a rest. Could I drop by? Would you mind?'

She said she didn't mind, and a few minutes later he pulled up in the little cul de sac outside her house.

She looked out of the window before he knocked and saw a large silver BMW, with an angry face. Ralph emerged. He looked older than she remembered, and realized she probably hadn't seen him for a couple of years, but in that time he had become a white-haired old professor, maintaining a youngness of demeanour about him by wearing a T-shirt with a slogan on it, and a New York Yankees baseball cap. He came in for tea. She asked him about Mary, his wife. He said they'd separated after thirty-five years of marriage. Williamina wondered if she should say, 'Snap!' But Ralph was keen to point out the coincidence.

'Perhaps there's something in the air, like in one of those Shakespeare comedies, when all the people who are betrothed to the wrong partners are separated and remarried to the people they were meant to be with all along.'

'Oh well, I'm certainly not getting remarried.'

She caught the inner twinge of disappointment on Ralph's face. It still had not occurred to her that he had come a-wooing.

'Really? No, of course, marriage is a bit of a thing . . .'

'I think we should both enjoy being single for a while at least. Don't you relish it? Being alone?'

'Yes,' he spoke hesitantly, 'of course. The freedom.'

He wanted to say, the freedom to start another relationship. 'At the same time, after so long, it does seem rather
strange. I think – there is something rather odd about it.'

She could see that he was struggling to say anything
to her – he had arrived bold and gallant, but had become childishly unconfident when alone with her. It
did not occur to Williamina that this man she'd known
as a friend for twenty years or more could harbour any
sexual longings for her.

'Why did you leave Gavin, if you don't mind my
asking,' he said, with such an innocent lack of tact she
could almost have answered him, but gathered herself
enough for a rebuttal.

'It's none of your damned business,' she said, brightly
and humorously.

'Of course not,' he replied, 'but it would be useful for
me to know if there was another man involved.'

'Useful?'

'Well, you know, it would enable me to take a step or
two back.'

'You mean you're here on the prowl?'

'Of course not. Look, I've just come here in a new
car, I don't know how to drive it yet, how to handle it,
and it crossed my mind that that was what my newly
single life is like – something I don't yet know how to
handle. When I realized you were single as well, I
thought perhaps we could have a talk about it, share
our experiences.'

'Well, that sounds very sweet. At the same time I

can't help thinking you've just brought that car over to impress me.'

'Well,' Ralph was affecting to be offended, 'if you think I am the sort of man who uses cars as some sort of display of male prowess, how can what I've said about my shortcomings as a driver square with that? To be honest I am frightened of the car. It's too powerful. I can't control it.'

'You need to tame it, break it in, like a wild stallion.'

'And I may not succeed. You should come out with me. Come for a drive in the car. Your presence will help soothe it.'

'After what you've just said about not being able to control it, I should fear for my life.'

'I was jesting. Of course I can control it, it's all just a question of feeling comfortable. At least come out and sit in it.'

'Why would I want to sit in your car?'

'It would make it nice for me. I've never owned a car like this before, Williamina. I've always owned used cars who've lost their edge, whose voomph has gone.'

'Like us?'

She went out to look at the car, more to get rid of him than anything. She was aware that she was being monitored from neighbouring windows. The car looked like a shark, its radiator grille like shining teeth. Its headlamps were rings of intense staring. But she refused to be seduced by the machine. Even as she looked in, she could see the seats still had their plastic showroom covers.

'It's got twenty-one miles on the clock,' said Ralph. He pressed his fob and the car seemed to give a yelp of pain, before yielding up its doorlocks. 'Get in.'

She thought – why not, and sat in the passenger seat, after Ralph had pulled the plastic cover off, which proved an awkward task, he had to use both hands to pull it up over the seat, and it snagged several times. Then he floundered for a solution as to what to do with it, for a moment it seemed the cover would scrunch up small enough to fit in the glove box, but it kept springing back into life, and becoming huge. In the end he threw it on the back seat, where it unfolded and sat, slumped, like a drunken second passenger.

Ralph started the engine.

'What are you doing?' Though even she, who had spent very little time in her life admiring cars, could appreciate the silky near-silence the engine produced. She was enchanted by the array of different-coloured lights that propagated in the smooth blackness of the dash. Soft notes were produced, nudging little sounds that warned of some very unlikely danger. Ralph reached over and pulled her seatbelt across and fastened it. The bleeping stopped. Williamina had expected a subtle groping, but he managed the manoeuvre without touching her at all.

'Are we going somewhere?'

'Just a little spin.'

'I don't remember agreeing to that.'

'I don't remember you objecting.'

'I don't remember you offering.'

'I didn't.' He was chuckling, and Williamina could see that he was thrilled with what he'd achieved. She'd been captured.

'I hope we're not going far, I've got to get back.' Despite herself, she was enjoying being whisked away like this. The car did have a sort of mysterious power of charm, but she was determined not to show this to Ralph.

'Oh, I'm sure you have lots of things you've got to do.'

'I have, actually.'

'Such as, anything I can help with?'

'No, and they're my business, nothing to do with you.'

The journey went on for longer than she felt comfortable with. When they started to leave the built-up areas altogether and began heading for open countryside she felt compelled to be firm and demand to be taken home.

'But there's this wonderful little pub I've found . . .'

'If you take me there I will cause such a scene the police will be called. You must take me home now, and I mean this minute. Stop the car and turn around now.'

He was a little shocked. She could see that he had meant no more than a harmless pub lunch and that she had probably overreacted, but she also saw that he was the sort of man who only responded to ultimatums. There was no point in going through the preceding levels. He did as he was told, turned the car around and drove her home. They were silent for most of the way. She could tell that he was stunned and lost for what to do, other than take her home. He had run out of every conversational parry he could think of. Glancing at him she wondered if he was tearful, and she thought that he was. As they neared her home he had nothing left to say for himself but offer an apology. She accepted it.

When she was out of the car he had one more go.

'Could I call you? We never had that talk.'

There was nothing she could have wanted less than to have to speak to him on the telephone, but she nodded anyway, and then went into the house aware, again, that she was being observed from all the other houses.

Ralph wasn't the only one. Men of a certain age were coming to life all around her. Half-forgotten acquaintances whom she had previously not dreamt would be interested in her suddenly made themselves known. Her vet, the man who had given her sickly spaniel a lethal injection four years ago, introduced himself in the supermarket. She had never seen her vet in a supermarket before, but then she was, since moving, using a new supermarket. Unwittingly, she had moved into her vet's home patch. Perhaps it was understandable then that he should strike up a conversation.

She found the vet attractive, and couldn't help being flattered by his interest, and amazed that he should remember her. She told him as much.

'Oh, I have a very good memory for . . . faces.' He

paused a beat, and had been about to say 'beautiful faces', or at least that's what she supposed, and she was very glad he hadn't played that card so early.

'Do you remember animals' faces too? Or does one Labrador look much like another?'

'Sometimes I'll see a dog in the street and recognize the dog, but I'll have forgotten the owner's face altogether.'

He was shopping with just a basket. Could he really be single, a man like him? In her world, such men were snapped up like two-for-one frozen peas – the analogy occurred to her because they met in the frozen aisle, a fact which she couldn't help finding a little embarrassing, why couldn't they have met at the delicatessen?

'Did you get another dog?' he went on.

'No. We only bought Bessie for the children – when they were little. Now that they're grown up we didn't feel the need for another one.'

She too was shopping with just a basket – frozen pizza, garlic bread, individual fruit tarts. She may as well have hung a sign around her neck.

'You don't miss having a pet at all?'

'No. Freedom. That's what I'm interested in at the moment. Having as few responsibilities as possible.'

He looked down at her half-empty basket. She looked at his. The metal wickerwork held meagre portions of their respective lives.

'What about company? Wouldn't you like a pet for company?'

'What makes you think I need company?' She said it in as theatrically affected and amused a way as she could, bending her knees, putting her hand to her chest, rolling her eyes.

'Well, I just wondered, you know.'

She made a mental note to do her shopping with a trolley from now on, no matter how little she was buying.

He asked her if he could call her, and to get rid of him she said yes. She wrote down her number for him, but at the last moment, transposed the final two digits. When she got home she regretted it, sitting by her silent telephone, and imagining the vet repeatedly calling the wrong number she'd given him, being baffled and wondering what had happened, never realizing that he was out by just two numbers. She wondered whose number she'd given him, and couldn't help but wonder at how delightful it would be if she had accidentally given him the number of her unkind, elderly neighbour.

Three days later she was startled to find that it was the vet's voice on the other end when she answered the phone.

'But how did you . . .' She suddenly realized she had incriminated herself by showing surprise. She should have been expecting his call.

'But you gave me your number, didn't you?'

'Yes, of course.'

'As a matter of fact you gave me the wrong number. But I figured you might have got it wrong because you've just moved house. So I tried out a few permutations, on the off chance. Swapped some digits around.'

He didn't tell her that he had methodically tried every permutation, and that he had made hundreds of calls, before landing on the right number. Nevertheless, she suspected he had.

'That was lucky. How stupid of me.'

He too had become gauche and clumsy when dealing with conversations beyond the opening parries. On the phone he seemed to have nothing to say, and to be waiting for her to offer him something but she held firm.

'I was just wondering,' he said, 'this sounds a little unexpected, I know, but I was wondering if you'd like to go out for dinner.'

She reluctantly agreed. He would pick her up from her house the following Friday. When she gave him the address he jokingly asked her if she was sure it was the right house number.

He arrived on time, in another impressive car, but with a similarly angry face. Once more she felt observed as the man with flowers escorted her from her front door down to the vehicle that sat tiger-like at the kerb. He took her to an Italian place she hadn't seen before. The safest of all possible food choices, she thought. But he was surprisingly awkward in the restaurant. He clearly didn't understand what some of the dishes were, and was too embarrassed to ask for elucidation, from either herself or the waiter. She sensed he took no pleasure in food, and she was surprised by how much this lowered him in her estimation. When he was able to give his full attention to it, her husband had eaten her meals with enjoyment and was always interested when she tried out something new on him. She suddenly realized how empty that part of his life must have suddenly become, when he lacked the ability to cook. He was always stocky, but he was always fit. Her vet looked thin, suddenly. Thin and pale. Hollow. She realized how much she would have to teach him – about food, art, books, music – before she could have anything to do with him. And he wouldn't be worth the effort. She had known that from their first meeting in the supermarket, and it was only confirmed during the meal at the Italian, when he proved so profoundly uninteresting. Perhaps I should just steer clear of scientists altogether, she thought.

The vet proved difficult to shake off. He wouldn't take the hints when she turned down his invitations without a good reason, nor of his unreturned calls. He was doggedly persistent and emotionally blind. When he did catch her on the phone he talked crossly, even when she made it plain that she didn't want the relationship to continue. 'You haven't given me a chance,' he would say, in an incredulous tone, 'how can you make a decision based on one meal? This is the rest of our lives we're talking about.'

It culminated with a doorstop confrontation. He called round one evening. She didn't let him in and couldn't contain her anger at being confronted in such a way. She threatened to call the police. They shouted at each other, then he became whiney and weepy and finally, he left. The very next day she got a letter through her door, unstamped and unfranked. She assumed it was from him, at first, until she noted the clumsiness of the handwriting, like a child's, but trying very hard to look adult, and the fact that her name wasn't on the envelope, but just the number of her house.

The letter was barely legible, the handwriting shaky, fussy and full of odd mannerisms, learnt decades ago and rigidly adhered to ever since. It was from the old lady next door.

> *To the woman at No. 4*
>
> *I have reported you to the council for noise disturbance. I have also reported you to the council for allowing your clematis to overgrow into my garden. I cannot be expected to prune back this plant, at my age, nor can I afford to employ someone else to do the same. And it is cutting out my light. I have taken legal advice and the responsibility is yours. You must cut back your clematis or face legal action. You will be receiving a letter from my solicitor detailing the same.*
>
> *Yours sincerely*
>
> *Geraldine Smethwick (No5)*

Just then, as if to give emphasis to the letter, a bolt of noise shook the house as Mrs Smethwick launched herself on her stairlift and worked her slow way upwards through the architecture of the cottages. It has begun, she thought. At the back of her mind she had been wondering when, precisely, the campaign to dislodge her from her haven might begin.

The letter from the solicitor did come. It was short and nasty, and made it plain that she had no alternative but to comply with their client's demand that she cut her clematis back. It gave her a date to fulfil this obligation, and stated that if she didn't, she would face prosecution. Her first inclination was to ignore it. The letter was full of legal bravado, but she suspected there was not much of a case, and that if she so wished, she could counter with a letter from her own solicitor (when she found one), and put up a lengthy fight that would be too much for Geraldine Smethwick. But at the same time she knew she would not have the heart to get into a long legal battle with her elderly neighbour. There was something distasteful in the mere thought of it. Much as she had come to loathe Mrs Smethwick, she found the only way of coping with her was to pretend she didn't exist – a hard thing to do when every day, several times a day, her stairlift pulsed through the walls like an engine of unforgetting, but she was even becoming used to that, in the same way people who live next to railway lines get used to the thundering express that passes every hour. But she did mention it to Gavin, in one of their phone conversations. He was outraged, and urged her to fight back. He, of course, had fallen foul of the laws regarding overhanging plantlife, and was still smarting from his spell in a police station as a result.

'Do you want me to help? I've got some experience of the legal side of disputes like this. I know a very good lawyer.'

'No, I can handle it myself.' She could sense that he had been waiting for a moment like this, the moment when her life as a single woman fell apart for the want of husbandly support. He was waiting for her to ask him to step in, take control of things. But then his kind of help was the last thing she needed, climbing over garden fences, getting himself arrested.

'You shouldn't let people take advantage of you.' (She almost laughed out loud at this.) 'This woman has got no right – that clematis must have been there for years, why does she suddenly demand that it be cut down?'

It was an odd request. The clematis grew on a trellis above the fence. Cutting it down would only make her and her neighbour more visible to each other. Mrs Smethwick professed to be a keen gardener and lover of all things floral. In the spring the clematis had swarmed with pale pink flowers as beautiful as anything she had ever seen in her life.

In the event, she left it until the last possible day before she went out into the back garden with secateurs and gardening gloves and began cutting, pulling, disen-tangling what must have been decades of growth. The clematis grew close to the house and through the trellis she could see, as the plant was slowly cut away, right into Mrs Smethwick's house. This was the view that had opened up to her, and would be available always. Was that what the old lady had really wanted? Well, now she had it. Exposure. Next door was as different from Williamina's house as it was possible to be. Whereas hers was tiles, bare, varnished wood, pottery and books, Mrs Smethwick was wall-to-wall carpet, plastic and glass. A disabled rail support was screwed to the back wall next to the step. Everything was beige within. There was no reading matter visible. And there was Mrs Smethwick, her back to the window, oblivious to the sacrifice Williamina was making, engrossed in the screen of her laptop. She was playing some sort of video game.

The culled clematis filled five plastic bin liners, and left a trail of snipped leaves and stalks that littered the garden for weeks. She could hardly bear to be in the garden now. When before it had felt secure and private and impregnable, now it seemed naked, raw and exposed. She could plant something else, she knew. Something evergreen that would hide Mrs Smethwick behind a thick but non-invasive layer of pine needles, but even so, she felt it would never have that magical quality it had once possessed, of being an island in which she was the sole inhabitant.

In spite of herself she did, very occasionally, miss a masculine presence. She would have liked a man to have dealt with the clematis just as, if she had kept chickens, she would have liked a man to have dealt with the wringing of their necks. They were useful for the delegation of unpleasant tasks. What she found most attractive in a man was his confidence and ability at such tasks. She couldn't abide squeamishness in a man, or lack of practical sense. She knew she would be better off falling in love with poets or artists, and they were attractive in some ways, but unless they could manage those physical tasks as well, they always ended up seeming to her rather pointless. It was not a quality she appreciated in herself, because she knew that the problem with her marriage had been just that lack of a creative, empathetic and thoughtful side to her husband. And she was so anxious about getting entangled with someone like that again that she thought it best to avoid men altogether.

The man who came to look at her boiler had nothing attractive about him at all. He was bald, small-eyed, nervously polite. It seemed he, like many tradesmen these days, had been rigorously schooled in political correctness, and was terrified, when alone with a female customer, of accidentally overstepping the bounds. A single complaint of sexual harassment could probably spell the end of his career. So they danced a cautious dance around each other. He politely refused her offer of tea, seeming as shocked at the offer as if she'd suddenly appeared in a negligee. He kept all conversation on a strictly business level, to the extent that she thought he must know about nothing other than boilers, that he had no life at all beyond central heating.

Yet when he left she felt the house had changed some-how. A layer of foreboding had been removed. The boiler – she had seen him strip it down to its intestinal innards – held fewer fears for her now. Whereas before it had been a machine of fearsome powers and difficult temperament, liable either to explode or cease function-ing altogether (nothing between those two extremes), now it seemed something that could be easily handled. The engineer had been so undaunted by the machine, had casually flipped the hinges she had been far too terrified even to touch, had talked about it with an easy, almost disrespectful, almost contemptuous tone – it was an old boiler, but could be good for another ten years, he said. She was rather disappointed when he used the neutral pronoun. Had they even been schooled so far as not to refer to boilers as 'she'?

She spent a while imagining that such a person, such an attitude, could be brought to bear on any type of problem – that he would have tackled the problem of her discontented neighbour with the same practical swagger, inspecting her inner workings, tapping her sadly on her rusted panelling and muttering something about her being on her last legs, but not to worry, she can be made safe.

She knew the effect wouldn't last long. The immediate afterglow, in which she felt she could happily apply a pair of pliers to a fuse box or gas fitting, would slowly fade and the machinery of the house would resume its quietly threatening mystique. In such moods she could feel amazed that her fridge, or her washing machine, so full of energy, so volatile, didn't just get up and bang its fists on its chest and rage about its unfair lot.

But the men hadn't finished with her. There was another visitor, one afternoon, a short slim man standing on the doorstep, her age, perhaps a little older, though in rather good nick, apart from a balding crown. The rest of his hair, and his closely trimmed beard, was a resolutely dark brown. Blue eyes, kindly and amusing, stared at her, begging recognition. It took her a few moments because she hadn't seen him for ten years or more, and then the hair had been full to the brow. It was Toby, her brother-in-law.

'I only just heard about you and Gavin,' he said, 'bit of a shock.'

'It wasn't a shock to me.'

She realized he was waiting to be invited in, and stepped aside to let him through.

'Hope I'm not disturbing you . . .'

His voice was quietly husky, as it had always been, very different from his brother's voice, but that, she supposed, was the point. They had always striven to be as different from each other as possible, in every possible way. Toby was artistic, gregarious, irreverent. She had always disliked him because of his casual swearing. She remembered actually telling him off once, when the children were small, about using expletives in front of them. How can he be Gavin's brother, she remembered wondering, when he is actually working class? It was true that Toby had a different accent from his brother. His husky voice was full of glottal stops and rather quaintly old-fashioned proletarian slang, a building-site vernacular that she supposed he must have picked up during a summer season working in such a job, and had felt so comfortable with he had spoken it ever since.

'I don't want to intrude . . . what a beautiful room.'

Of all the men who had visited, he was the first one to be complimentary about, or to even notice, the little house that she cherished so much. He inspected everything, stooping to read the titles of books on the bookshelves, scrutinizing her paintings and making little exclamations of delight. Automatically she went to the kitchen, which was barely separate from the living room, and began making tea.

'Really lovely little place you got here,' said Toby. He was wearing horrendous-looking shoes, big army boots that looked horribly sturdy. She had made a rule for herself that she would always remove her shoes at the door, and anyone else who came in other than for the briefest of visits would have to do the same. She longed for the boots to come off and stop indenting her carpet, but she couldn't help feeling it would be a risky manoeuvre, allowing him to be bootless in her house. She didn't entirely trust him.

'So what are you doing here, you just want to inspect my new house?'

'No, well . . . How long is it since we last met?'

'I can't remember. Not since the children were quite small.'

'I'm bloody ashamed of myself. What an uncle I turned out to be. How old is your youngest . . .' He evidently couldn't even remember their names.

'Jane is twenty-one.'

Toby sighed and shook his head. 'Last time I saw her . . .' He put out a hand to indicate how small she was, exaggerating grossly, because she was probably almost as tall as him, at eleven. This was another way in which he differed from Gavin, in height. 'They grow up so fast now, don't they? Ridiculous.'

'They just grow at the rate they've always grown. What you mean is, *how time flies.*'

'Yes, you're right. I'm talking in fucking clichés, as usual. It's the nerves.'

'Why are you nervous?' She did her best to ignore the expletive, handing him a mug of tea, which he seemed uninterested in.

'Well, after all this time, visiting you alone, not as my brother's wife but just as . . .' She had expected him to say 'a friend' or something equally bland, but instead he said 'a woman . . .', which gave the word an oddly threatening feel. The sentence remained unfinished.

'Have you seen Gavin?'

'Talked to him on the phone. In fact, he phoned me to try and solicit my advice, about what to do about you.'

'Oh, so that's why you're here. Trying to talk me round to going back to Gavin.'

'No, not at all.' Toby seemed to notice the tea in his hand for the first time, and looked at it with a puzzled frown on his face. 'Quite the opposite, actually.'

'What do you mean?'

'Well, for God's sake, Bill. Would it offend you if I said I've always wanted to fuck you, and now you've left Gavin, I think this is my best chance?'

Williamina was so shocked she couldn't speak. At first she thought it was one of his crude jokes. She knew how he talked about women. She'd once eavesdropped on a conversation at a party and had heard him passing judgement on various women of their acquaintance. He'd referred to her own sister – she recalled the exact words – as 'a serious piece of arse'. It had sickened her at the time, as much for the surprised tone of his voice, as for the colossal presumption of the man to feel he could pass judgement so definitively and casually. Then there was the vile synecdoche of the phrase he'd used, as though her sister was nothing more than a hunk of protein hanging on a butcher's hook. Her best response now should be to throw the tea in his face, curse his cheek for penetrating her house and making such a declaration and march him out there and then. But in the end the only response she could make, after what seemed like several minutes during which Toby waited patiently and hopefully for a response, was to laugh. It was a type of laugh she hadn't given in years, a laugh through half-closed lips, a spray of laughter, a rasping, incredulous laugh, the sort of laugh she used to give to her children when they said something absurd, it seemed to have a dissolving effect, rendering everything in its path inert, neutral.

'Toby, that is the funniest thing anyone has said to me since I left Gavin.' She could only just manage to get this sentence out between fits of laughter.

'I'm serious, Bill.'

'So am I!' And another stream of laughter came from her lips.

'I wanted to fuck you the first time I saw you. I wanted to fuck you at your wedding. I wanted to fuck you even when you were carrying your kids in your arms.'

She realized this was a kind of assault. By repeating the phrase, he was causing the image to form in her mind of her and Toby having sex. She realized now that laughter had been the worst possible response. He had taken encouragement from it, and his speech was delivered half-laughingly, and with a pixyish grin that formed pleasingly dark vertical lines in his cheeks. Not dimples exactly, more like gills. But she couldn't let him get away with it. She couldn't let him think that it was permissible for him to talk like that, so she slowly cut off the laughter, and shook her head incredulously.

'Well, Toby, I'm very disappointed in you.'

'You won't be, I can promise you.' He was still talking as though it was a big joke, as though they were at a party, or in a teenage disco, but they were in her quiet living room, empty of everyone apart from them.

'I think you'd better go now.'

'But I haven't finished my tea.' A look of mock surprise on his face.

'I'll finish it for you. Go now, I'm fed up with you.'

'I didn't mean to offend . . .'

'Of course you did.'

'No – you know. It's just how I talk. You know I'm harmless. All I want is a chat and a cup of tea.'

'Not today.' She had taken the tea out of his hands, feeling as though she was handling the situation rather well. Toby was harmless, but needed to be treated like a spoilt child – firmly but with good humour. He yielded the mug of tea without protest, and tried to put a brave face on the event of his being forcibly ejected from the house, if the delicate laying of Williamina's hand on his shoulder could be called force.

'I realize I've put my foot, or my mouth, right in it again,' he said, turning on the doorstep, 'my remarks were totally inappropriate. I'll make it up to you, I promise.'

She waved him off, closed the door and returned to the living room. She sat on the couch and burst into tears, and cried for about an hour.

What she had not expected, on leaving Gavin, was the sensation of loneliness. That was because she thought she already knew what it was, through her marriage. But this loneliness was different. The presence of another person in the house, no matter how distant one felt from them, was a form of companionship. But here, there was not even that token. Instead there were empty rooms, and hostile neighbours on the other side of the walls. She had no real friends, she realized. The people she had previously thought of as friends were people she only knew through her marriage, and were not people she could approach as a single woman, unless it was to ask for advice on how to retrieve that marriage. Other friendships had died. There were some old friends she saw once every few weeks, friends from her school days, but she didn't really like them, they were not confidantes or soul mates. No one she could open her heart to. Despite her loneliness now, she shrank from the very idea of contacting them, to have them offer their advice, to congratulate her. One of her friends, Mandy, had been divorced three times, each time with an increasingly lucrative settlement. She was quite open about her strategic approach to her relationships. She never expected any of her marriages to last a decade, and was quite adamant that she deserved a handsome payout for her troubles when the marriage was over. It had shocked Williamina. Mandy seemed to regard marriage as nothing more than a very long-term form of prostitution. And she had done very well out of it financially, living in a big house with its own long drive. She could imagine the looks of pity she would get if Mandy were to ever see the tiny workman's cottage she lived in now.

Her children were disappointing. She had had phone calls from both the girls, both very disapproving. Her youngest, Jane, had sobbed on the phone. 'Where am I supposed to go for Christmas?'

'Wherever you like,' Williamina had replied. She had meant it as a genuine offer of openness – she didn't mind if she went to her father's for Christmas, or her mother's, it was up to her. But Jane had taken it as a statement of indifference, as though her mother couldn't have cared less where her daughter went for Christmas. 'No, I didn't mean that, sweetheart. I meant I don't mind if you go to your father's or come here. I really don't.'

'Well, you should mind.'

'Well, come here then. But the trouble is . . .' How could she put it delicately. 'It's only a one-bedroomed house. I wouldn't be able to put you up.'

'Don't bother,' her daughter had said, and put the phone down.

She felt guilty after that. She should have thought of something more to offer her daughter – but what could she do? Put her up in a hotel? She thought about hiring a many-bedroomed cottage somewhere nice and having the children there, but it seemed pointless.

Her other daughter, Gillian, who was the oldest in the family, was less whiney. Her work as a lawyer meant she was very good at putting emotions to one side. It also meant she was very good at bossing people around.

'You need to think very carefully about where this is going, Mother. If you want a proper divorce settlement you might get nothing, on grounds of desertion, and you have no evidence of any mistreatment on Father's part.'

'You don't actually know what you're talking about, do you, Gillian? You're not a divorce lawyer, you've never been divorced.'

'Well, I think I'm a hell of a lot more knowledgeable about divorce law than you.'

'Anyway, I've never said I wanted to divorce your father.'

'Then what on earth are you doing?'

'I just wanted to live in a house of my own. That's all.'

'But you've got a house of your own.'

The children all loved the house they grew up in. When they phoned she wondered if it was the house they missed, rather than her. Or rather, that they regarded her as an integral part of the house, whose absence altered it irrevocably for the worse. In this case she was on the same level of existence, in their eyes, as an attractive chest of drawers, or a piano. They would get just as cross, just as upset, if a favourite piece of furniture was sold without their knowledge.

'I've been through all that with your father. Sharing a house isn't the same as having a house of your own, no matter how big it is. I have never had a place of my own in my whole life. I went straight from living with my parents to living with your father.'

Her son didn't even phone her. She had to phone him.

'Oh, I heard something about it. You've left Dad.'

Heard something about it, as though it was a vague piece of gossip. The apparent indifference was a great relief to her however, though she wondered if he was just putting on a show.

'I have left him.'

'Is it permanent, then?'

'Well, unless your father makes basic changes to his personality, but I don't think that's ever going to happen.'

'How do you know? And what sort of changes?'

'Well, you know, if he transformed himself, somehow, into a completely different person, almost the opposite of the sort of person he is now, then I might consider it.'

'I suppose that is asking a lot.'

'Yes, and he will realize, if he ever attempts it, that he can't keep it up, and that it wasn't worth the effort anyway.'

She realized she was talking to her son in a far more confiding and pleasurable way than she had with her daughters, with their cries of abandonment and their useless advice.

'David, promise me you will not use my marriage to your father as any kind of role model for your own relationships. You think you came from a stable home, but it was a stability that was dependent on one thing – me holding it together. There was never any love between your father and me. He thought he was in love with me but he didn't understand the meaning of the word . . .' She paused, thinking she might have taken the confiding too far, even for David. She had, because he changed the subject, and they spent the rest of the conversation talking about some trivial new aspect of his job.

Ralph phoned again.

'I was just wondering if you would let me make it up to you for getting things off on such a bad footing the other month.'

Williamina sighed. She was so bored by Ralph that the mere thought of refusing him made her feel tired. On the other hand, she was bored with her day when he phoned, and so she allowed him to come round in his car again, to take her to the pub he had intended they visit the last time.

He was very different. He seemed more confident, he could talk more fluently, and flowingly, but mostly about things that failed to interest her. He had got it into his head that they shared an interest in wildlife. It was true that Williamina loved birds and flowers, but Ralph seemed to treat the whole thing as some sort of competitive sport. When she remarked on the prettiness of a pied wagtail (pleased with herself that she could name it), Ralph responded with a list of wagtail sightings, facts about wagtail reproductivity, European varieties of the species that he had spotted as far east as the Carpathians. On a visit to Japan he had seen an emperor's wagtail, and so on and so on. Like her husband he had gone on long treks in search of wildlife, he had stood as still as a statue for seven hours for one glimpse of a rare species, only to have the creature devoured by a sparrowhawk before his eyes the moment it appeared. For her, being interested in nature meant sitting in a meadow with a good book and a bottle of wine, occasionally lifting one's eyes up to catch the colourful flitter of a butterfly. She couldn't understand this obsession with counting, documenting, recording, compiling. 'I love nature, but I don't really care about how it works,' she once said to Gavin, after he'd explained the elaborate pollination methods of some rare alpine plant. Now she wondered if there was some deficiency on her part, whether she lacked an essential curiosity.

They had a nice lunch, although she suspected her roast lamb wasn't as fresh as the pub proclaimed. It was just a dead sheep. Ralph behaved himself, and drove her back to her cottage afterwards. She didn't invite him in but there was a sudden awkwardness as they departed, an awkwardness which she felt she could only resolve by kissing him lightly on the cheek.

A few days later he phoned again. He wanted to tell her how much he had enjoyed their lunch, and he seemed anxious for her to express the same. She had enjoyed it, though she decided not to mention anything about the limpness of the meat. He ended the call with what she thought another odd request.

'You won't mention any of this to Gavin, will you?'

'Won't mention what to Gavin?'

'Anything about us.'

She took a moment to order her thoughts.

'What do you mean "us"?'

There was a quiet laugh at the other end of the phone, a knowing laugh, as though she was being deliberately obtuse.

'Well, you know what I mean, Bill. Gavin is still a colleague of mine.'

'Well, if I thought there was anything worth mentioning to him, I would take your request seriously, but as there isn't . . .'

'Bill, if Gavin finds out we've been . . .'

'Been what?'

'Seeing each other.'

'We haven't been seeing each other. You've taken me out to lunch once. That's it.'

'Well, twice – almost.'

'Once. The first time doesn't count, because you tried to kidnap me.'

'But I hope there will be other times, soon. Don't you?'

'Well, I'm not really sure, Ralph, to be honest. Since you've put me on the spot like this, forced my hand, as it were, I'll say it was very nice of you to take me to lunch last Thursday, but I'm in no hurry to have the experience repeated. You're talking as if we're in the middle of a full-blown affair. What's the matter with you?'

There was a short silence at the other end of the line.

'Well, I rather thought, after you'd, you know, when we said goodbye . . .'

The kiss, obviously, had been a mistake. Poor old Ralph, who probably hadn't been kissed by an attractive single woman for more years than he could remember. She remembered now the look in his eyes, the gratefulness, the shock, the relief.

'Please, Ralph. Don't think that by taking me out to lunch I'm duty bound to serve your every need . . .'

'But we're both living alone, for God's sake.'

'If living alone was the only criterion, I might as well be having an affair with my next-door neighbour, and she's in her eighties and uses a stairlift.'

She sometimes worried about the absence of sex in her life, not because she particularly missed the twice- or thrice-weekly assault on her body, but she wondered if there was something of a more chemical nature that she might be missing. She had, to think in her brother-in-law's crude terms, been fucked with an unfailing regularity for over thirty years. And she looked better than almost anyone she knew of a similar age. Her skin was almost wrinkle-free, her body still slim and firm in the right places, her hair still dark. She could easily pass for someone ten years younger, or even more. Could it be that that had something to do with the regular fucking? She thought this when she noticed some grey hairs on her head. Might there not be some truth in the idea that the sex act causes the body to release certain beneficial hormones, or other chemicals? That her body might be surging with oestrogen, or testosterone, or adrenaline, regularly oiled by those substances that keep all the parts of her working smoothly, and now, with the sudden absence of that stimulant, her body might be drying out as a result. There were lines appearing where there had been perfectly smooth skin before.

Unable to bear the thought of total isolation, she had done her best to get involved in local activities, to meet people in the area that surely must be more friendly than her widow neighbours. She tried various things – she went to an oil-painting class, a crochet class, she joined a local choir that was putting on a performance of *The Creation*. She had supposed she possessed some abilities in crafts, and that she would pick up the new skills rapidly, but crochet turned out to be horribly complicated, and her eyes were not as good as they'd been. To her dismay she discovered that she was one of the slowest in the class, and that many of her fellow students had already had some crochet experience. She felt foolish and gauche and older than her years. With so many grandmothers among her fellow students she felt as though she was being inducted into the sisterhood of the elderly. At the coffee break they chatted with her, the grey seniors. One of them, a stooped, blue-rinsed, ape-faced old dear, turned out to be only five years older than herself. Did she look as young to them, she wondered, as they looked old to her? Or did they see her as one of them? What difference is five years at this end of the lifespan? They remembered the same paraphernalia of childhood, the same political events, the same radio programmes. Oh it was disheartening. And then they asked her, as she had been asked before, as she was nearly always asked when in the company of her only-just-elders – 'Have you had it all taken away?'

At first the question had puzzled her. Have I had what taken away? Oh – you know – down there. They meant a hysterectomy. Not just that but the whole works – womb, fallopian tubes, ovaries, the entire reproductive kit, lifted out like a deflated balloon with attached streamers, as though the children's party in her body was now finally over, and the decorations were being put away for good. 'You know – pre-emptive move. Once it falls into disuse it can only get in the way of things, why hang on to it? Imagine getting ovarian cancer when you're eighty, what a pointless way to die.' She would no more think of having her womb cut out than she would consider having a lobotomy. But then it seemed that all the older women she met had had it all taken away – they were red and plump and glossy as a result, oh they were vivid and bouncy, these women, possessed of strength, savage. Beyond childbearing capacities the female body seems to realign itself, becoming shapeless and heavy. On these women's bodies there was no distinction between neck, breast, midriff and rump – all there was was a series of stacked volumes, amorphous, interchangeable. Their faces were fierce, creased. But somehow without emotion at the same time. They seemed to boil without getting hot. They had nothing to lose, these satisfied women, widowed or into their fourth decade of marriage, the world of courting, of dating, of mating rituals so distant they had literally forgotten about them, forgotten what it meant to flirt, to be attracted and attractive.

She found herself in friendship against her will with a sprightly, plump seventy-year old, one of the choir. She was of the glossy, roseate kind, bright blue eyes, hair that had been golden, and still had a vestige of its metallic hue, now subsumed by silver. She was over-complimentary. Everything Williamina did was praised by her.

'Oh, I don't know why I'm doing this,' Williamina said to her at one rehearsal break, 'I can't sing. I'm fooling myself.'

'But you have the voice of an angel, sweetheart,' said the woman. When she came close Williamina could actually feel the heat coming off her. She put a hand on Williamina's arm and squeezed it. They always sang together, standing side by side. Williamina had wondered about the prospect of meeting men, but she had forgotten how the sexes are separated in choirs, and all the men were sectioned off in another part of the church, their baritone voices booming and echoing from a distant transept. Instead, she was stuck with Audrey, as she was called, week after week. The choir was part of a community project to get ordinary people involved in classical music, and to make the music of Haydn available to the masses. They were to stage a public performance in the cathedral, and to everyone's surprise the choir was booked to do a small tour over the Christmas period, to some other towns and cities in the region. Williamina was beginning to lose interest by this time but she felt obliged to Audrey, who was so enthusiastic about the choir, and kept praising her. Williamina was angry with herself for feeling anxious about Audrey's friendship. She was sure that the woman was a lesbian, but she would talk endlessly about her children and her grandchildren, and her husband. Why has he never come to any of the rehearsals, Williamina wondered. Oh, he hates music. It is very sad when a human being can't appreciate music, but Nigel is tone deaf and always has been, always will be, a sad fact of life. So, she was a repressed lesbian, had spent her entire married life suppressing her desire, stifling it for the sake of her marriage and her children. When the time came for them to go to the other city to perform *The Creation*, Williamina was horrified when Audrey said they could go together in her car, could stay in the same hotel. She booked it all without even consulting Williamina. And she was still angry with herself for worrying about Audrey's sexual intentions. I can never be satisfied, she thought – I berate my neighbour for her hostility, and I berate Audrey for her friendliness – how can I be satisfied? Well, if only people would respect boundaries, that would be a start. She couldn't believe that Audrey would make any sort of physical pass at her, but she felt very uncomfortable when it came to them sharing a room.

'Would you like me to brush your hair for you?' said Audrey.

'No thank you,' said Williamina, a little too quickly.

'Oh, please. I would love to. I used to brush my sister's

hair when we were little. I thought I would be able to do it with my children, but what can I tell you – we had three boys. I love them dearly, but they never had hair that could be brushed, not the sort of long hair that you have. How do you keep it looking so beautiful?'

Williamina reluctantly allowed Audrey to brush her hair. As she did so, Audrey took care of it for her as though it was the most precious thing she had ever been given charge of. Electricity sparked in Williamina's mane. She was sitting before the dressing-table mirror, and could see Audrey reflected. Her face seemed as hard and as round as a Victorian doll's, and had a look on it she had not seen there before – a tinge of fear perhaps, and awe, as though she was in the presence of something godly. Then suddenly she stepped back, still holding the hairbrush at arm's length, and then parrying it like a dagger at her own reflection in the mirror. 'I think we should take up fencing,' she said.

Williamina for a moment wondered if she meant the type of fencing that involved hammering posts into the ground. 'Why would we do that?' she laughed.

'Well, it's a way of keeping fit and supple. I used to do it when I was at school. In fact I was the inter-schools champion for 1958. I've always wanted to take it up again but never seem to have found the time.'

'Oh, I think we are too old for that sort of thing.' Poor Audrey, bright and glossy though she may be, her body could not possibly survive being clad in a fencer's outfit, how ridiculous she would look, her bulk dressed out in white padding, she would look like the Michelin Man. But suddenly Audrey was all over the room, hopping and leaping with her hairbrush held forward, demonstrating the moves she remembered as a teenager. She gave a running commentary on what she was doing, and as she was wearing her nightgown by this time, her enormous tits were bouncing and swaying with great ungainliness, rolls of fat concertinaed, yet she hopped and parried, shaking the floor. In a few seconds she had worked up a sweat whose sharp perfume filled the room. Williamina, having turned to watch her friend, suddenly felt a great sadness weigh on her. Audrey was so profoundly imprisoned within herself; these little hops and leaps, they were nothing more than attempts to escape her own body, her own self, as though she could skip out of that heavy outer shell and emerge as something light and shimmery. Shortly she concluded her demonstration of fencing and returned to the dressing table. Williamina turned to the task of applying face cream while, to her dismay, Audrey resumed the pointless task of brushing Williamina's hair. Williamina moved her head around as much as possible, turning left and right, bending over, shifting from side to side, to show that she was not being accommodating to Audrey's attentions in any way.

Then she suddenly remembered an experience with her youngest daughter, who had suddenly, at the age of thirteen, expressed a fear of dying. Not a fear exactly, so much as a sense of disappointment, of irritation – she'd said the phrase 'I don't want to die' in the same way she might have said, 'I don't want to go to school.' And though the sentiment had grown out of a conversation about cosmology, about why and how the world had come into existence, about the Big Bang and why it had happened, and the acknowledgement of the transience of life had been dismissed by them both as nothing to worry about as it was so far off, and by that time they might have found a cure for all known diseases, including ageing, they felt an unacknowledged but profound fear that they could only assuage by singing nursery rhymes to each other. Her daughter by then was beyond the age of nursery rhymes, and they both had forgotten many of the words, but nevertheless they persisted in singing to themselves the half-forgotten rhymes, neither of them noticing any connection between the conversation about death and the singing of the rhymes – they sang the rhymes as though they were on to a new subject entirely, and that did indeed seem to dispel the fear of death. But when she thought back to it now, Williamina was saddened by the early arrival of the fear of mortality in her daughter's mind, but at the same time she was also rather impressed by it. It showed an early awareness of a complex kind of reality. Now, looking at the mirror, at the sight of round-faced, varnished Audrey, she feels like the child who has just discovered death. She feels she is about to be eaten. She feels over-simplified. And she can't quite believe it when Audrey, having treated her hair as though every single one of the hundred thousand follicles is a precious tree of gold, and having wrought a parting of the hairs in an almost perfectly straight line down the centre of her scalp, so that a strip of its whiteness was exposed, and after many murmurings of how she must dye it, it can't be quite so dark through any natural means, bends her face down, first as if to sniff it, which would have been quite bad enough, but then, to touch the naked scalp that shone in the division of her hair with her lips, to plant a kiss on the crown of her head – yes a kiss. A kiss. The touching of lips against skin (is that the definition of a kiss, Williamina found herself time to wonder, yes, surely just that, the pressing of lips against skin). She found the naked line of her head and kissed it. And it wouldn't have been quite so bad had Audrey simply kissed the thickest part of her hair, in which case the hair would have acted as a sort of shock absorber. No, it was far more significant that Audrey had created that line of nakedness in her hair, a line of cocaine, she suddenly thought, who had never seen a line of cocaine in her life, apart from that one time at a party in about 1979, the friend of Gavin's, the junior lecturer, at a time when most botanists were seen as having a specialist knowledge of drugs, since most drugs seemed to come from flowers of some sort. No, Audrey came at her like a good, queenly bee, a pollinator, stirring the follicles with her lips, right at the top of Williamina's being, the highest part of her, the crown of her head, not just her scalp but that precise square inch of it that was, when she was standing erect, furthest from the ground. Her summit. And the kiss sent a bolt of sensation through her, as though she'd been nailed from above, a single nail piercing the very tip of the skull and with a single blow sent right down to the toes. The kiss was like having a sudden weight placed on her head. She felt bowed under its mass. She felt her spine bend. But it was hideousness. It was wrongness. Williamina had never once entertained the thought of physical pleasure with another female, at least not since her school days, and she had long since consigned such memories to those which are never to be examined too closely again. And the kiss from Audrey was too long, as well. The lips in contact with bare, naked scalp for a horribly gluey moment . . .

Afterwards Audrey brushed the hair again, as though vigorously wiping out any trace of the kiss, and rearranging the pattern of her hair she was able to cover her traces. And as if realizing she had gone too far, she started talking about her children. Audrey's children were much older than Williamina's. Audrey was a grandmother, as Williamina had been told many times. She had three, including a set of twins. 'I feel it is slightly cheating to say I have three grandchildren, when two of them are twins. I have only had two deliveries of grandchildren, you might say. But that's the wonderful thing about twins, isn't it – my daughter-in-law said it – you get two for the price of one. One labour. One pregnancy. One round of morning sickness. But two babies.' Williamina was prompted to ask many questions about Audrey's grandchildren, and duly obliged, and Audrey duly elaborated on every aspect of her offspring's lives. It seemed to work, and Audrey's passions were put back in their place, and the rest of the weekend passed without any further embarrassments.

Back home Williamina spent long hours thinking of ways to escape the friendship with Audrey, but could think of nothing that would not lead to ugly scenes and difficult confrontations. Instead she resolved herself to endure Audrey's friendship, and her passions, for as long as it took for the passion to die away. She was convinced it was the wrong thing to do, and that she was only doing it out of cowardice. She couldn't bear to reject Audrey, or take any action that could be interpreted as rejection, even though, with every subsequent encounter, her discomfort increased.

But she berated herself that this was wrong, and it was exactly the same course of action that led to her being married to a man she didn't love for thirty years. Her capacity to put up with unhappiness was one of her strongest qualities, she decided. The patience to endure the boredom of marriage to someone with no inner life. For the sake of the children. Her ability to endure this kind of suffering was a virtue of some sort, and had given her strengths in other areas of her life – that was how she rationalized it to herself. But just occasionally the counterargument emerged, and she thought about how foolish she'd been, how weak, indecisive, cowardly. All of these were qualities that held her trapped in an unhappy marriage. But what about loyalty? Wasn't that another strength? Loyalty to her husband, her family. Had she knowingly thrown away that virtue?

He called one evening, livid and loud, bursting in through the front door as soon as she'd opened it.

'Right, where is he?' he shouted.

'Where's who?'

'Don't lie to me.'

'I'm not lying, I asked you a question, how can that be a lie?'

'Because you're pretending you don't know what I mean.'

He was showing her the face he hadn't shown her for nearly thirty years, the angry, raging, furious face. In the early days of their relationship he had shown her this face a few times. It was clearly something he'd developed as part of a male-dominated family, where the appearance of being in a white-knuckled, barely controlled physical rage was a very useful disciplinary tool. And she remembered, rather surprisingly, how she had been thrilled by that face. She didn't find it frightening, any more than she found the face of Joe Frazier frightening – she remembered those great boxing bouts of the seventies suddenly as things that defined a certain period of their lives, the nights they stayed up to watch boxing matches, a sport she'd never been interested in before or since, but for the life of Cassius Clay and the poetry it contained. She had thought about Gavin in those terms for a short while, as a gladiator, but without an opponent, as an athlete, but without an event to compete in, a warrior, a slayer. For a time it seemed the great American boxers bestrode the world, could lift it onto their shoulders, and it was always their shoulders that captured her attention, not their fists or those great cobbled torsos, but the shoulders, the broadness of them, the roll of them. That was how Gavin was posturing now, as he filled the house in search of an adversary.

'There's no one here, you fool,' she said, laughing. 'And who were you expecting to find?'

'Do you deny that you've been seeing Ralph Richards?'

'Ralph? Ralph? You know where he lives, why don't you go round there and ask him, instead of barging in here.'

'Well. Have you?'

'Not in the way you think . . .' She was about to go on to point out that he had been pestering her, but thought better of it, it might send Gavin off on some mad mission of retribution.

'What way, then?'

'I've seen him twice, the first time so that he could show me his new car, and the second to go to a pub for lunch. That was it. Not that it has anything to do with you, and look what you're doing to my carpet.'

He had left traces of black stuff, mulch or mud, on the white pile.

Suddenly, silently, he ran upstairs. Williamina followed him again, still laughing. 'Do you really expect to find him hiding up here? Are you going to check the wardrobes?' To her amazement, he did. She heard the wardrobe door being briskly opened, the metallic scrape of hangers being pushed aside. Then the door being slammed shut. 'And what would you do if you found him?' she said, as she joined him in the bedroom, where he stood, brooding. 'Just what would you do?'

He looked at her for a moment, trying to control his breathing, focusing his eyes hard, trying to redirect his energies. 'I would tear his head off,' he said quietly.

Ridiculous though the statement may have seemed, she could not say with confidence that he would not have done as he said, if such a thing was physically possible.

'I want you to leave now,' she said.

He walked past her, and would have knocked into her, she thought, had she had not stepped aside. He walked into her bathroom. She thought for a moment he was continuing his search, and she tried following him, but he shut the door behind him, and locked it. Shortly there was a sound of running water, and the house was full of the hum of the hot-water pipes. He was, it seemed, filling the bath. Suddenly worried that he was preparing for some act of self-harming, she knocked on the door. 'Gavin. Don't be silly. What are you doing in there?'

'I'm going to have a bath,' he called back through the door.

'A bath? Now?'

'I need one. I just do. I won't be long.'

She waited on the landing a while, as if to make sure,

by the sounds that were coming through the door, that he was doing as he said, and having a bath, and after a while she supposed that he was, she could hear the quiet splashing, the slow trickling and the periods of silence that characterized the sounds of someone bathing in a slow, relaxed way. There was one period of long silence which did prompt her to worry, in fact it went on for so long that she couldn't prevent herself from knocking on the door and calling through it, 'Are you all right in there?' Which caused the water to reply firstly with a loud splash and gush and then a rippling of liquid that she supposed was caused by a reposing body suddenly uprighting itself. 'Of course I'm all right – what are you doing standing outside the door, have you been there all this time, listening?'

'No, I haven't,' she lied, 'I just came up to check and couldn't hear anything.'

She could just make out a sigh of impatience coming from the bathroom, but otherwise he didn't reply, and she went slowly downstairs, remembering how Gavin used to take his baths, how he would wallow in the bathtub for what seemed hours, a damp flannel over his face, stretched out, submerged up to the neck, achieving a stillness you only normally see in cold-blooded creatures like lizards and newts, or in the insect world. It was the only time he ever properly relaxed, given that he was a restless, fitful sleeper.

Downstairs in the kitchen she wondered what to do, or even if there was a need for her to do anything. The silence from the bathroom was unnerving. Unwittingly it seemed she had allowed him into her life and he had arrived on a pretext of fury only to gain access to what could give him peace, her bath. She waited. Then after a long silence, there was the sound coming from the pipes again, this time of water pouring through the waste pipe, of the dirty bathwater collapsing down the thin drainage tubes and into the sewers. She peeped up the stairs from where there was a partial view of the bathroom door, which opened as she was watching, and her husband emerged, unaware that he was being observed. He was completely naked, though he was carrying a towel bunched in his hand. He walked across the landing and into her bedroom, and she had the briefest glimpse of his genitals, which were shrivelled and retracted, and then his buttocks as he turned, a shiny, ruddy glow in each one from where he'd been sitting in the bath. He looked surprisingly healthy. But what was he doing walking about naked in her house – she would have asked him this but didn't want to confront his nakedness full on. She wondered if he thought she was in her bedroom, and that he had gone in there in search of her. It was not unusual for him to walk naked in the old house when they were together, to dry himself off in the bedroom, and it would often lead to sex if she happened to be in the bedroom at the same time. Out of habit, it seemed, he was following the same routine, and had wandered into her bedroom to dry himself off and check out the possibility of a quick fuck, while he was clean. Cautiously she peeped again. He came out of the bedroom and went back into the bathroom, this time to get properly dressed.

When he came downstairs he seemed calmer, more composed and relaxed, but he was very quiet. He was always a quiet man, rarely speaking unless he had something important to say, he was not a man for small talk, never had been. At least when he was angry he was full of words, but in his calmness he resumed the familiar beetle-like silence.

'Do you want any tea?' said Williamina, feeling cornered into making the offer. In fact the thing she wanted more than anything was for him to leave immediately and without any further fuss. To her relief, he shook his head. But then he focused on her and said, 'You don't know what you've done to my heart.'

'You don't know what you've done to mine,' she replied, immediately.

'No, I'm not talking about love. I mean my heart, the physical thing. I get pains in my chest.'

'Do you?'

'Yes. They don't go away. An ache, right in the centre, behind the breastbone. And then pains in my arms. I can feel it now.'

'Well, you know what to do.'

'Oh, what'll the doctor do but tell me what I already know. I have a strong heart. I went for a check-up only last month. My arteries are good. But I lie in bed at night, and I can hear my heart beating, and feel this ache, and realize what a knot you've tied me in. I could go just like that.' He snapped his fingers, or tried to, the snap didn't quite come.

'We all could,' said Williamina.

'But I can feel it in my chest. I can feel how little there is that is keeping me alive – just the flow of liquid through some thin tubes, that's all it is. And that red liquid is what keeps the universe visible to me. Stop the flow, turn off the tap, and everything becomes darkness, for ever.'

They were silent for a moment, looking at each other, Williamina wondering where all this was leading.

'If you are trying to make me want to live with you again, you are going quite the wrong way about it. Do you think I want to spend my time listening to you worrying about your heart?'

He looked surprised at this, and then blushed. But it was a blush of anger. Williamina went on, 'You come round here, talking about decapitating people, you slosh around in the bath, probably playing with yourself at the same time, then talk about your heart like it's the centre of the universe . . .'

'Well, I might have known it would be a waste of time talking about hearts with you,' he suddenly snapped. She didn't say anything to stop him as he marched out of the cottage, slamming the door behind him. But after he'd gone she suddenly felt faint. The room spun gently, she had to sit down. And then she felt the same ache in her chest, almost as though a bone at the front of her ribcage had slipped out of place and was pressing on her heart. She felt she was going to die, that she was within minutes of it. She could just be sitting there on her little two-person sofa and she could just let the blackness envelop her. And how long before she would be found? It could be days. Days and days. And Gavin. What if he was to die when he got home, if his heart just suddenly gave out, how long before he would be found? Even longer, possibly. They would both be dead in their different houses, waiting for someone to find them.

LEGOLAND

I got the phone call about 4.30 on a Saturday. The well-spoken, hesitant voice threw me for a moment. It didn't sound like the usual cold caller.

'So sorry to disturb you. I am a consultant neurologist at Hill Hospital. We have a patient here who was brought in to us suffering from severe amnesia . . . Are you still there?'

'Yes, I'm here.'

'Well, this patient of ours, as I say, he is suffering from a very severe form of amnesia. He can't remember his name, or where he lives, or anything about himself at all. He has no means of identification: no wallet, driving licence, credit card, nothing. The only thing that has been found on him is a playing card on which is written your name and telephone number. So I am phoning to ask you if you can help identify him.'

This was quite a lot of information to take in, and I asked the consultant neurologist to go through it again. He did so, providing a little extra detail. The patient he was talking about had been found wandering along the hard shoulder of the M3 just outside London. The man had, apparently, seen a sign for Legoland and, intrigued by the name but having no idea what it was, had decided to go there and find out. The playing card puzzled me. Was my name and number written on the back or front of the playing card? On the front, I was told. And what card was it? It was the three of hearts.

'Could you describe the man?'

'Yes, he is five foot eight, medium build. I'd say he is in his early thirties. Brown eyes. Short brown hair. No particular distinguishing features, though I would say . . .' here the consultant gave a short pause and a half laugh, 'I would say he is a rather handsome chap . . .'

Most of my friends, when I came to think about it, were pretty good looking.

'It doesn't ring any bells,' I said.

'Perhaps you'd like to speak to him?'

This threw me again.

'What, right now you mean?'

'Yes.'

'You mean you've got him there sitting next to you, all this time while we've been talking about him?'

'Yes, he's been following the conversation with interest. I'll hand you over.'

There was a moment of telephonic fumbling; the dry, crisp breathing of the consultant was replaced by the shallow gasping of another man. I could hear a tremor in his breath even before he spoke, and I was expecting a rough, croaky voice to emerge, but instead it was soft, clean and polite.

'Hi,' it said, in an empty sort of way. There was no warmth at all in the voice. No sense of expectation either. It was like he didn't think I would bother to reply. As if he'd sent his greeting out into the void.

'Hi,' I replied. Then, sensing that it was up to me to carry on the conversation, 'So . . . we might know each other?'

'Yeah. I had your number on me.'

'Right. On a playing card.'

'Yeah. Three of hearts.'

'You play cards much?'

'I don't know. You?'

'I've never played cards, not since I was a kid.'

There was a pause.

'So you've lost your memory,' I said.

'I suppose so.'

'That must feel pretty strange.'

'It feels weird.'

'You don't know where you live, what your name is . . .'

'They say I've got a London accent, but that can cover quite an area beyond London these days, so I'm told. You've got a London accent as well . . .'

'Your voice, it doesn't sound familiar at all, but I suppose if you've got my name and number we must have met at some point . . .'

'What sort of places do you go to?'

I tried to explain how many people I meet face to face in an average week – the stream of people who pass through the office, the people I meet in the pub every lunchtime (mineral water for me, usually), or in the cafe after work, the people I meet on the train to and from work, the people I play football with on Wednesday evenings . . . It must run into thousands. I give out my number sometimes, if there's a useful contact to be made, or a potential client. But I don't usually give out my home phone number. That was odd.

'You haven't lost a brother recently,' the amnesiac said, in a half-joking tone, the first sign of emotion I'd noticed in his voice.

'No. I don't have a brother. I've got two sisters.'

He paused for a moment and then said, 'That's nice.' There was another rather awkward pause and then the amnesiac continued, 'Well, Mr Stern is asking for the phone back, so I'd better say goodbye.'

'Goodbye,' I said.

'Goodbye.'

The brisk, efficient breathing of the consultant returned to the mouthpiece.

'This is Mr Stern again. Did our patient sound at all familiar to you?'

'Not really,' I said. 'I don't think we've met.'

Mr Stern seemed prepared for my lack of recognition.

'I know this is a lot for you to take in,' he said, 'but do you think you could find the time to come to the hospital and see our patient face to face? His voice may sound different as a result of the amnesia. If you saw his face . . . Or perhaps he might recognize you, or if not then at least it might trigger something else in his memory, anything. We are rather desperate, you see. We have no other leads at all as to this man's identity, and until we do, we can make no progress.'

I couldn't really say no, but I told the doctor I couldn't make it for a couple of days. I was going over to my girlfriend's place on the coast that evening and staying all day Sunday. I wouldn't be able to get to the hospital until after work on Monday evening. The doctor seemed put out by this, as though he'd expected me to drop everything and come in straight away, but it was only a case of memory loss, it wasn't as though he needed a new kidney, surely he could wait a couple of days. Anyway, I thought, if I delayed a little, perhaps he would recover his memory in the meantime, or perhaps someone else would claim him.

But I should have gone straight away. I couldn't get him out of my mind while I was down at Gemma's flat. That empty little voice speaking into my ear, hoping that I might recognize it. How had my name and phone number found its way onto a three of hearts playing card?

Gemma had a tiny flat right next to the beach. All it lacked was direct access to the pebbles. For that you'd have to climb out of her bedroom window and swing down a rope to avoid the downstairs garden. We went for a walk along the shingle and hardly spoke a word to each other. Gemma had had one of her nightmares and was in a sombre mood. Then we found a strangely shaped piece of metal sticking out of the mud that Gemma decided was an unexploded mine. If she was so sure, I said, we should call the coastguard. But we didn't. We just went home again, silently.

I didn't tell her about the amnesiac.

So it was rather a relief for me when Monday evening came round and I made my way to the hospital. I thought I could get this business over and done with. Once I'd convinced the amnesiac that there was no connection between us, that we didn't know each other after all, I would at least be able to stop thinking about him.

He was in a room of his own, off the neurological ward. As the doctor had said, the amnesiac was a good-looking man, roughly my age, perhaps a few years younger. He was sitting in a chair beside his bed reading a broadsheet newspaper. He had that dense sort of stubble that leaves a shadow even after close shaving. He was lean, healthy-looking. He had soft, brown, very gentle eyes. The nurse who showed me in explained that Mr Stern, the consultant, was not around at the moment. She said she would try and find his registrar. This meant I spent quite a while alone with the amnesiac. He stood up politely when I came into the room and we shook hands. His grip was firm, and I could sense the urgency in his eyes as he searched for something to recognize. For my part I could tell straight away that we had never met before. There was not the slightest trace of familiarity about him. I could sense, however, that the amnesiac was not so sure. His eyes fixed on mine and wouldn't let them go. He looked at me constantly, unwaveringly. I felt like I was a magnificent portrait in a gallery and he had travelled across the world to view me. He didn't want to waste a moment of his looking time. He even began mirroring my movements. If I looked at something in the room, he looked at it as well. If I went over to the window to inspect the view, he did too. I nodded at the pile of newspapers on the table in the corner.

'Trying to catch up?' I said.

'Yes,' he said, in his polite, soft voice. 'One of the staff had saved all their copies of *The Times* for the last few weeks and brought them in for me. The trouble is I always need the previous day's paper to make sense of the one I'm reading, and so it just keeps going, back and back.'

'You really can't remember anything? Not even who the prime minister is?'

'No. The other day they showed me a lot of photographs of people. I thought they were just showing me pictures of their folks, but apparently they were pictures of the Queen and the royal family.'

'But you can remember how to talk . . . ?'

'Yeah. Good job.' (He laughed nervously.) 'I can remember what they call generic memories. So I can remember that a tree is called a tree and that there's a sun and a moon and that people have to wear clothes and that you don't touch things that are hot. But I can't recall things that have happened to me, things that I've done. Experiences. It's all just gone.'

I shook my head and blew out my cheeks, doing my best to express sympathy for his awful predicament. I needed to prepare the way for the worse news I had for him.

'Well,' I said, squaring myself up, 'I'll have to say straight away that I don't recognize you. You don't even look vaguely familiar to me.'

To my surprise the man expressed irritation at this. He jerked his head, frowned and tutted, as though I'd said something grossly unfair. I wasn't expecting that at all. I was expecting a shrug. He was a shrugging sort of man. This sudden burst of irritation annoyed me.

'Oh come on,' he said, loudly, 'you've been in the room five minutes. You haven't even given it any thought.'

'It doesn't matter,' I said, raising my voice to match his, then quietening it. 'You can tell straight away with a thing like that. You either recognize someone or you don't . . .'

'But maybe I look different – I don't know – maybe I used to have a beard. Maybe I always wore a suit – not this . . .' He tugged at his loose-fitting T-shirt. 'Maybe . . .' He couldn't think of another example, but then reached into his pocket and produced the playing card. 'So how do you explain this?'

I took the playing card, interested to examine it. There on the front, sideways beside the three hearts on the face, was written my name, and my phone number.

'It's not my handwriting,' I said. I believed this was true. It was too small and neat to be mine. 'I didn't write this. Someone else has written it for you.'

'What do you mean?' The man snatched the card back and examined it. The thought that I might not have actually written it myself didn't seem to have occurred to him.

'Someone has written down my name and number for you. I don't know why . . .'

'What do you do?'

'I'm a designer.'

This seemed to cause the amnesiac a momentary problem of comprehension. He gave a barely perceptible shrug.

'So if someone gave me your number, what would be the most likely reason?'

'That you were looking for someone to design a lighting system for your home, or your office.'

He looked at me in a lost sort of way.

'That's my area,' I said, feeling slightly as though I was having to explain myself, 'lighting systems. Or, more specifically: intelligent, energy-saving lighting. Lights that come on the moment you walk into a room, and go out as soon as you leave. Lights that don't have switches, but come on at the wave of a hand.'

The man was looking despondently at the floor while I said this. He looked up when I'd finished.

'That must be impressive,' he said, wistfully, 'lights coming on on their own.'

We each considered the implausibility of the amnesiac having had a need of my lighting design services.

'I'm sorry I can't be more help,' I said, wondering how I was going to make my exit. The man seemed deeply crestfallen, and had returned to staring at the floor. I held out a hand, saw that it wasn't going to be taken, and so quickly morphed the gesture into a shoulder-pat instead, 'I hope you find out . . . you know . . . I'm sure someone will . . .' It was very difficult to find the right words. What I wanted to say was, I'm sure that someone will claim you. Like he was a piece of lost luggage, a carelessly discarded umbrella. The man clearly wasn't going to ease my passage out of his realm, so in the end I just left.

I realized, as I was leaving, that I hadn't seen Mr Stern, the registrar, or anyone else. I hadn't officially denied a relationship with the amnesiac. My non-recognition of him had not been witnessed by anyone in authority, and this fact bothered me as I drove home.

Two days later Mr Stern phoned again.

'Sorry to trouble you. I was wondering how the meeting with our patient went the other day?'

'Has he not told you?'

'He's given me his account of it. I'd like to hear yours, if I may.'

'Well, I'm afraid I wasn't much use. I didn't recognize him at all. As far as I know, we have never met before.'

'Oh.' Mr Stern sounded surprised and disappointed. 'That's not quite what our patient said.'

'No?'

'No. He said you looked familiar. He said he was sure you'd met some time in the past but he couldn't quite remember how, or where . . .'

'He didn't say that when we met.'

'Well, his memory is in a very fragile state. It can take him a very long time to process information.'

Again I didn't know quite where this conversation could go from here, and was anxious to end it. But Mr Stern had already thought ahead.

'I wonder if we could ask a very great favour,' he said. 'I would like to bring our patient to visit you at your home. He says he has this vague recollection of you but can't quite place it. Perhaps if he saw you in your usual surroundings it might help him. Something in your home might trigger memories . . .'

'No, I'm sorry. As I've told you, I'm quite sure that we've never met. I would certainly remember if he'd been to my home . . .'

But of course, I agreed. Mr Stern was so very polite and so very persuasive. But I managed to put him off for a couple of days. It was Gemma's turn to stay with me midweek. She arrived looking stunningly, almost stupidly sexy. She'd had her hair streaked red and blonde, she had on this new leather coat, and she had her shirt unbuttoned so that she was displaying as much cleavage as possible. It was to her left breast that my attention was immediately drawn. As she came towards me to give me my greeting hug I noticed that amid all the familiar freck-les there was something else.

'What's this?' I said, amused. 'You've stuck something to your . . .'

Something small and red, like a sticker dot, seemed to be attached to her breast. I bent down, partly to gain closer inspection, partly to nuzzle my face in the soft skin down there, and saw that it was a little red heart. Gemma giggled.

'Do you like it?' she said.

'Wait a minute. You've tattooed it on.'

'Yes. You know I've always wanted a tattoo. What's the matter? Don't you like it?'

'It's a tattoo,' I said, unable to conceal my shock, 'I mean, that's sort of permanent? This thing's there on your breast for ever.'

'You're saying you don't like it?'

'Well, that's just it. It's there for ever, so if I like it or not is irrelevant, I'm going to have to live with it.'

'But do you like it?'

'I would have liked some warning. It's going to take some getting used to.'

'It's just a tattoo, for Christ's sake,' said Gemma, buttoning up her shirt, 'I'll cover it up, you won't have to look at it.'

'I'm not saying that . . .'

I couldn't say what I wanted to say, that the tattoo looked horrible. It was because of the colour. From a distance it looked like a stab wound.

Gemma buttoned herself right up to her neck and then looked at her watch.

'I can still get the last train back if I leave now. I'll give you a call some time . . .'

'No, don't go, Gemma, don't be . . .'

I could have chased her down the stairs, and out into the street, begging her to come back, but I didn't have the will. In a way I was glad to be left on my own. I needed to think about things. The shock of seeing the heart tattooed on Gemma's pretty breast stayed with me all evening. I still hadn't told her about the amnesiac. She knew nothing about the three of hearts playing card, his only link to another human being. To see one of those hearts on her breast felt like a terrible intrusion.

The amnesiac was delivered to my house two days later by a young woman whom I presumed was a nurse or carer of some sort. The amnesiac wasn't quite holding her hand but he seemed very dependent on her, almost as if he was blind and she was his guide. But when she asked if he would like her to wait outside, he nodded slowly and thoughtfully, and she went out to sit in the car.

'Would you like a cup of tea or coffee?' I said, treating him as normally as I could.

'No,' he replied, absently, then, 'I mean, no thanks.'

He was looking much smarter than when I last saw him. The T-shirt and jeans had been replaced by a blue shirt with a collar, and a double-breasted jacket. He carried these simple clothes with extraordinary elegance.

He had an innate sense of style, just in the way he walked around the room, the way he stood. He could have been a male model. It certainly looked as though he came from a well-to-do background.

He pointed suddenly to the light bulb that was hanging from the ceiling in the middle of the room.

'You don't practise what you preach,' he said, as though talking to the light bulb itself. Then I realized what he meant.

'Oh, you remember what I said about hidden-source lighting. No – when do I ever get a chance to work on my own flat? Anyway, this place isn't mine, it's rented.'

'You could ask your landlord.' He waved his hand vaguely around the light. 'I was hoping I would be able to switch it on and off like this.'

'Do you want to sit down?' I said, still not sure how to deal with the amnesiac. It was like hosting a party for a single, very awkward guest.

'No, I'd rather walk around. Do you mind if I take a look? Mr Stern said I should take a good look around your place, see if there is anything that triggers a memory.'

I had still not met Mr Stern. I imagined him as the classic consultant type – tall and thin with grey hair and half-moon glasses.

'Help yourself,' I said, waving generously at all four corners of the room, 'I'm going to make myself a cup of coffee.' The amnesiac busied himself with a detailed examination of everything that was on display. He looked at all the spines of the books on the shelves, the paintings on the wall, the photographs on the mantelpiece.

'Who's this?' he called, picking up a framed photo.

'That's my girlfriend, Gemma.'

The amnesiac laughed, incredulously.

'She's not really a girl, is she? How old is she?'

'No, she's thirty-five or thirty-six. Thirty-six.'

He considered the photo for some time and I thought he was going to come out with a brutally honest assessment of her appearance, but he seemed to sense what embarrassment this might cause, and ended up just nodding approvingly as he put the photo back. I continued making coffee while the amnesiac wandered into the bedroom and bathroom. He returned a little while later holding something in his hand.

'Hey, I thought you said you hadn't played cards since you were a kid.'

He showed me a pack of cards still in their cardboard sleeve. He threw it over for me to catch. I didn't recognize it, though there is a lot of clutter in my flat – things piled up in what Gemma calls a very Bloomsbury way. It was just possible that he had found something I'd forgotten about.

'I'll let you look inside, see if there's a three of hearts in there.'

'You're joking,' I said.

'No, go on. Have a look.'

The pack was very old, the cardboard sleeve was creased and torn in places. The cards themselves had furred edges that made the pack seem thick and soft, like an old pocket Bible. The pattern on the back was the standard pattern that you see on lots of card packs. I turned them over and fanned through them. I looked through them three times. There was no three of hearts.

Now it was my turn to shrug.

'OK,' I said, 'I don't want to suggest that you are so devious, but obviously you could have removed the three of hearts just now, before you showed the pack to me. Or this could be a pack that you've brought with you. I've never seen it before. And I certainly haven't played a game with it, not within recent memory anyway.'

'I didn't think you'd believe it,' he said, taking my rejection quite calmly, 'but at least it proves to me that I've been here, and that we've met.'

'No, I can assure you, I'm absolutely positive . . .'

But I realized that, no matter how certain I felt about it, I couldn't prove that I didn't know the amnesiac. All I could do was deny any knowledge of him or the pack of cards. I could deny it all I wanted, but I couldn't actually prove it.

But I'd had enough by this time.

'Listen, why don't I go out and call your nurse in and she can take you back to the hospital and you can forget all about me. We have no connection whatsoever. I can't explain the card – maybe you looked me up in a phone book at random and wrote it down yourself – who knows?'

'No.' The amnesiac's tone changed dramatically as I

walked to the door: the unbecomingly cocky self-assuredness that had crept into his manner during his visit was now replaced by the more familiar tone of helplessness and innocence. 'I'm sorry, I don't mean to put pressure on you, I'm really sorry, don't go out there, give me just a few more minutes.' He was tugging at my sleeve by this time. 'You don't understand the situation I'm in. If I don't find someone who remembers me, they're going to keep me in hospital for good. They might even section me. They tell me I won't survive in the outside world on my own, and that until someone claims me, I have to stay there.'

'I'm really sorry,' I said, 'but there's nothing I can do.'

'There is. You can say to Mr Stern that you know me. If you say that, they'll let me go . . .'

'I can't say that.'

'It'll do no harm. Then I could stay with you, just until I find a job and then I can get a place of my own.'

'Live with me, you mean? Are you out of your mind?' I paused, embarrassed by what I'd just said.

'OK, not live with you. That would be a terrible imposition. But look – what if I just spent a few days – or a week, perhaps, with you. Maybe if I tagged along with you for a few days, going to the places you go, meeting the people you meet, someone would recognize me, or I would recognize someone . . .'

The difficult thing was explaining it to Gemma. We had made up after our row about the tattoo, and we were on our way to an opera. Neither of us had ever been to an opera before but we had always thought, at the back of our minds, to try it, in case we liked it.

'Why haven't you told me about this guy before?' she said, as we ate in the little spaghetti place we both hated.

'I don't know,' I replied, which was true, I didn't really know why I hadn't told her about the amnesiac, 'I suppose I just thought it would blow over. After the first phone call I didn't really think anything would come of it, I thought I'd just fail to recognize him and that would be it. But it doesn't seem to have worked out like that . . .'

'And now he's coming to live with you.'

'Not "live",' I corrected as emphatically as I could, 'not "live", "stay". He's coming to stay with me, just for a few days.'

Gemma gave me a pitying look, and laughed as though charmed by my naivety, as though I was a poor victim of that old trick – the lost-memory routine – the one where somebody claims to have lost their identity, moves in on some sympathetic, unsuspecting mug, and then takes over their life.

'Come on,' I said, 'the poor guy needs a chance. Imagine what it must feel like to not know who you are.'

Gemma stared into the middle distance for a moment.

'Well,' she said eventually, 'will I be allowed to meet him?'

'Would you want to?'

Gemma gave one of her childish shrugs.

'Depends. Would you want me to meet him – perhaps you like keeping him to yourself.'

'You're being a bit . . .' I wanted to say melodramatic, but I had used the word so many times throughout our relationship that it had had lost its value, and besides, we were on our way to see an opera.

'Maybe I would remember him,' Gemma said, suddenly brightening, pushing aside her hardly eaten dinner, 'if he ever did meet you, perhaps I met him too?'

This was quite a good point.

When we made love that night, doing our best to make up for the terrible disappointments of the opera, my helplessness in the face of her tattoo was doubled when I found that there was now a second heart on her breast. I couldn't help, as I approached to suckle, commenting on it.

'Well, you said you liked it on the phone, so I had another one done. To keep the first one company.'

The first heart had looked solitary and poignant. Two hearts looked happy and buoyant, side by side.

'It represents us, of course,' Gemma said.

'Let's just leave it at two,' I said, 'no more,' and smiled.

The amnesiac arrived at my flat a week later, looking far more confident than I had ever seen him.

'I remember this place,' he said as he rolled in, picking up a pear from my fruit bowl, smiling widely. 'By the way, I've got a name.' He seemed about to take a bite out of the pear, but then thought better of it, and put it back in the bowl.

'Oh yes?'

'Yes. It's Terry.'

'Terry? You mean that's actually your name – you've remembered it?'

The amnesiac – Terry – laughed, as though I'd fallen for a joke.

'No – well, maybe it is, but I don't remember. No – I just gave it to myself. I named myself. I got fed up with not having one, everyone calling me sir, or mate (even worse). So I'm Terry. What do you think?'

'I don't know. You don't really strike me as a Terry.'

'Don't I?' He looked genuinely hurt.

'I'd say you're more a Giles or a Miles or a Rupert. Alexander perhaps. Toby, at a push.'

'I've got a second name as well.'

'Let's hear it.'

He delivered the name with his two hands delicately raised, as though holding either end of a piece of string.

'Hartley,' he said.

I must have looked rather blank.

'Do you get it? Three of Hearts. Terry Hartley. Not quite an anagram, but it sort of works, don't you think?'

Terry fitted very neatly into my life. He came to work and shadowed me for a day. Everyone was charmed by him. Despite his awful predicament, his lack of a place in the world, people felt at ease with him, especially women. He was naturally attractive, but the men enjoyed his company as well. He had quickly relearned his social skills. (What must he have been in his previous life, some sort of PR genius perhaps? A spin doctor? A company lawyer?) It was like seeing all the manufactured charm stripped away from someone, to leave a core of genuine human warmth. He joked with people at the bar at lunchtime, he watched me playing football on Wednesday evening, and in the pub afterwards chatted happily with burly goalkeepers. On Thursday he came with me to a consultation for a Docklands firm that was looking for innovative lighting systems. Normally I would have been very wary of taking someone with me to meet a client, but Terry was positively an asset. I began to feel rather proud of him.

And Gemma was as charmed by him as everyone else. We had dinner together, the three of us, one evening at my flat. Terry cooked it, a French-cut rack of lamb encrusted with spices. Gemma and I both thought this indicated he must have been a chef in his previous life, because it was cooked to perfection, but Terry laughed it off, saying all he'd done was follow a recipe in one of my rarely used cookery books.

He brought out a side in Gemma I'd never seen before – a shy, bashful, demure side. At the end of the evening, when Terry was in the bathroom, she said:

'I feel like I've known him all my life. But I don't remember him.'

No one remembered him. No one at work, no one in the pubs and bars we went to, no one in any of the offices we visited. They loved him, but they didn't remember him. For two weeks I took him to all the places I could think of, all over London, and all the time we were longing for that moment when someone would call out, 'Hey, ******, haven't seen you for ages, how are you?' Or some such, but nothing like that happened. And Terry was getting more and more despairing as the days went by. In company he was still charming, but when we were alone he gave expression to his deep anxieties and fears.

'I'm sorry, Terry,' I said to him eventually, 'I'm going to have to phone the hospital. You can't stay with me for ever . . .'

For a while I thought perhaps he could blend in with my circle of friends and acquaintances, perhaps he could charm one of them into renting him a room, or giving him a job. But it was difficult for anyone to do this for a man with no identity, no National Insurance number, no bank account, no birth certificate. There must be some sort of provision the authorities can make for people like him, I thought, to enable someone to start afresh with a new life and a new identity. But it didn't work like that. Supposing he was set up with all the paperwork for a new life, the reasoning went, and then, later, he remembered who he was. He would then have two identities, and be able to exploit one or the other for any number of purposes.

They were difficult days. Terry was irritable and sad by turns, snapping at us one minute, weeping to himself the next. I feared that he would be very resistant to the idea of being handed back to the hospital, that he might even become violent. Then one day Gemma had a thought.

'Terry, you know you were found on the M3, walking along the hard shoulder – why do you think you were doing that, were you trying to go somewhere?'

'It was Legoland,' said Terry, 'I'd seen a sign for Legoland and I was following it.'

'But why?'

There was quite a long pause.

'I don't know. It just sounded – interesting.'

It was rather a long shot, but Gemma went on to suggest that perhaps there was a deeper reason for Terry's interest in Legoland. Perhaps if we went there, he would see something that would trigger memories. Perhaps he used to work there, who knows, (Gemma went on) perhaps he used to be the manager, or perhaps he was a theme-park designer . . . I was laughing at the idea, but Terry wasn't.

And so we took Terry to Legoland. He sat in the front seat while Gemma sat in the back. We passed the brown tourist signs on the M3 that said *Legoland*, and Terry pointed to the exact spot where the police had picked him up.

'That's where my new life began,' he said, as the nondescript piece of hard shoulder rushed by. I was feeling nervous. The nearer we came to Legoland, the more certain Terry seemed to feel that he would find the answer to his identity in the theme park.

'That was such a good idea of yours, Gemma,' he said over his shoulder, 'I don't know why I didn't think of it before – but it's so obvious now – Legoland. I was going to Legoland . . .'

There was a long queue. It was a warm Saturday and the whole world's children seemed to have gathered in one place. Terry's tetchiness increased as we waited. He kept walking up and down the line, shaking his head, unable, quite, to understand why we had to wait, when our quest was so much more important than everyone else's. Gemma bought him an ice cream from a nearby kiosk, and this seemed to calm him down for a while.

Once through the gates, the familiar sense of disappointment returned. Terry had really been expecting to recognize things this time. And he tried his hardest to find everything familiar, but he couldn't keep it up for long. We'd stared at miniature cities and tame little roundabouts for long enough. He had to concede he didn't remember a thing.

'It must have just been the name,' he said, despondently, 'that was all. I must have just been interested in the name.'

He had spoken to a few members of staff, a happy young woman selling balloons, a grandfatherly type in a restaurant, people who looked well established in the park, and would have known everyone who'd worked there for long. No one remembered Terry.

'Well,' I said, trying to be cheerful, 'at least we've had a nice day out.'

Not having any children, Gemma and I tended to steer clear of places that attracted them. We were both surprised at how much fun we were having. We didn't go on any of the rides, but just watching everyone else having fun was enough. And hearing the laughter. I don't know why, but Gemma and I, we both felt a strange thrill at that sound.

Terry had given up hope of finding out anything at Legoland, and we were thinking of starting back. Then he suddenly had an urge to go on the big roller coaster. There was only one big roller coaster at Legoland, all the other rides were rather small and slow, designed for young children. He was quite happy to go on his own, while Gemma and I waited on a bench. We watched him as he queued. He would cast occasional serious glances in our direction. He looked a little bit scared.

'I think you should go on with him,' said Gemma.

'Don't be silly. He's a grown man.'

Eventually we lost sight of him as the queue rounded a corner. We knew it would still be a long time before Terry got his ride, and we began to feel restless. A strange fidgetiness overcame us. We had to stand up, walk around. We found a viewing point close to the track, where the first drop of the roller coaster descended below the path. Every minute or so another car would rush past. It was an odd thing to be so close to these people in the midst of a near free fall, yet just a few feet away. The roar of the car, the breeze from it, the brief burst of screaming, wide-open faces, trailing hair, and then they were gone. And then another car, then another. The cars only held up to six. Mostly they contained whole families. This meant families were falling past us, one at a time, continually. It was as though we were on the end of the conveyor belt at the family factory, watching the new ones coming off the assembly line, to be dropped into the world.

We were watching this for so long, mesmerized, that we'd forgotten to look out for Terry. We hadn't kept track of the time – should he have had his ride by now? Had he been among the many screaming, wide-eyed faces that had been falling past us for so long? We'd strayed from our seat and if he'd come off the ride, he wouldn't know where we were. Would he have the sense to stay by our bench, or might he wander off, become lost again, among the many thousands in the park?

Gemma was already panicking. She ran round the side of the roller coaster, through the snaking slaloms of the queue, pushing her way right up to the front to see if he was still there. He wasn't. And by now enough cars had emptied for us to know he wasn't on the ride itself. Looking in every direction about us, there was no sign of him.

'We've got to tell someone before he wanders off out of the park,' said Gemma, 'get them to make an announcement.' I told her not to worry. We were out in the middle of nowhere, we'd find him in the car park probably, if not before. I tried not to remember the vastness of those car parks, the endless rows of family saloons, like a whole planet of cars. And I thought it would be absurd to have an announcement made – would they ask him to go to the room for lost children?

And then there he was. He'd been to a kiosk for some candyfloss, and had a pink ghost of it on a stick, and some sugar round his lips.

'It wasn't very exciting,' he said, not noticing our panic.

Gemma went up and hugged him. Really hugged him tightly, like she never wanted to let him go. I gave him a hug as well. We were both so pleased, so relieved, so glad that we remembered him.

ASTRONOMY

As far as he knew, Clark had never expressed any interest in astronomy. Why, then, did his wife, on the occasion of his thirty-second birthday, buy him a telescope?

'So you can see the rings of Neptune,' she said, then, 'is it Neptune?'

'Don't ask me,' said Clark.

'Saturn,' said their daughter, Kelly, who was nine, 'you mean the rings of Saturn.'

The telescope looked impressive. Marianne had taken it out of its box and had assembled it herself the night before, while Clark was in bed.

'All by yourself?' said Clark, incredulously, because Marianne had always expressed an exasperation with technical things, and liked to present herself as someone permanently flummoxed by gadgetry. 'You didn't put this together by yourself.'

'Anyone can follow instructions,' said Marianne, handing him the manual, a thick glossy document that Clark leafed through, to be instantly lost in its jargon – *equatorial mount, azimuth, declination, finderscope*. He looked up from its pages at Marianne, who was standing in front of him, her arms folded, resting her weight on one hip, and nodding her head towards the telescope, which was standing in a similar pose at the other end of the living room. If it had arms they would almost certainly have been folded. Its three tapering legs were prim and stiff. Angled and poised, it suddenly struck Clark how out of place the thing looked. Everything else in the room – the brown velvet couch, the bookcase full of DVDs, the bloated, frowning, too-realistic dolls that the girls liked to play with – they all seemed fat and clumsy in comparison to the telescope. It was as though a ballet dancer had frozen mid-pirouette. An impression enhanced by the big puffy bow of scarlet ribbon that was tied around its main shaft.

'Well,' Marianne said, 'aren't you going to . . .'

'Going to what?'

'You know. Look through it? Do some astronomy?'

'Oh . . .' Clark thought for a moment. He was about to say something like – Why on earth have you bought me this bloody great telescope, Marianne? I've never once in my life expressed the remotest interest in the stars. Was it that you meant to buy me golf clubs, and somehow got things mixed up? Just tell me. But what he actually said was, 'Perhaps I should wait until it's dark.'

'Dark?' Marianne looked exaggeratedly puzzled.

'Yes, I think you can only do astronomy at night.'

Marianne tutted, as though astronomy had just been

revealed to be a big scam – all those expensive telescopes, and they were useless for half the day.

'Well, you make sure you use it tonight,' she wagged a mock-stern finger at him, 'I don't want to see her going to waste, after all the times you've said how much you wanted one . . .'

'I never . . .' But Marianne had silenced him with a kiss on the cheek.

'Happy birthday,' she said.

That was in the morning. They went their separate ways for the day, as usual. Clark worked for a food company. Marianne was a care assistant. In the evening, when Clark came home, he had almost forgotten about the telescope. Kelly and her little sister, Jodie, were already home, and were watching television in the living room. The telescope had been moved, because it was blocking the view. It was in the corner now, next to the DVDs, and looking slightly resentful, so Clark imagined.

The children had forgotten it was their father's birthday. When he reminded them, they said, without taking their eyes off the television, 'Where are your presents?' Clark said that he'd only had one present, and that it was standing in the corner, watching them. The girls looked around them in mild alarm for a moment, before realizing what he meant.

'Oh, the telescope. We had to move it, we couldn't see the TV.'

'Is that all?' Jodie said.

Clark cast a weary look around the room, as though there might be a pile of gifts in another corner somewhere. There wasn't.

'Looks like it,' he said.

Marianne came downstairs. She'd got changed and had glammed herself up. The babysitter was coming at eight, she said. She'd booked a table at the new seafood restaurant, the one everyone was talking about.

But Clark was hungry now. He didn't say this.

The children groaned when they heard the babysitter was coming. They didn't like her, Pauline, a dumpy teenager with hoop earrings, who gave her opinion loudly on everything. So unlike the telescope, Clark thought.

'Well?' said Marianne, nodding again at the telescope, and smiling knowingly. 'It's dark now.'

So half an hour after getting home from work, still in his work suit, and as hungry as hell, Clark found himself in the back garden, on the lawn, manhandling a telescope. No, he couldn't just stick it out of a window. Not even out of a skylight. It was too big for that. And the instruction manual said it had to be taken outside. Astronomy was an outdoor activity. This was the first thing he learnt about the subject. So he'd taken the telescope outside, carrying her, with her three legs sticking out, knocking against doors, as though waltzing with an elegant robot, onto the lawn, as far away from the lights of the house, and the other houses, as he could.

The others didn't come with him. He asked the children, but they weren't interested. Neither was Marianne. 'No,' she said, 'you're the astronomy nut. We'll stay indoors like normal people.'

He had wanted to remonstrate, to deny that he was an astronomy nut, to emphasize that he was as uninterested in the stars as he was in most other things, apart from golf. But to have done so would have been to show terrible ingratitude, for the money, trouble and time Marianne had spent. So he dutifully did his thing alone in the back garden. It was the first time he could look at the telescope closely. It was an extraordinary thing, he had to concede. A three-and-a-half-inch reflector. The main shaft was held by a pair of ring clamps to the equatorial mount, which had a counterweight fixed to it, so that, when balanced, the telescope could be moved with the gentlest of nudges. The mount itself was a heavy piece of metalwork, with dials and gradations that corresponded, so he read (under torchlight), to the hours and degrees of the heavens, the Earth's angle of tilt, and Clark's position on the surface of the Earth.

Lifting his head from his close reading of the manual, Clark felt a need to take a look around him, to get his bearings on his familiar surroundings. The backs of the other houses. Then the houses the other way. Was anyone watching him, wondering what on earth he was doing? He saw a red light bobbing near one of the houses, a smoker banished to a patio. Must be that old devil whose name he didn't know, three doors down, who left little notes on his windscreen that were full of clumsy irony – *'Thanks again for taking our parking space'* or *'Please feel free to park outside our house any bloody time you like'* – that Clark would read once before screwing up and throwing in the gutter, but whose words, even after such a brief reading, stayed with him.

Clark turned back to the telescope. He imagined it speaking to him, standing there impatiently on its trim little legs. 'Well, bully for you, you've got me out here. Now what are you going to do?' He looked up at the sky. A clear night, no moon, but not many stars. Most of them were blotted out by the orange glow of the city. When he came to putting his eye to the eyepiece, he felt as gauche and as inadequate as a boy stealing his first kiss. He didn't know where to put his hands. If he put them on the telescope, she moved, making it impossible to see anything. But there was nothing to see. A big fuzzy blackness. Clark took the lens cap off and had another go. Nothing again, but this time an orange sort of nothingness. He had been expecting to be dazzled, to see a jewelled vault up there, a firework display of comets, planets ringed and in the grip of colourful storms, but there was nothing. Clark turned the focusing knobs, but all that seemed to do was to make the nothingness sharper. But then a star did come into view. A weak little thing, twinkling feebly with blue light. No brighter, no more interesting than the stars he could see with the naked eye.

Clark stepped back, wondering if he'd done enough

astronomy to clear his conscience. Did that tiddly little star count? He was starting to get cold. His attention was drawn again to the backs of the houses. He realized he had never been down to the end of his garden in the dark, and so had never seen this view before, the living rooms and bathrooms of the street glowing. He was surprised to see next door sitting down to a civilized meal. All he knew of them, through the dividing wall, was a stream of ferocious arguments. He imagined that they lived in some sort of cavern with blood-splattered walls, the children cowering and undernourished, feeding on scraps in a corner. But no, they were eating beneath the light of a little chandelier, and the children, he could see, were happy. Next door again he could see someone in a bathroom. It was the woman he fancied, who'd just got rid of her husband and had, about a month ago, come on to Clark as he was leaving for work one morning. They'd met in the street and she had made a passing comment as she walked an eager little Scottie dog down the road, 'I like a nice, clean pressed shirt on a man.' Barely acknowledging him as she walked by, so she might have been thinking out loud, but he couldn't help feeling flattered, even a little proud. Now he could see her naked body, though blurred by frosted glass, and barely recognizable as a human form. Clark was astonished at how much of his neighbours' lives was visible, that they conducted them so openly, illuminated and uncurtained. But then, of course, they had all assumed the back gardens to be empty at night.

The thought crossed Clark's mind that he should redirect his telescope at that bathroom window. His Skywatcher (as it was called) was capable of a hundred times magnification. Even through frosted glass this might be able to render detail. The woman in the bathroom a hundred times life size – what would that be like? Six hundred feet tall, a giantess the size of a skyscraper, drying herself after a shower. Should he try it? Would it work?

The telescope moved easily against its counterbalance. By slow degrees Clark lowered the angle until it was nearly horizontal, poised like a rocket launcher, with its gaping mouth, aimed at the bathroom window. Was he doing anything wrong? If caught out, if the banished puffer on the patio should spot him looking through his three-and-a-half-inch reflector at an exposed bathroom window and call the police, how would it sound? I was looking for the rings of Saturn and I lost my way. Pretty lame. But then he was a novice astronomer, a first-timer. An astronomy nut.

When he looked through the eyepiece this time, there was dazzle. It was filled with light, unfocused so that it broke down into thousands of smaller pieces that stirred and blinked and shivered. He looked again, feeling that he was peering into the centre of something magnificent, desperately trying to focus, to make the nothingness into something. The eyepiece was nearly fully extended before he got a sense of something moving against the light. The edge of a body, a horizon of flesh, a sense of blushing pinkness – then everything went dark.

Clark looked up. The bathroom light had been switched off. It was over. And now he could see that there was something happening at the back of his own house. The garden door was opening, children were spilling out. For some reason they were interested now, as Clark quickly redirected the telescope so that it was back into the vertical, pointing at the sky. Kelly, Jodie, their mum behind them, even the lumbering babysitter who must have just arrived. Was it that late already? It must be. They were all coming down the garden towards him.

'Have you seen anything?' the children were asking. 'Can we have a look?'

'Pauline said you should be able to see the edge of the universe,' said Kelly.

'Can you see as far as that?' said Marianne, doubtfully.

'Pretty much,' said Clark, wondering why his hands were trembling so much as he lifted his youngest daughter to the eyepiece. 'Even a bit further.'

VICE

There must have been some little job that needed fixing, or why else would he have bought it? Or perhaps it was more than a little job; perhaps he'd had something bigger in mind, something more ambitious and complicated. Perhaps he was going to bind books, make furniture, or toys for his friends' children. Whatever it was for, he had it now. He had a vice.

He could clearly remember buying it. It had been a sunny Sunday morning. He'd walked down Locks Hill to the DIY shed near the station, and he had bought a vice. For some reason he remembered feeling slightly ashamed, as though he'd sidled into a sex parlour. There was a young woman on the till. He felt embarrassed, couldn't look her in the eye as he heaved the heavy vice onto the counter. She had trouble getting at the bar code underneath, and he had to help her. A bang of bleached hair fell across her pierced eyebrow, and she seemed to wink at him. Then she sprayed his vice with infrared light, and swiped his credit card through the till.

'Would you like a bag?' she said, chinking a studded tongue against bright incisors. 'So that no one will see my vice?' he wondered. A brown-paper bag? 'Maybe you'll need two,' she went on, shaking out two thick carrier bags, 'but you'll have to help me.' That wink again. The flash of tongue. She held the plastic bags open while he carefully eased the vice inside.

It was a long walk back up Locks Hill. Why hadn't he taken the car? The sunny morning had been too seductive, making him think that he'd like a nice morning walk. But he had forgotten this simple fact – vices, even if modestly sized, are bloody heavy. It was like carrying an anvil home. The vice strained at the plastic carrier bags, stretching the handles, threatening to break them. His fingers began turning blue. Then, when he finally got home, the task of explaining it to his wife.

'You been shopping already?' she said, as he arrived in the sunny kitchen of their breeze-block bungalow. He was so heavily laden she must have thought he'd bought a whole week's shopping, but no, he'd bought a single thing. Already he'd forgotten why.

'What is it?' She peeped inside the carrier bags that he had, with difficulty, placed on the kitchen table. Looking at the object in its bag didn't seem to answer her question. It needed to be completely uncovered before she could guess what it was.

'You've bought one of those things – what's it called. A lathe? It's a lathe, isn't it?'

'No,' he said firmly, 'it's a vice.'

'Right, a vice.'

The vice sat squatly on the table. Husband and wife

contemplated it thoughtfully. The vice was about the size of a cat, and as neatly constructed. Black and glossy, with brushed-steel jaws, and a chrome handle that clinked prettily when turned, it looked somehow pleased with itself, pleased with all the important space it was taking up, pleased with its weightiness, which meant it couldn't easily be moved. It gave a whiff of workshop grease, and Jane wondered why she'd allowed her husband to place it on the table. The trouble was there seemed nowhere else to put it. She folded her arms and looked from the vice to her husband and back again, repeatedly.

'Well?' she said.

'Well what?'

'What have you bought a vice for?'

'You know . . .'

'No, I don't know.'

He gave a sigh of exasperation.

'How many times have we talked about it? How many times have we said we need a vice?'

'Hmm, let me see,' said Jane, pretending to tot up the times on her fingers, 'not once.'

He took his jacket off; he was still sweating from the walk back. He waved a hand dismissively at Jane.

'Don't start,' he said.

The vice remained on the kitchen table. There was nowhere else to put it. There was nowhere in the living room, the bedroom. They didn't have a garage or a shed. He had a small study, but the little table in there was already taken up with his computer and printer. He could have put it in the loft, but what use would it have been up there? Neither he nor his wife seemed in a hurry to dispose of the vice, not without some thought, at least. What to do with a vice, where to keep it, these were decisions that couldn't be taken lightly. Its own weight was a problem in itself. A moment's carelessness could mean a broken foot. Lift it without due regard for its weight and you risked throwing your back out.

So Gordon and Jane had their breakfast, lunch and tea at the table with the vice in between them, taking up the space normally occupied by a vase of flowers. They exchanged glances over its smooth metal back, smiled at each other, smiled at the absurdity of their situation, an ageing married couple, with a vice in between them on the kitchen table. Gordon had given up trying to remember why he bought it. He had no other tools anyway. He was not a handyman.

'You know,' said Jane after a month, 'if this vice wasn't here one day, I'd feel that there was something missing from my life. I've grown so used to seeing it.'

Gordon lowered his newspaper and nodded.

'It's like one of the family,' he said.

'A pet,' said Jane. 'It's like a pit bull that doesn't bark, or bite.'

'Oh, he can bite,' said Gordon, warningly, 'he can certainly bite.' Then, after a moment's pause, 'So are you pleased I bought a vice?'

Jane looked carefully at her husband, considered for a moment all his faults – his lack of humour, libido, intelligence or looks – and decided that the vice somehow made up for all of them.

THE UNDERHOUSE

I first got the idea for the Underhouse when, as a child, I would stand on my head in a corner of the living room, and thereby find myself in a different house entirely, one where the furniture hung from the ceiling rather than stood on the floor, where light bulbs grew at the tops of tall, thin trees, and where doors had to be passed through like stiles, one leg at a time. I desperately wanted to explore this exotic house, and was profoundly disappointed every time I uprighted myself (at the behest, usually, of my exasperated parents, 'The blood will pool in his head!') to find that it had vanished.

Then, as a grown up with my own house, I noticed how the cellar, which was underneath only one room (the living room), exactly matched, in shape, the room above it. And then I thought how the horizontal boundaries of rooms, unlike their vertical counterparts, change their essential nature depending on which side you are viewing them from. To put it more simply, a wall is a wall no matter which side of the wall you are. But a floor, when viewed from underneath, becomes a ceiling, which is a very different thing. Do you follow?

Standing in my cellar one day, looking up at the boards which provided a floor for the living room, I had the turn-around thought; what if I refused to regard this thing above me as a ceiling – what if I decided to call it a floor also? The thing is, it looked like a floor. It was made of wooden boards supported by joists. The only difference was that the joists were foremost, and the boards were rough, dirty wood, whereas on the floor above they'd been varnished and draped with rugs. Dimensionally the only real difference between the cellar and the living room above it was to do with height. The cellar had much less height than the living room. I had to stoop whenever I went in there, though in fact this was an unnecessary precaution, for when I measured it it turned out to be six foot five inches from floor to floorboards (i.e. ceiling), and six foot exactly from floor to joist. At five foot eleven I had plenty of headroom, but still I felt the need to stoop.

The dissimilarity in height between the cellar and the living room became something of an obsession, and eventually I had to do something about it. It was a very simple thing. All I had to do was to lower the floor of the cellar by exactly thirty-seven inches, and the two rooms, above and below, would be perfect spatial mirror images of each other. I suppose it was something to do with symmetry.

So I took a pickaxe to the floor of the cellar. It hardly needed it. The floor was a ropy thing made of asphalt under a thin layer of concrete. A garden fork could just as well have done the job. It yielded, under its crisp shell, thousands of sticky black grains that I had to scoop into a bucket and carry upstairs and out into the back garden. Beneath the asphalt I was into the raw earth of the world under my house, which I dug down into. Then when I had gone far enough, I levelled off and finished with a layer of good cement. It was hard, aching work, and took me several weeks. (I'm not as strong as I was.) But at the end of my work I had a room, below my living room, that was its proportional twin.

It occurred to me then to set about duplication of the room above in other ways. I started with the walls. Bare brick in the cellar, I plastered them as best I could (I'm no handyman, really), and after a reasonable period of drying out, papered them with the rose pattern I had so long lived with (and which was very, very hard to find). The paintings that hang on them were also difficult to reproduce, and I had to try my hand at copying one of the simpler ones myself, the result of which endeavour surprised and pleased me.

Next I bought floorboards to nail over the joists of the cellar ceiling to form a perfect replica of the floor above. In effect I now had two floors back to back. Onto this upside-down floor I tacked rugs identical to those in my living room, and in the same position. I bought furniture identical to the furniture in my living room, and placed it on the upside-down floor of the cellar, in identical positions once again. This was a harder task, and one I could only just manage on my own. Bolting a settee to the ceiling of a cellar is work for a strong man. I will not go into details about how I managed it, except to say that I adapted techniques I read about in an account of the building of Salisbury Cathedral. Nor will I detail the many journeys I had to make in order to find chairs identical to those that furnished the living room. But the exquisite delight I felt when I achieved my aim, when I found my replica suite, my coffee table's double, the lampstand's long-lost and long-forgotten twin, in some distant junk shop or car-boot, was indescribable. Though perhaps it is not unlike that experienced by an actual twin, who has been deprived of the knowledge all his life, to find himself reunited with his brother from the womb.

I now had everything on the floor of my living room reproduced exactly upside down on the ceiling of the cellar, bolted fast, the cushions of the seats stitched to them, and all other precautions taken to make a convincing upside-down room, identical to the original.

It took me several years of hard work to reproduce everything in the living room. One thing I couldn't reproduce, of course, was the view from the front bay window. I had to satisfy myself that drawn curtains would do. Eventually I worked out how to make them hang convincingly, which involved a hidden rail at the bottom of the curtains, so that in reality the curtains hang downwards into the pelmet. I succeeded very well, I think, in giving them a convincingly unfastened look.

The most enjoyable touches were the two light fittings (one a chandelier) that in the real room hung from the ceiling on thin lengths of flex. Again trompe l'œil was involved in producing flex that would hang upwards and support a shade; moreover, I fashioned a modest chandelier, just like the one above ground, and managed, with glue and solder, to make the crystals hang upwards instead of downwards. I think if there is any true crowning glory to my upside-down room, it is in the upside-down chandelier, with all its crystals pouring casually upwards as if there was nothing untoward in their world at all. Of course, I wired the lights up to work just like the lights in the real living room.

Completed, my project gave me many moments of unspeakable joy. Just sitting in my armchair, knowing that beneath the floor there was another armchair, hanging, in a room where everything else hung that should have stood, and which stood that should have hung, just knowing it was there, was enough to cause delight. It was as though my life was a reflection in a pool, into which I could actually enter. It was as though Narcissus could indeed embrace his own reflection.

The experience of descending the cellar stairs into the inverted world below, to suddenly find oneself the only upright thing in a room turned upside-down, to be given the sense that gravity pushes upwards rather than downwards, to feel oneself floating, in fact, was an experience of delirious, dreamy delight.

And one I had to share.

So that is how I came to bamboozle acquaintances I met at the Earl of Chatham, the rather innocent, almost destitute young men who frequented that once family-friendly place, and who could easily be bought drinks. I would invite them home, after many reassurances that I was not an old queen, and they would accompany me back, usually because they had nowhere better to go, and not much prospect of a roof over their head for the night. I would sit them in the armchair, plying them with Jim Beam and playing Count Basie on the record player, until they passed out in a drunken swoon. Then I would carry them down to the cellar, lay them down on the floor (the ceiling), and leave them alone to wake up, but still with Count Basie playing on the now upside-down record player (I won't bore you with details of how I made a record player work upside down). I would return to the right-way-up room, and wait. It could take a long time, but eventually there would come a cry from downstairs. 'Jesus Christ,' they might say, 'Holy Jesus, get me down, get me down,' and I would go downstairs into the cellar, peep at them from round the corner and see them writhing on the floor (the ceiling), aghast at their weightlessness, terrified at their defiance of gravity. At first I would hang from the stairwell and peek at them upside-down, as if I too were part of the upside-down world, to increase their sense of being on the ceiling.

'What's the matter, old chap,' I would say, 'feeling a bit light-headed?'

They would stare at me with about-to-be-shot eyes, hyperventilating, unable to find words, pressing themselves to the floor (the ceiling).

'You should be pleased, old chap,' I would say, 'you've learnt how to fly. Aren't you the clever one?'

I would then reassure them that it was simply something they'd drunk. I would tell them to close their eyes and let me take care of them. Then I'd carry them back upstairs, plonk them down in the right-way-up living room, tell them to open their eyes again. From their perspective they had not left the room at all, merely descended from its ceiling to its floor. The look of tender alarm on their faces, as they felt about the arms of the chair, and the floor with their feet, to ascertain whether they really were back on the ground, and the way they looked up at the ceiling, apprehensive of the horrible notion that they might, at any moment, plummet towards it, was something to cherish.

I have plans for extending my Underhouse, so that the whole house, every room including the loft, should be duplicated. It would be a work of many, many years, and one I may not live long enough to complete. To open up so much empty space beneath my own house could be dangerous. I have this peculiar thought that, having completed my duplicate upside-down house, and having weakened the foundations of the right-way-up house, the latter will eventually collapse into the former. If the right-way-up house fell down into the upside-down-house, one must suppose that the two would cancel each other out, and that both houses would simply disappear. And if I happen to be asleep in my bed (right way up or upside down – how would I know?) what would become of me? I would have folded myself out of existence.

A rather attractive thought.

I'd better start digging.

GLUE

Dawn and Lana were sisters, born two years apart. Dawn, the older, was a legal secretary for a small firm of solicitors who had a High Street office in the quiet Midland town to where she'd moved with her husband Tony, a commercial photographer. Lana was an artist who lived in the East End of London in a flat above a noisy market street. She was a lesbian, and had had a string of short-term relationships, the longest of which, a three-year involvement with a formerly straight married woman, had recently ended. Childless herself, she was godmother to Dawn's two girls, Annie and Petula.

Neither sister was religious, and so Dawn hadn't given much thought to what the role of godmother meant, and she hadn't expected Lana to either. It was a token relationship, she thought. A sign of family closeness. A way of saying that Lana was more than just an aunt.

To Dawn's surprise, Lana seemed to have a much stronger idea of what a godmother was. Shortly after Dawn had mentioned, in as casual a way as she felt capable, that she would be very happy if Lana would be

239

Annie's godmother, Lana sent her a letter thanking her very much for the role, and that she would do everything she could to look after Annie's spiritual well-being, and enclosing, already, a small painting to be framed and put on the child's bedroom wall. The painting was rather difficult to decipher. Dawn had never felt that her sister had any special artistic talent, and that although she could make striking images, she couldn't actually draw or paint anything that resembled what it was meant to be. The painting enclosed with the letter was a murky water-colour that seemed to depict a winged mythical creature, a sort of gryphon-type thing with two heads, wings and breasts. Since Annie, at only a few weeks old, was still too young to respond to an image like that, she put it in a drawer and forgot about it.

The sisters had fallen into a routine of visits that had grown less and less frequent. They satisfied themselves that the reason for the decline was Dawn's move away from London. Now they saw each other, at most, once a year. Dawn hadn't expected the birth of Annie to change this pattern greatly. Lana visited shortly after Annie was born, and Dawn didn't think she'd ever seen anyone so uncomfortable with a baby, or so confused by the sight of one. It didn't help that Annie, at their first encounter, was wearing a mask of pumpkin puree and mucus. Lana clearly had been expecting something more beautiful and pristine, and had visibly recoiled. Nor, when Annie had been briskly cleaned with a damp towel, had Lana seemed ready for a person so emphatically small, so resolutely miniature. 'She moves like clockwork,' was her first amazed comment. And later – 'How does the human race survive, when we all start off so small? How do we not get trodden on, or lost down the backs of settees?' It seemed to her that the simple weight of the social world, the jostle of the populace of already existing and fully-grown people, should crush the child out of existence. But no – she grows within days of being born, and is soon taking her place in that jostling world.

Lana had that look, when she held Annie, of someone unsure of how they are supposed to react, or of what they are supposed to feel. There was delight and tenderness in her expression, but there was also an awkwardness, a bewilderment. In the end she handed Annie back to her sister as though she was a broken thing she couldn't mend, though not for want of trying.

And after that brief visit, Dawn didn't expect to see her sister again for another year or more. But to her surprise, she turned up again only six weeks later. Dawn tried to conceal her surprise when Lana invited herself up, and tried to refrain from asking her if there was a reason for her visit, though Lana supplied one unasked. 'I didn't want Annie to forget me. I wanted to make sure we bonded, otherwise how can I be a good godmother to her?'

She had brought her a present – a set of paints. Dawn couldn't help laughing. 'You can't give a six-month-old baby paints,' she said, 'she would eat them, or drink them.'

'I know, I know,' said Lana, 'of course I know that. But when she's old enough they will be there waiting for her.'

Dawn thought that Lana was lying – she could see in her face that she was disappointed, and that she felt stupid for not realizing young babies can't use paints. Dawn also slightly resented the idea that, but for her godmother, Annie might never have contact with painting materials. Of course they would be buying her paints and brushes and paper and crayons and all the other stuff as soon as she was old enough to handle a paintbrush without putting it in her mouth. She didn't say any of this of course, but the paints were put away in a drawer, like the gryphon, and forgotten about.

There were several more visits during that first year, and the frequently repeated invitation to bring Annie down to London. Dawn didn't mind the visits, but was looking forward to a time when their frequency might become more bearable. She visited London twice with Annie as a baby, and both times it was an ordeal. Lana lived in a flat-cum-studio, with little to mark the boundary between the two. It was a pretty flat but quite filthy, with plates of leftover food on the floor, cold cups of coffee, dust everywhere, fragile objets d'art – if that's what they were – teetering on narrow plinths. And then the studio area itself, a terrible mess of things piled on top of each other without any apparent sense of order – drawings pinned crookedly on the wall, drawing pins on the floor, scalpels, scissors, sheets of glass, engraving tools, rolls of wire, Sellotape, pots of white glue, even a blowtorch. It was impossible to let Annie crawl around. She had to be kept in her high chair for the whole visit, or else had to be carried about. And this made Annie frustrated and she became hot and bad-tempered, and so the visits ended in confusion and bad spirits.

'I'm sorry, Lana,' Dawn wrote, 'but I can't bring Annie to visit unless the flat is made safe for her. She can't be kept in her high chair the whole time, and with it being such a long trek to London I don't think it's practical for us to visit at the moment.'

Even though she'd hoped Lana would understand, it became clear that her sister had taken this decision as a judgement on her lifestyle. She claimed that other friends brought their babies round, and would let them range freely about the flat. The babies had come to no harm. 'They all agree it is a very stimulating place for a child,' she wrote, 'and the children love it. They have a lot more common sense than you seem to realize.'

Common sense? Little babies? That is exactly what they don't have, that is why they need protecting. They would eat a razor blade as though it was a lettuce leaf, they would stroke a candle flame as though it was a bright butterfly. But Dawn couldn't be persuaded to visit Lana in London, and this seemed to make Lana all the more determined to visit her as much as she could manage. She seemed to think that, deprived of the stimulation of Stanley knife blades and countless choking hazards, Dawn's child was trapped in a sterile darkhouse robbed of all motivations to thrive.

When Petula was born, the process started all over again. The visits, just starting to tail off as Annie grew older, resumed their earlier frequency. Lana visited every few months all through the girls' infancy. She always brought gifts – colourful, non-plastic things when they were little, arty craft sets and creative toys when they were older, or things designed to stimulate their interest in the world of knowledge – formicaria, wormeries, sea monkeys, skeletons, natural history detective kits, none of which, Dawn was half-pleased to note, gained preference over the computer games and traditional dolls that were the girls' favoured playthings. She also took them out on visits to art galleries and museums. It was good to have the children off her hands for a while, but it annoyed her that Lana assumed they would not go to such places otherwise, and pointed out, whenever she could, that they had already visited that particular gallery some time in the past. At other times Lana would just play with them, but with far more vigour and energy than was really needed. 'Overplaying,' her husband had called it. Out-childrening the children. She ran round the garden like a demented dog, did head-over-heels with them, turned cartwheels, fell over. Yes, I would have the energy to do that as well, if I only saw my children once every three months. I could turn somersaults too if I didn't have to get them their food, wash their clothes, give them a bath. But you, you can just swan in and out of their lives whenever you feel like it, enjoy the children in the way that I want to enjoy them, if only I had the time and the energy.

She did try her best not to feel resentful, but the last straw came when she read an interview with Lana in one of the Sunday papers. By now she had achieved a modest level of fame, enough to attract some attention as a promising new artist (at thirty-seven!). In the interview she talked about her lesbianism, and the interviewer asked her if she would ever like to have children. 'No, I am comfortable with the fact that I will never be a mother, but I have two beautiful godchildren, and I make sure that their lives are as creative and as stimulating as it's possible for them to be.'

How good of you, Dawn thought, to take the trouble to make sure my children don't turn into brainless idiots, which I am sure they would do otherwise, without your regular visits to take them to the cultural hotspots of the world. Of course, it made it all the more difficult that the children loved Lana and looked forward to her visits. But that was because Lana let them do what they liked, and when they were on their gallery visits would buy them almost anything they asked for. She wouldn't rebuke them for bad behaviour, in fact she even seemed to encourage it. Once, after one of her sister's visits, when Dawn had asked Annie to do her homework she had replied, in a merrily bright voice, 'Fuck you, asshole.'

It took a lot of pain and crying and heartache to wipe that phrase from Annie's vocabulary, and it wasn't the only occasion. Nearly every visit from Lana left behind it a mark in the girls' behaviour that would take weeks, sometimes, to eradicate. One visit had resulted in Annie becoming more destructive with her toys, making her dolls fight and break things. Lego towers were constructed and then bombarded by Lego missiles. Dawn supposed there was a sort of expressive creativity in the play, but it was so noisy and disruptive it had to be stopped. Then there were the experiments with clothes and daring make-up. At nine years old Annie was making herself up like a little Goth. Again, the more physical process of erasure was long and heartbreaking. No, you can't go around like that, it's OK at home but I'm not taking you out looking like something from *Carry On Screaming*.

All through these childhood years Dawn had managed to maintain the ban on visiting Lana in London and her hazard-filled flat, but eventually she moved into new premises. Her increasing success as an artist meant she was able to rent a proper studio and buy her own house, a proper house with separate rooms, where work and home lives didn't overlap. She had a new partner, a stolid and respectable lawyer, so she understood. Lana had described a sane and stable home life. Surely now the girls could visit, who were long past the age of putting inappropriate things in their mouths anyway. And so a visit was arranged. Lana proposed that the girls stay for three nights, during the first week of the Easter holidays. She would come up on the Thursday to collect them, and then Dawn would come down to London on the following Sunday to take them back.

Dawn could find no way out of this arrangement. She understood that Lana's domestic life was no longer the hazard it had been, and yet she couldn't help feeling that she was putting her daughters in danger. She couldn't say what that danger was, and told herself off for being unreasonable. Lana was her own sister and loved the girls more than anything. Why was she so worried? She was coming up on Thursday morning with her partner, Jeanette, and they would stay for lunch and then take the girls down to London in the afternoon. It was a two-hour drive each way, if the traffic was good. Lana felt sick with worry.

She didn't warm to Jeanette, despite the fact she was nothing like the tall, intimidating lesbian lawyer she'd been expecting, but turned out to be small and round with a pageboy haircut and a rather piercing way of looking at you, as though she'd seen right through whatever front you were putting up and was thinking – *Nice try, darling, but I can see you for what you really are.* She walked through the ground-floor rooms of their house as though she was a prospective buyer, sizing everything up, noting the quality of everything. She had not met the girls before, but greeted them as though slightly bored by long acquaintance, seeming pointedly uninterested in them. It was a clever strategy. The girls instantly relaxed in her presence, and seemed willing to do anything she asked.

And so the girls were taken away in the back of this stranger's car (Lana had no car of her own and had never learned to drive), and Dawn could do nothing but wait.

The house Lana had bought was a small brick terrace in a recently gentrified quarter of the otherwise rough part of London she'd been living in for years. Jeanette answered the door wearing a novelty apron that depicted a large-breasted, lingerie-clad torso, the comic volup-tuousness of which was not so very far from the reality of the body beneath, Dawn supposed. She was silently impressed by the comfortable domestic interior of the house, everything was stripped wood and tastefully dis-tressed, with lots of artistic paraphernalia everywhere, though unlike the old flat it was all framed or fastened securely to the walls, or hanging from the ceiling. She followed Jeanette, who seemed a little red and flustered, into the kitchen. The girls were not ready, they had not packed, and the whole – she hesitated to use the word to herself – family was gathered around a baking activity. Dawn had already noticed Jeanette's floury hands, more floury at the ends, so that it looked as though she was vanishing. The children were utterly absorbed in their cookery, Petula was holding a rolling pin, Annie a knife. It took Dawn a moment to realize that her sister was absent from this complicated kitchen scene. The girls were alone with the little round lawyer. They only gave their mother a brief acknowledgement, over-the-shoulder glances and half-smiles. If she had been inclined to feel self-pitying, Dawn would have thought the girls were a little disappointed to see her. Of course, they never had the time to do anything like that at home. Dawn couldn't remember the last time she did any baking.

'We're making strawberry tarts,' said Annie, turning her messy face towards her mother. Dawn winced when she saw how Annie was slicing a strawberry with what seemed to be a very sharp knife. No one was taking any notice of her, and Annie was clearly not concentrating very hard, and was not even looking at what she was doing, but carried on slicing while looking over her shoulder at her mother.

Dawn stepped over and took hold of the hand that was holding the knife, 'Careful, darling,' she said. Then, to Jeanette, 'Where's Lana?'

'Oh, she had to go away.'

'You mean she's not here?'

'She had an unexpected last-minute problem with an exhibition that's due to open on Wednesday. She had to go and sort it out.'

'So she'll be back later this evening?'

'Hardly. The exhibition's in New York.'

'New York? She went to New York today?' Dawn couldn't help but laugh at her sister's new lifestyle.

'Not today. She went on Friday morning.'

It took Dawn some moments to frame the next question, during which time she expected the woman before her to provide a more detailed account of their weekend, but a few seconds' silence told her she thought no explanation was necessary. In fact she pointedly carried on as if nothing was amiss, and as if she wasn't there, burrowing deep into her dough, rolling it out with a rolling pin, and showing the girls how to do the same with their own rolling pins.

Dawn hadn't even been offered a cup of coffee.

'I'm sorry,' she said, suddenly losing her patience, 'are you telling me that the girls have been with you alone since Friday?'

'Don't worry,' said Jeanette, rolling her eyes and throwing her head back, as if to mime being hit by the tidal wave of Dawn's indignation, 'I'm perfectly capable of looking after them on my own.'

'That's hardly the point. Listen . . .' Suddenly aware that what she needed to say should be said out of earshot of the girls, she tried to contrive a way of removing them from the scene. But the task of separating them from their cookery, when they were up to their sharp little elbows in flour, butter and strawberry juice, seemed too great, and in the end she managed to have them cook alone for a little while (knives removed), while she and Jeanette went into the living room.

'This is all very melodramatic, isn't it?' said the lawyer. 'I hope the trust I have won from the girls won't be damaged by this cloak-and-dagger stuff.'

'But this is absolutely outrageous. My children have been in the care of a stranger for two full days. Why wasn't I informed?'

Jeanette looked aghast, unbelieving, and shook her head slightly.

'Informed of what?'

'That Lana had gone away, that the children would be on their own.'

'But they haven't been on their own.'

'Listen, with the greatest respect – I'm sure you are a wonderful person – but I had not met you before Thursday, and I don't know anything about you.'

'You know I am your sister's partner. Do you think your sister would entrust her godchildren to the care of someone who would be likely to harm them, or let them come to harm?'

'Frankly I have been uncomfortable with many of the choices Lana has made in her life. Like I said, I don't know anything about you . . .'

'And so you suppose that we have to let you know every detail of our arrangements for the weekend, that we have to consult you on every little thing we do?'

'Going to New York for several days is hardly a little thing. And yes, they are my children, they are still very young, and I think it's my right to know exactly what is going on when they are in someone else's care.'

'Well, would you like to see some qualifications? References? These are the godchildren of the woman I am in love with and have chosen to share my life with.'

'Yes, but they are not your godchildren.'

'What difference does that make?'

'What difference? All the difference in the world, I would have thought.'

Jeanette sighed. 'Lana said you would be like this.'

'Well in that case she should have known to tell me.'

'And have you storm down to London and take them away from us? But you haven't had to sit up all night comforting a woman because she's so distressed at not being able to see her own godchildren. You haven't had to wipe the tears from her eyes as she weeps with the pain of separation. She has told me how difficult you've made it for her to see them, that you think she is a bad influence on them. She has been waiting for years for them to come and be allowed to visit her. Would you like me to take you upstairs and show you the special bedroom she has made for them? She spent a year painting those murals.'

Dawn was taken aback.

'We never deliberately made it difficult. We live a hundred and fifty miles apart.'

'This is the first time they have been allowed to visit in eight years, Lana told me. Eight years. That's a whole childhood. Instead she's had to traipse up north every few months to look after their well-being.'

'Look after their well-being? I think I can manage that on my own, thank you very much.'

'Without a single book in the house? Without a single original painting on the walls, not even one of Lana's, but cheap poster reproductions of Jack Vettriano? The children tell her, every time she visits, that they haven't been to a single museum or art gallery since her last visit. If she didn't do her work as godmother they would be starved.'

The presumption of this woman, her readiness to believe anything Lana said over anything Dawn might say in her defence, was breathtaking. Anything Dawn might say by way of retaliation – about the fact that her house contained hundreds of books, all of them upstairs, about the fact that her walls were not adorned with her sister's art because her sister's paintings were, quite frankly, frightening – could do nothing to chip away at her presumption. Dawn realized she had been the subject of many long tearful conversations in this little house, and they had pinned her down as a certain type of person – a philistine heterosexual. A *normal*, as Lana called them. In the end she didn't need to say anything, because they were interrupted by a sound so intrusive they assumed it to be some sort of car or burglar alarm in a very nearby house, and it was a few seconds before they gathered themselves enough to realize that the sound was produced by a human larynx, at a shocking pitch and volume.

They ran next door to find Petula wandering about the kitchen with her fist held aloft, as if giving a thumbs up sign to someone in the distance, except that the thumb had come away, and blood was pouring down her arm. Annie was pressed against the corner of the kitchen counter, as though trapped by an invisible force, and her face was grey with fear. Jeanette, too, seemed struck dumb and motionless by the sight, and it was only Dawn who seemed capable of any decisive action. She bore down on her child with reassurances and motherly medical knowledge. Dawn had never been able to tolerate a child's pain. Pain to them comes unregulated, uncalibrated, so that what to an adult might feel like an irritation to them feels like the deepest, most searing agony. Having held her thumb aloft like a trophy when her mother was absent, now she stowed it and wouldn't let her mother look at it, as if she feared the very act of looking might increase the pain. Dawn found a way through the swirl of bodily anxiety that her daughter had become to find the thumb tucked away in the centre of her, covered by her other hand, as if beneath a lid. Only with the gentlest, most delicate prising could the lid be lifted and the damaged thumb exposed, and even so it seemed suspended on a continuous note of distress that came from her daughter's mouth, her voice like a tripwire whose snagging would close the lid instantly. Dawn got a long enough look to see that the cut needed medical attention. She felt pain herself as she looked at it, the way the cut neatly bisected flesh and thumbnail as though there was no difference between them. Another few millimetres and the top would have been severed completely, but in fact there was a sort of hinge that held it together.

For a moment the injury brought mother and daughter together in a chemical, molecular way. It was almost as if her daughter had deliberately cut a door into herself that her mother could enter. Noticing Jeanette, Dawn saw her as if from the window of a house of flesh, and suddenly felt sorry for her that she could never know her daughter this way, and then felt guilty for the way in which this made her feel superior to her sister's lover. You can never know a person like this, she said in her mind, as something moulded from your own self. She shook the thoughts away again. There was a time in her past when she would have cringed at such sentiments and would have been on Jeanette's side against the normals of this world. But nothing could change her back now. Jeanette was outside, irredeemably, for ever.

At the hospital, to Dawn's surprise, they seemed delighted by Petula's injury. The staff seemed to relish the opportunity to extend sympathy to someone as deserving as a young girl, when they spent most of their time having to force sympathy on undeserving drunks and incompetent handymen. They slipped her through the fast channel, crowded round her, stroked her hair, inspected her cut, told her not to worry, that everything would be fine, that there was enough blood supply to save the semi-detached portion of the thumb, all they needed to do was to glue it back on. Yes, glue. They were using glue. Dawn and Petula laughed as the nurse explained about the special surgical glue. No need for stitches. No pain. No discomfort. The glue would do its healing and then dissolve as if it had never been there. It only took a few minutes, and Petula's thumb was bound in a stiff bandage with a plastic casing that would have to stay on for two weeks.

It was nearly ten years later that Petula told her mother the truth about that evening. By that time Dawn and Lana had settled into lives of contented separation from each other, at ease with their distance, and respectful of it. Lana's influence on and interest in the children had waned as they'd grown older. Now that they were at university and studying non-arts subjects (microbiology for Petula, computer science for Annie) they saw nothing of their famous godmother, and didn't expect to, unless they happened to be at home during the annual visit. Lana and Jeanette split up after three years. How could a lawyer and an artist ever live happily together? She was living with a writer now. A poet, ten years younger than her. She still loved to shock Dawn, and believed she still could. But she wasn't the force she once was. She never made much money as an artist, and was now a part-time lecturer at an art college.

'You remember that time I cut my thumb at Aunt Lana's, when that woman was there?'

'Yes.'

'Well, I never told you at the time, of course – but I did it on purpose.'

'What? You cut your thumb on purpose?'

'Yes.'

Dawn didn't know what to say. She looked carefully at Petula, trying to discern the reason for the disclosure.

'That was a silly thing to do.'

'I realize that now.'

Dawn felt an uprush of affection for her daughter. It was as though she had been given a gift ten years ago and hadn't opened it until now. The sacrifice her daughter had made that night, to help her win the battle against the dreadful Jeanette, the person whose claim on their lives had proved so flimsy. Though she could tell by Petula's expression that she felt guilty about how effectively she had acted against Jeanette. 'I didn't do it to help you win your argument. I did it to stop both of you shouting.'

'I know,' said Dawn.

'You were very cross with Aunt Lana, weren't you?'

'No, I was cross with that woman. It was all out of proportion. I thought she was stealing you, even though she hadn't done anything really.'

'She was nice,' said Petula, 'I thought you were being unfair to her.'

'Maybe I was.'

'We should visit, sometime. Soon.' Petula lifted up her hand and examined her thumb, as if all her memories about Aunt Lana were written on it. Then she looked, just for a second, as though she was going to suck it. The thought had crossed her mind, her mother discerned. Then she put her hand down again, and picked up the book she'd been reading, a huge scientific textbook that in a secret moment, the night before, while Petula was asleep upstairs, Dawn had flicked through, trying to understand it.

The Flag

On the day our country was invaded, I was surprised how many of our neighbours expressed an allegiance to our invaders. Their flag suddenly appeared in the windows of people who, we were sure, only a few weeks previously had spoken of them as dogs, or rats. They greeted the passing tanks with cheers. Some threw flowers. The new flag hung from many windows and balconies. They were not just showing support for the invaders, but claiming to belong to them, to be of their kind. What surprised me was how carefully they'd kept that fact secret until now.

They had invaded us before, but the last time was one hundred and fifty years ago. That time there had been much cruelty. There were executions and mass graves, public hangings in the town square. Resistance movements were ruthlessly quashed, their leaders tortured for days. Anyone who spoke out against the invaders was paraded naked through the city, their body painted green, red and yellow, the colours of the invaders' flag.

This time the invaders promised things would be different. Along with the tanks came armoured vehicles from which men in white uniforms addressed the city through loudspeakers. 'We are your friends,' they said. 'Our two peoples have always been friends. Only history has put a border between us. The old regimes were built on fear and distrust. But we have a new regime now, with good men and women sharing power through a central committee. There will be no more greed and despotism in either of our great nations. We will share everything for the good of all of our peoples.' I can't remember it word for word, but it was something like that.

My mother came into the living room where I and my two sisters were watching the endless procession of military vehicles, along with my father. She had brought some pieces of material with her – a large bed sheet, a green tablecloth she had found in the attic, and an old yellow curtain, though it looked more orange than yellow.

'Look, we can make a flag. Children, help me cut them and sew them together.' My mother had scissors sticking out of the pocket of her apron. Her hair had come undone and was falling across her face.

My father looked at her disapprovingly.

'Take a look at yourself,' he said, 'think about what you are doing. You look ridiculous, trying to make a flag.'

'But everyone else is doing it. They're probably making a note of all the windows that aren't showing the flag.'

'Well then, they will have a big task because most

houses have no flag at all. It is just because the flags are so bright they make it seem as though there are more than there really are. Have a rest and look out of the window at this cavalcade.'

We lived in a ground-floor apartment on the Marin Boulevard, and so had a perfect view of the procession. It seemed to have been going on all day, so many tanks and armoured lorries, more than you'd have thought the city could contain. There were people out on the pavement now, cheering and waving smaller versions of the invaders' flag. Where had they found so many, so quickly? Then I noticed that the invaders themselves were distributing them, throwing bunches of them out of their vehicles as they passed.

Marin Boulevard was one of the main roads into the city centre, broad and tree-lined; it could have been designed for military processions. The fact that we lived on the ground floor made me feel nervous. If the invaders began calling on the residents, they would start with those on the ground floor. But we were surprised. It did seem as though it was to be a peaceful invasion. The residents of the city were not being troubled by the invaders at all. But what had happened to our government? What were they doing? Had they fled?

'It's like a carnival,' said my father, still incredulous, 'like a festival – look at these.'

He was pointing to some vehicles in the military procession that I thought at first were some sort of rocket launchers but when I looked again I realized they were fairground rides packed up and loaded on the backs of lorries. A waltzer, a Ferris wheel, a ghost train. And later that day I heard that they were setting up a funfair in the main square. I wanted to go and have a look. My mother told me not to even think about going out now, while the city was full of foreign soldiers.

The rest of the day passed quietly. We didn't leave the house, not even when the parade of vehicles had finished and the boulevard had returned to normal. We stayed inside, but kept a constant eye on what was happening out in the street. It seemed that we expected something to happen, for there to be a knock at the door, or some official announcement on paper put through the letter box, or proclamations by loudspeaker. But there was nothing. Occasionally a military vehicle would be seen driving down the boulevard, but alone, as though it was on a routine errand. There were children in the street still, milling about, as if waiting for something. I asked my mother – why can't I go out on the street when there are other children out there? Their parents were stupid to let them out, she said.

Later, in the evening, as the sun set and the lamps came on, there seemed to be a relaxed and easy atmosphere. Couples were out walking arm in arm, families strolled in a relaxed manner with little dogs on silver leads. Some of the children were carrying paper windmills and stars on sticks, and lots of toys in orange and green colours. They must have been to the funfair in the city square.

We had dinner in silence. Whenever anyone spoke the conversation led almost immediately to the invaders, and our father silenced us whenever that subject came up. And so we soon gave up even trying to say anything.

We did wonder what we should do tomorrow. Would schools and factories be open as normal? Would the shops be open?

'Why not?' said my father.

'Because everything has changed,' said my mother, 'nothing can be taken for granted, we have new rulers and new rules – but we don't know what they are.'

'If there are any such big changes they would have told us.'

'How? They can't knock on every door in the city. Oh, you should have gone out today, and then you might have picked up some news. But no, you had to keep us locked up in the house all day long while everyone else was out chatting on the pavements.'

'And at the funfair. We could have gone to the funfair,' I said. 'It's still on.'

'You're not going out now, it's too late and it's too dangerous,' said my mother.

'Tomorrow I will go to work as normal and the children will go to school, though you should take them, dearest, I don't want them going on their own.'

And so the next day we set off for school with my mother guiding us. I was a little disappointed because, being the eldest, I was usually guiding my sisters, and it wasn't until my mother guided us that I realized how much I enjoyed the responsibility, and missed it now.

'It's like a different city,' said my younger sister.

'Don't be silly,' said my mother, 'it's exactly the same as it's always been.'

'No, it's different.'

She was right, but none of us could have said in what way. The flags of our invaders still hung from some balconies. And the boulevard did have something of the strewn quality of a post-carnival atmosphere, with colourful litter hanging from the trees and silting up by the kerbstones. I was amazed, when we crossed the road itself, how the mighty procession of tanks that had travelled that way yesterday hadn't left some sort of permanent mark on the carriageway – that there should be the impression in the cobbles themselves of those great caterpillar tracks – but there was nothing. And looking around us, we could see not a single military vehicle or person in uniform. And in fact there were not many people at all, because our hunch was right – the school was closed and the day had been declared a holiday. Everything was closed.

There was no sign to that effect on the school gates, but the gates were firmly shut and padlocked, and we had to turn around and walk all the way home again. We should have felt happy to be on holiday, but on this day we would rather have been at school. We wanted to see our friends and our teachers and ask them about what was happening, and what the invaders would do with us, we wanted to share news and make sure all our friends were safe, but now we would have to go home and make do with knowing nothing again.

When we got home we found that my father had already returned home. The factory was shut. And he hadn't met anyone else – it seemed that everyone else knew that the factory would be closed, and so had stayed at home, which meant he didn't meet anyone at the gates, and so had no news.

What were we supposed to do? It was a holiday, but it didn't feel like a holiday. It just felt like a nothing day. It was as though someone had just switched our lives off, and we could do nothing but sit at home and think about what might be happening in the world outside, but with no real idea if we were right or wrong.

'Maybe nothing will change,' said my father. 'Why should it?'

'Because yesterday we were working for ourselves. Tomorrow we are working for them,' said my mother. 'Who knows what that might mean. Less pay? Higher taxes? They will look after their own people first, and ensure they have the higher living standard, and we will be paying for it, one way or another. I don't like to think about it.'

The conversation went on like this for some time. Out of the window we could see little sign of change. The streets were nearly empty of vehicles, because of the holiday. But still the flow of people walking to and from the city centre continued, families walking there, the children full of excitement, and returning some time later, laden with prizes and cheap toys, their eyes red from having stared for so long at wonderful things.

'I refuse to go to the fair,' said my father, 'until we are told what is going to happen. Let us be told what is to be done with things, then we can accept their entertainment, but I am not going to be so easily bribed.'

I saw one of my friends from my window, walking back from the fair with his parents. I called out to him and he waved at me, full of excitement and happiness. He managed to tell me, before his parents pulled him along, that everything at the fair, all the rides and all the stalls, was free.

Some of the flags were still out. My friend was carrying a hand-sized one. Later I told my father about how everything at the fair was free, but he was absolutely resolved not to go to the fair until he'd been to work.

The next day, we went to school as normal, but things had changed. A person I didn't recognize was standing at the entrance, a tall man with a dark beard and glasses. He told my mother to wait in the playground while I went in to the school. When I went to my classroom I was surprised to see that there was no room for me, and that someone else was seated at my desk. My teacher told me that I was going to be put into a different class. She said this in a very kindly and apologetic way, and tried her best to reassure me that this was just because 'the school was being reorganized' to make it more efficient. 'We are having smaller classrooms.' I was very upset. I didn't want to be put into a new class. When I asked where it was, my teacher said that they hadn't organized the new class yet, and that I would have to go home and wait until a new teacher could be found. I returned to the playground where my mother was still waiting. I told her what had happened, and she went up to the bearded man who was still standing at the entrance. He seemed to understand what had happened already, and apologized again. He was, he said, the new temporary headmaster, and that he was sorry but they were reorganizing the school to make it more efficient. 'You should go home,' he said, 'until the reorganization is complete. Then you will be informed, and can come back.'

My mother was outraged by this. Why did I have no place in the school, when so many others did? Why did I have to go home? The man with the beard patiently explained that it was just a matter of reorganization. Everything would be sorted out soon. There were other mothers and their children in the playground, and they were being told the same thing. My sisters, too, had been excluded from their classrooms, and had to go home as well. The new headmaster made it obvious that he was not to be argued with. We had no choice but to go home. My mother was crying, as much from anger as anything else.

When we got home, we found my father sitting in the kitchen, with his jacket off, drinking tea.

'You? Why are you here?' my mother said.

'Guess,' my father said.

'Surely they haven't fired you?'

'Not in so many words. They said I should return home. They are restructuring the factory. I will be told when I am required to return to work.'

'And are they still paying you?'

My father paused.

'It's ridiculous, but I didn't think to ask.'

'Of course, you know why this is happening, don't you? Because we didn't put up a flag and we haven't been to the funfair. I told you they would notice. They've been taking note of everyone who hasn't done those things, and they are going to make life impossible for us. You have lost your job, let us face it, and you won't find another one.'

'Don't be stupid. If they wanted to sack me, they would have said, "You're sacked," not, "We're rearranging things and we'll call you later." '

'Because they don't want a bloody revolution on their hands, of course. They'll make it seem as though it's just a temporary thing – and then, when it's too late, you'll realize you have lost everything.'

'What can I do? I have no choice but to wait and see what will happen.'

'We can't just sit here waiting. I bet no one else is just sitting and waiting. Look out into the street and see how everyone is coming and going, looking contented, as though they have no troubles.'

Although the window was behind them, curtains

open and displaying a panoramic view of the boulevard through net curtains, neither of them turned round to look into the street. Each knew what they would see.

Later that day my mother went out to visit the shops. We needed bread, milk and eggs. She also planned to buy some meat and vegetables. None of us knew what the situation with the shops was. Surely they would be operating as normal, but we couldn't help worrying that something would be different, that there would be shortages, or new rules, or rationing. My mother was gone for more than two hours. Normally a shopping trip wouldn't take her much more than an hour. We all realized this meant problems – that she had been forced to shop further afield than normal. By the time she finally returned we were all in a state of silent agitation, no one wanting to actually voice their anxieties about my mother's long absence. She came in looking tired, and her shopping bag didn't look very full.

'The butcher's had nothing. I queued for an hour and by the time I was served, everything was gone, all he had left was some fat and some bones. I refused but the woman behind me bought some – what was she going to do with it? She said she would combine it with gravy powder and make it into a stew. I walked all the way to Royal Quarter but the butchers there had closed at lunchtime. Everyone was saying they are going to start rationing. Others were saying no, there is plenty of food, it's just that people have been panic-buying since the invasion, and the shops have been emptied. They will be back to normal in a day or two. Who do you believe? I couldn't buy any bread either, but I did manage to buy some flour, and we have bicarb in the cupboard, so I can make soda bread. They had some old margarine in the grocers. And I managed to buy some potatoes and cabbage and eggs.' She didn't want to worry us children, but it was clear she was worried about the fact that we only had enough food for one more day. If the shops were empty again tomorrow, we would begin starving.

'I heard a lot of people chatting about the fair,' she said. 'They have food there, hotdog stalls. I wondered, you know, whether it might be a good idea to go up there. I looked in some of the cafes and restaurants along the boulevard. They are either closed or they are charging ridiculous prices. They can't get ingredients either. But the hotdog stands at the fair, they are full, and they are giving them away for nothing.'

At first my father acted as if he didn't need to say anything, but then, when my mother refused to turn away from staring at him, he was forced to say, 'The world is falling apart around our ears and you want us to go to a funfair?'

And nothing more was said on the matter for the rest of the day.

The next day, we waited. No one really knew what we were waiting for. Well, we knew that we were waiting to be told when to go to school, when to go to work, but we didn't know how that information would arrive, nor if it would arrive at all. Would they send a letter? If so, when would they be likely to send it? And was the post operating normally, or was that being restructured as well? At heart, I suspected my parents didn't expect anything to happen, and that we would have to go back to school and try again to find out what was happening.

We ate all the food that Mother had bought the day before, and by the end of the day all we had left was half a loaf and three eggs. We could have breakfast the next morning, but Mother would have to try again at the shops. They will be restocked by then, we thought, hopefully.

She went out again after breakfast and was gone all morning and didn't return home until lunchtime, when she looked very weary and in fact almost collapsed in the hall. All she had in her shopping bag were two small and very spongy beetroot and a small tin with no label on it. I took charge of the tin, and both my sisters followed me. 'Don't open it now,' my father shouted, 'leave it until this evening, when we will be properly hungry.' 'But we're properly hungry now,' said my little sister. 'Don't be stupid, you've still got your breakfast in your stomach. Don't waste that tin by eating it now.' 'We only want to find out what it is.' A long argument ensued. My father insisted that the tin shouldn't be opened until dinner time, otherwise the temptation to eat its contents would be too strong, and if we ate it now, we might not have anything to eat again until the next day. In the end we agreed, and the tin was put away on the top shelf of the larder, where it sat looking rather precious in its shiny silveriness.

'They are closing some of the shops to all but favoured customers,' said my mother. 'Unless you are a regular they won't even open the door for you. But all the shops where I am a regular are empty already. It's no good, if they don't have fresh stock by tomorrow, then we'll be finished.'

'Don't be silly. Where can all the food have gone? It's a supply problem, nothing else, there are still the same number of mouths to feed as there have always been.'

'They've taken it. They are taking all our food back to their own country – can't you see?' My mother quietened, realizing how she was frightening me and my sisters. 'I know what I'll do. I'll set off early tomorrow. We won't have anything for breakfast anyway. I'll set off at seven o'clock and be first in the queue.'

That evening we sat around the table while my mother prepared dinner in the kitchen. By 'prepared' I mean she opened the tin that had been sitting in the cupboard all day. She served the contents on a plate. It was a pink, rectangular block of something that looked, at first, like meat, but when my father cut it with a knife it crumbled into a grainy slush. My father seemed quite pleased because he recognized it as cod roe, probably mixed with tomato paste to give it a pink colour. We had it with the last of the potatoes – roughly one small potato each. Even as I ate the roe I realized that in normal times I would have found it disgusting, but now it tasted as good as anything I'd ever eaten. Salty. My father said it was very nutritious, and would do us good.

My mother had made an odd sort of cake for dessert, but which tasted like a very heavy, slightly sweet bread. It was filling, that was the important thing.

It was the last food my mother was able to get from the shops. When, the next morning, she set off at 7 a.m. to be at the front of the queues, she found that some shops had started selecting their customers, and that her custom was refused in all the shops she tried, even those at which she'd been a regular customer for many years. Every shop she tried. She came home with her shopping bag as empty as when she left.

'What do we do now?' she asked my father, who had spent the morning trying to find out if he still had a job at the factory. As he'd expected, he wasn't even allowed to get through the reception area. New people on the desks said they couldn't find his name in the employees' register. He said to them – Have I been sacked? No, they replied. According to our records you have never worked here. 'Go and try to take the boy to school tomorrow morning, the same thing will happen. They will have erased his name from the register, they will claim he never had a place there. Do you see what is happening? They are casting us out. What'll be the next move? We'll have to go to the city hall and ask to be registered. Registered in our own country! And they will give us forms to fill, then lose the forms, then we will have to fill them out again, then they will lose them again, meanwhile our landlord will throw us out because we can't pay the rent. The bank will say they can't find any trace of our names – not that I had any money in there anyway.'

It had been nearly a week since the invasion, but it felt to us like many months. I couldn't even remember the old life. When we became sure that the old life would never return, it seemed impossibly distant, as though it had been a different life altogether, populated by twins of ourselves. I couldn't even remember the school, my friends, if they were ever friends. My mother said we were better off without them.

Until now my parents had tried to shield us from the things that were worrying them, but now, with the prospect of no food or money, we were included in the family discussions as much as anyone.

'What have they got planned for us? Will they come and take us away? Perhaps we should be leaving.'

'How can we leave? We haven't got any money for a train. I heard you need warrants to be able to buy a ticket.'

'Then perhaps we should go into hiding somewhere, there must be friends we could stay with . . .'

My father gave a hopeless laugh at the suggestion.

'I met Mr Brownlee yesterday. He claimed to not even know my name. And we worked side by side for twenty-seven years.'

'Where did you see him? You should have asked him what was happening. Asked him why he's got a job and not you – what's the difference, you're the same religion, race, background, age. What's so perfect about him?'

'What does it matter? He has done something right.'

'He displayed the flag. That's what he did. I bet he did.'

'No one cares about the flag now. You've heard them saying how we are all friends. But the most important thing now is, how are we going to eat?'

'There is only one thing we can do. Go to the funfair. It might not be on for much longer. I heard someone say it was finishing tomorrow. It is the only place that is serving free food. Anyone can go. Anyone can get something to eat.'

'But that's not a permanent solution to our crisis, we can't rely on a funfair for food.'

'I don't care. I'm hungry, the children are starving, we have no choice.'

And so, that evening, we left the flat as a family for the first time since the invasion. We had put on our best clothes, as though we were going to church. My hair had been washed, and my father had spent nearly an hour shaving. My mother had found her old fur coat with the snow fox collar, which she hadn't worn for years, in fact I don't think I had ever seen her wear it, I had only ever seen it hanging on a hanger in the hall cupboard. My sisters were dressed in their best frocks and their hair done in plaits and ribbons.

On the boulevard, we joined the stream that had not ceased flowing since the day after the invasion, the current that carried families to the funfair and back again. It felt reassuring and comforting, just as, when swimming in a real river, you feel connected to all the water in the world, so here we felt we had re-joined the population of our fellow citizens, after having been stranded on an island of doubt and uncertainty for nearly a week. There was a strength to be taken from this sensation, and even though we were starving, we felt an energy (I think I speak for all of us) that passed through our joined hands like a form of electricity. We noticed, also, that people were looking at us in a new way. On the few times I'd been out of the house I had the feeling that I was invisible, because no one's gaze seemed to settle on me, even for a moment, but now I was seen, we all were. People nodded acknowledgement at us. And no one out on the street seemed to be suffering the same anxieties or deprivations we had been. It was permanent Sunday afternoon out here, under the leafy trees, through which an unusual sun was shining. There was no sign of hunger in anyone's eyes, no sign of fear.

I had forgotten how long the boulevard was, dead straight into the heart of the city, long enough to land a Jumbo jet. It led directly to the City Square, and it was there that the funfair was sited. If we stood out in the centre of the boulevard, which was still closed to traffic, you could just make out the structures – the helix of the helter-skelter, the long slender jib of something that rose and fell, tiny from here but up close must carry its twirling passengers to terrifying heights. I tried to hurry my family along, fearful that what I could see in the distance, impossibly remote at the far end of a river of human heads, might disappear by the time we got there. It had a mirage-like quality.

The crowds thickened as we neared the funfair. Against our flow the happy families came, laden with prizes and joy, some were carrying large fabric animals, others puzzles that they had already taken out of their boxes and were mulling over as they walked along. I couldn't decide if I was hungrier for toys or food.

My father was still anxious. He was convinced that we wouldn't be allowed in to the fair, and indeed when we arrived at the square we could see that the funfair was fenced off, and that there was a security gate, similar to an airport customs channel, and it seemed that some sort of documentation was being checked as people passed through. It was a free fair, as advertised, but that didn't mean you could just walk in. There were soldiers here as well, wearing the uniform of the invaders, and it was their flag that was prominent everywhere. Our own flag was nowhere to be seen.

The fair itself seemed immense, filling most of the square, a city within the city. It seemed, in the encroaching twilight, like a single elaborate machine, a vast contraption of wheels and levers that worked furiously to remain in the same place, emitting jets of steam, sudden spinning dervishes that tilted and, to my amazement, actually seemed to carry passengers. People were all part of this machine, at one with it; they threaded through it like film through a projector, or like fuel through the pipes of a motor car. I had never, in my life, seen anything so exciting, seductive, bright and mysterious as the funfair in the town square. I didn't care if there was food there or not, I just wanted to be in amongst it.

But the rest of my family hesitated. My mother first, she stopped fifty yards short of the entrance.

'I don't like it,' she said, 'we don't know what the rules are. We might be putting ourselves in danger.'

My father, too, seemed uncertain, but saw no other option. 'It is too late to think about things like that. We have to put ourselves in their hands. We have no choice.'

There was the familiar, beautiful scent of funfair food, frying onions, popcorn, candyfloss, hotdogs, wafts of burning fat smoke, that we had smelt from way back, and was now intense as we reached the gate.

There were several tables at which men in uniform were standing. Before us, visitors were being questioned, their documents inspected. Some were sent through, others detained for more questions, or their bags were searched. We went into this security area expecting to be thoroughly questioned, but the uniformed men barely acknowledged our existence, and we walked past them, not quite able to believe the operation was so easy and simple. And then we were in. We were in the funfair.

Moving through a small avenue of trees that were lit from below in spangly purples and oranges, we entered the complex itself, countless stands under striped conical awnings, the towers of several helter-skelters, it had all the rides and attractions you would expect, the dodgems, waltzers, ghost trains and Ferris wheels, but everything was larger, faster, more acute than anything I remembered from our own funfairs. It was, as my father suspected it would be, a brazen assertion of economic superiority – this is how the invaders understood fun, this is what their greater economic strength enabled them to do.

We had expected long queues at the food stalls but there were so many stalls there was no need to wait, we could go straight up and order what we wanted – and it was, indeed, all free. We went to the hotdog stand and my father, nervously at first, ordered five hot dogs. When they came they were enormous, a foot long, if not more, the sausages thick and meaty, we fell upon them like starving wolves, and I thought I would have eaten dozens of them, but it took me twenty minutes just to eat one, it was so big, and I felt as though the hunger of days was being dealt with in this single meal. My sisters chomped and chewed at theirs, their mouths became greasy and red, but they didn't finish them. I could see their spirits lifting as the food filled them, the colour returned to their faces, their eyes glistened, their hair began to shine, as though they were wonderful temples being switched on from the inside.

I went straight to the candyfloss stall and ordered my own stick, which seemed as bulky as a bright pink sheep when it was handed to me. It was so big my sisters and I realized they wouldn't need their own, and we all fed on mine, standing round in a circle as I held the sweetened wool, and we stood there picking tufts of sugar away, and we all did so with a sort of seriousness and concentration, as though we were weavers of a sacred cloth, except in reverse. The sugar filled our hearts and we entered the main part of the funfair with renewed enthusiasm. We saw people we knew, and they waved to us, greeted us, people we hadn't seen for years. My father saw some old friends from the factory and they chatted away as happily as if they were still working together, and he also saw some old relatives he'd thought long dead. What seemed unusual, even to me, was how friendly these people were. It was as though we had died and gone to heaven, all our sins had been forgiven, and everything was starting afresh.

We went on the Ferris wheel, the five of us, filling a gondola and having it to ourselves. We were slowly ladled into the air above the fairground, climbing to a much greater height than seemed likely from the ground, we soared into the air so high that the sounds of the funfair became distant, almost, and we could look down and see the illuminated spread of the complex, so bright and dazzling that it blotted out the lights of the city surrounding it, so that it seemed only the funfair existed, churning its delights in empty space.

'I'm glad we came,' said my mother, holding my father's hand suddenly. My older sister was suffering a little from vertigo and clung to my father's other hand as though she was about to die. My mother's words seemed to have the opposite effect from their intention, for they seemed to throw my father back into his previous mood of caution and suspicion.

'We have eaten well,' he said, 'but we can't come here every day for our food. This place is not a solution. In fact it is a problem, more than anything.'

My mother didn't answer but drew a tissue from her sleeve and wiped her nose. We had gone through one revolution, had passed through the noise at ground level, but straight through it, as though into a river, before we climbed again.

'That music,' my father said, 'you hear it?'

It sounded like typical fairground music, on an organ, jaunty, merry piping.

'I don't recognize it, but it sounds nice. Happy,' said my mother.

'It's their national anthem,' my father said, 're-arranged.'

No one seemed sure if this was an ominous thing or not. It was their funfair, why would it not play their music?

We had stopped at the top of the wheel, and hung for a while in the colder air up there. I looked down, startled again by how high up we were. The funfair sprawled beneath me, the main drag looking like a blazing motorway, people thronging it in both directions, stopping at the shooting galleries, the Arabian Derbies, the coconut shies. Looking further afield, beyond the awnings, I caught a glimpse of an area behind the stalls and rides, a darkened area near the lorries and generators that was shadowy behind the fair, and I couldn't be sure, but I saw a commotion going on, some people, ordinary people, families with children, were being roughly treated by men in uniform – or were they just doing something behind the scenes, fixing a generator, pegging down a guy rope – it was hard to tell – but then the families were pushed away so that I couldn't see them, and one of the soldiers pulled something from his pocket – was it a pistol? And then several cracks that could have been gun shots, a puff of smoke. Then the Ferris wheel began moving again, and the scene was removed from my field of vision, and we began our descent.

I was numbed by what I'd thought I'd seen. Looking along the main drag again, I saw someone at a shooting range, and realized how easy it would be to see people as his targets, rather than the triangles of tin cans, that he was quietly carrying out executions. Back on ground level, what I had seen lost its realness, and I wondered if I had witnessed anything at all. I scrutinized the faces of all around me, trying to see if the laughter was genuine or false, whether it was an act, whether this fairground was instead some sort of detention centre, a place we would never be able to leave.

'I want to go home,' I suddenly said to my father, but to everyone else as well.

'Already? We've only just got here,' said my mother.

'I feel sick,' I said.

'I knew you shouldn't have eaten such a big hotdog.'

Her concern with a mundane source of my sickness was comforting in itself.

'I want to go home now.'

I had begun pulling at my father's sleeve. He seemed reluctantly to agree, but we dawdled for a while, wondering if there was anything else we could try before we went, as this might have been the last time it was here. Should we try and ask for food to take home with us, but since my sisters had not finished their hotdogs and my mother had the tissue-wrapped remainders in her hand bag, we decided we should leave with just those.

It was as we approached the gate where we'd entered, through the colourfully floodlit trees, that we realized leaving might be harder than entering. Before us we could see a gathering – people were not leaving freely, but seemed to be going through another checking process. They were segregated, some pulled aside. I thought again of what I had seen from the top of the Ferris wheel, and felt a painful coldness sweep through me. I suddenly felt we had come to the end, that we had been lured into the sweetest, most fragrant and joyful trap that could be imagined, and that we had all been utterly stupid in falling for it. But there was no other way out. I appealed to my mother, I couldn't help it, I just came out with the question, 'Are they going to kill us?' No one else heard me but my mother, because I said it closely in her ear. I had wanted her to laugh at the idea, to tell me off for being silly and fanciful, but she just looked at me nervously, and didn't say anything.

By now we were among the throng being sorted. I pleaded with whatever forces watched over us that we would be allowed free passage to the outside and back into the city. I held my mother's hand tightly, she held on to my father, the girls were all arm in arm. One of the guards pulled us aside, drew us across a stretch of muddy carpet to a long desk, behind which were other men in strange uniforms. My father was a little ahead of me, I could hear that he had begun pleading with the guard, trying to explain himself, to justify himself. We were a good family, he was saying. We have never done anything wrong.

We were made to stop behind a rope barrier while my father was taken forward to the desk. There he was questioned for a short while, before being allowed to return to us.

'What did they say?' my mother asked.

'We are free to go home.'

'Are you sure?'

'Yes. Everything will be all right. Come on, let's go.' He headed towards a smaller side gate that was less crowded, but that led back into the city. He hesitated, and turned to us. 'We have to carry these, that's all.' He revealed that in his hand he had a bunch of little flags in red, green and yellow, the flags of our invaders, on short wooden sticks. 'We should carry these, and hold them out on display, all the way home. That's all. Here . . .'

He handed out the flags, one for each of us. I wondered why my mother didn't seem delighted by this. She had wanted to have the flag all along, right from the beginning. But now she seemed disappointed. My father gave her an encouraging smile, waved his flag close to her face, so that she flinched a little. And then we walked through the gate. We joined a stream of others, waving our flags, smiling brightly, thinking how lucky we were, how colourful everything was, even in the darkness.

NEIGHBOURS

There was a soft, scraping knock at the door. I was relieved when it was followed by a voice, the soft, scraping voice of Mrs Bredell, from the apartment across the landing. It almost certainly meant there was a minor domestic malfunction she needed help with – she wouldn't even change a light bulb on her own. I suspected this was not because she was incapable, but because she saw it as a job for a man. Strictly speaking, all such repairs, even the most minor, should be carried out by the block's caretaker, Mr Anderbolt, but he was useless, according to Mrs Bredell, and would make her wait for ever. And apart from that, he wasn't readily available at weekends, and would only take emergency calls. I wasn't sure if Mrs Bredell's current problem counted as one of those or not.

'I think baboons have moved into Mr Caro's flat.'

'Really?'

'Yes. I can hear them.'

Mr Caro was away on business and had left his flat empty. He had once tried subletting it while he was on one of his long trips, but it hadn't worked out, and this time he had just decided to leave it vacant.

'What can you hear?'

'Come with me – can you spare a moment? Come with me and listen.'

Mrs Bredell wasn't the sort of person you could easily say no to. Once she had decided on a course of action, there was no turning back for her, and she expected people to follow her lead. And so I dropped everything (not that there was much to drop) and followed Mrs Bredell across the landing and into her flat.

It was a place I was beginning to know well. Like some cunning piece of trickery her bleak little front door opened into a warren of country house trappings – Persian carpets, refracting crystalware, stuffed birds under glass domes, pinned butterflies, tapestry wall hangings. These were the scraps of her old life, when she had indeed lived in a grand country house. Widowed, she had edited that life down so that it would fit the new apartment block she was forced to move into, but she had retained a sense of stateliness and elegance. It smelt venerable and unsanitized in there, like a museum. Sometimes I would look at a curio and expect to see an explanatory label next to it.

She took me into the living room and asked me to listen at the wall. The apartments in our block were well known for their poor soundproofing. It was the commonest complaint of the tenants, that they were disturbed by noises from next door. Sometimes it is like living with invisible companions, voices without bodies, who conduct their lives as though you were the invisible one. I lived through the entire course of my neighbours' divorce as though it was my own. And they lived through mine, I suppose.

But in Mrs Bredell's living room I could hear nothing from next door. Mrs Bredell herself put her ear up to the wall, and listened, her eyes wide open and scanning left to right as though looking for the evasive sound. But if it required such close listening, it can't have been that loud to start with.

'They come and go,' she said. 'I purposefully waited until they were at their most noisy before I came to get you,' she said. 'Oh, wait.'

It seemed rather intrusive and underhand of me to put my ear to the wall, though I confess it wasn't the first time I'd done such a thing. I once had a neighbour who was so maddeningly sparing with his noise-disturbance that I was drawn into a paranoid need to monitor his every sound. I once spent an hour with my ear to the wall even though I could hear nothing, then to hear a loud cough behind the plaster, so loud it buzzed in my eardrum, and indicated to me that my neighbour was doing exactly the same as me, and we were, ear to ear, mirroring each other either side of the dividing wall.

Though this time, in Mrs Bredell's living room with my ear to a tumbler and the tumbler to the wall, there was nothing.

'If the baboons are there,' I said, 'they are being very quiet.'

Mrs Bredell was not convinced the flat next door was empty, and produced a loud *Shhh!* as I spoke, and she pressed her ear more closely to her tumbler.

'They're in there, I can hear them. Can't you hear them? You're not listening properly.'

'But really, Mrs Bredell, if they are making a noise, it is such a quiet noise I really wouldn't be concerned . . .'

'I'm not concerned about the noise, you stupid fool. I'm not complaining because the baboons are being noisy, I'm complaining because they are baboons! I don't want to live next door to baboons whether they are noisy or quiet. They could be completely silent baboons who do nothing but sit around all day, I still don't want them living next door. You stupid fool, thinking I was worried about the noise. It's the baboons!'

'Yes, of course, I take your point, Mrs Bredell. And I agree, something should be done about it if they have moved in. We'll have to contact Mr Anderbolt, and he'll sort it out.'

It was, of course, the only reasonable course of action. Mrs Bredell asked me if I could go and see Mr Anderbolt on her behalf because she thought he was a bit funny with her. 'He thinks I'm a silly old lady and he doesn't take anything I say seriously.'

So I said I would, but I would have to wait until Monday, because Mr Anderbolt wasn't available on weekends. There was a number to call if there was an emergency, but this wasn't an emergency, was it?

'Not an emergency? Baboons living next door to you and you don't think that's an emergency? You think they can stay there all weekend and then on Monday they can just be turned out? What'll they have done to Mr Caro's flat in the meantime? They will have torn everything to pieces, defecated on everything, eaten everything.'

I agreed it was a problem, but what else could we do? One thing we could do, of course, was to take an outside view – go down and out into the street and see if we could see if the windows were open in Mr Caro's flat. Mrs Bredell said that was a very good idea, and since she didn't feel up to going outside at that particular moment, I went on my own.

Our block had had a problem with baboons for nearly two years. At times it felt as though we were under siege. Some believed it was happening because of encroachments that were being made into their natural home, the forest at the edge of the city, where there had been much felling of trees and building of new housing developments. The forests had been officially protected until a few years ago. Now that the controls had been lifted, the trees were falling quickly.

No one could explain why our block in particular had come under attack. It was not unusual to see baboons in the city, but they usually kept to the open spaces, the parks, verges, and wastegrounds, where you could often see them foraging and generally exploring, or sitting around in groups. Sometimes they would ransack a dustbin at the end of someone's drive, or they would operate around the back of a supermarket and search for leftovers, but otherwise they steered clear of private property, and kept their distance from humans. But for some reason they had taken a different approach with our block. They began by scavenging our bins, but then they started to climb the walls and drainpipes, looking for windows that had been left open. In the hot seasons it is impossible to keep the windows closed, there is no air conditioning in our flats and the temperatures can be unbearable. The baboons take advantage of this, and will reach an arm into an opened window and extract whatever happens to be within reach. Sheets, pillows and blankets are their favourites. They have been known to pull curtains and blinds down from their rails. If a kitchen window is open they will grab cutlery, china, bottles of washing-up liquid, used tea bags, anything that comes to hand. They rarely find food.

The baboons, so far, have not been known to fully enter an apartment, though it has long been a subject of debate among the residents who wonder and worry about how far the baboons will go. Their invasion has been incremental, increasing with boldness and ingenu-ity at a steady rate. It is as though they are evolving before our eyes, at a vastly accelerated pace, and before long they will not just be visitors to our block, but full residents.

From the street below, looking up, I could see no baboon activity. Sometimes when I come home from the centre of town I look up and the baboons are crawling all over the face of the building. From ground level the block seems smooth, with very few ledges or visible handholds, so it can seem like the baboons are behaving like flies, somehow adhering through glue or suction, but in fact there are countless tiny crannies and crevices that the baboons can use to swing themselves up and across the walls and windows. A black, leathery fingertip is all that is needed, if it can find a purchase, then the baboon can pull itself up. Sometimes they take death-defying leaps from a window to an adjoining extension, and it looks as if they're flying. It is such a spectacle that we have become something of a tourist attraction, little crowds gathering when the baboons are at their most active. Families with children. Like it is a trip to the zoo.

The authorities don't do anything about them. Mrs Bredell is a tireless campaigner against the baboons. She used to try and rally support among the neighbours, but she was surprised, and a little disgusted, to find that her feelings about the baboons were not universal. I myself tried to remain as neutral as I could. I didn't worry too much about the baboons, but I didn't want to offend Mrs Bredell either, and this meant that she shared with me her true feelings about the baboons, and her neighbours.

Too many educated types have moved in recently, she said. People who don't understand nature and the coun-tryside, and think it must be protected and looked after at all costs, even at the expense of human freedoms. They see the baboons and think how sweet, how charming, and they don't think about the diseases they spread, or the damage they do to property. After many petitions against the city council, she believed their failure to act was part due to the fact that she didn't have unanimous support among the residents. So we just have to sit here and let the baboons walk all over us, and the tourists come and watch us like we're the ones in a cage. She had long been warning that things would eventually get to a point where the baboons would overstep the mark and actually move into the building, or start to physically attack the residents. There had been reports of baboons snatching shopping bags out of people's hands, but the baboon supporters said these were just rumours put about by the press, and others who were anti-baboon.

Now, on the pavement, I was starting to have trouble remembering which windows were Mr Caro's. Being round the back of the block, on the opposite side to my own windows, I was less familiar with the arrangements. I had to count up eleven floors from the bottom, then I had to do it again because I thought I'd counted the ground floor as number one. Then I wasn't sure how many windows along to count to Mr Caro's flat, and doubted that, from down here, I could be sure if a window was slightly open or not. When I saw a face appear at a window high up, I couldn't be sure if it belonged to a baboon or an old lady.

I returned to my own rooms, having told Mrs Bredell

that I couldn't be sure but that I didn't think Mr Caro's windows were open. She said that it didn't matter, the baboons were quite capable of closing the windows after them. I said maybe that was so, but it was unlikely that they would take the trouble to shut themselves in. Mrs Bredell muttered something but I made it clear there was nothing else we could do, and that she should come and get me if she thought she heard the baboons again. I shouldn't have said it, because it made it almost inevitable that she would hear something. Nevertheless I tried to make the best of my weekend at home.

It was my first weekend off work for what seemed like months, and I was determined to have a quiet day. A long stretch at work exhausts me, and I sometimes spend my days off entirely in bed. Then I regret my own laziness and the wasted day, and I feel no less tired for a day doing nothing.

After I had finished with Mrs Bredell I went to my bedroom with a glass of orange juice and yesterday's newspaper. But I couldn't concentrate. I too was now attentive to noises. When the baboons first began visiting our block, they never ventured much beyond the second floor and so we, on the eleventh, had thought ourselves above things, out of the way, beyond the reach of even the most intrepid baboons. I can remember the shock of first seeing a baboon climb past my window, when I was sitting on my living-room sofa watching an American football match on the TV. The windows behind the TV were uncurtained (there is no need for curtains really, eleven floors up) and gave their usual view, which was nothing but sky, when suddenly part of the window was filled with a lean, grey, long-limbed body, a naked body splayed with limbs stretched starfish-like, taut and tense, and a face that peered in with bright, circular eyes, as bright as two little spotlights, under a protruding, low brow that gave it a serious, frowning expression. The long, pouting muzzle, ridged and hard as a gourd, the lips drawn back to reveal lethal-looking fangs. Its face moved about with an efficient, mechanical rapidity, sweeping the apartment, taking in everything, it seemed, but me. For the few seconds that it filled my window our eyes did not meet. It looked through me and past me. What must it have seen? A cavernous space beyond glass, shapes arranged and stacked, inexplicable intricacies, myself among them.

I fell asleep for most of the afternoon, and in the early evening I had a long bath. This had the effect of reviving me, and I began to think I might go out for the evening. I could call a friend, see if they wanted to go out for a drink, or see a movie. I knew deep down that I probably wouldn't and that I would end up with a takeaway and a DVD, but just the notion of thinking that I might was a pleasure in itself.

I was at the window looking at the view. The city in twilight, lamps coming on, the sense of preparation for night time, the hills in the distance, low but powerful presences brooding on the edge of things. They mark the beginning of a forest that stretches for hundreds of miles. Thousands of square miles of uninterrupted forest, but that is not enough for the baboons, apparently. They may be felling the trees, but why don't the baboons go the other way, further into the forest, instead of into the city? In the far distance, beyond some parking lots I could see some figures in the shadows beneath the freeway. A little group of them, it looked like. It was hard to tell. Then the thought suddenly occurred to me – perhaps they prefer the city. Perhaps they like it here, with all the concrete and the tarmac, and the rubbish, and the noise. Perhaps they like the evolutionary future that is represented here. That agility, that curiosity, that boldness, eventually it produces cities like ours. They are exploring the fruits of the imaginations they have yet to acquire.

As I predicted, Mrs Bredell came back, knocking on my door at about 7 p.m., just as I was thinking about getting ready to go out. But her request surprised me.

'I was wondering if you would like to have dinner with me this evening? I don't have much, but I would very much appreciate not being alone tonight. I feel very nervous with the baboons next door.'

I thought – why not? When I arrived half an hour later I found that Mrs Bredell had a meal ready that she must have been preparing for hours. She had laid the table with silver cutlery and crystal wine glasses. Three candles were burning on a branching candelabra.

'So nice to have a reason to get all my pretty things out again.'

It was very civilized. That was the point, I suppose. Mrs Bredell seemed to be making a stand for civilization against what she perceived as an onslaught by our primitive past. She didn't say as much, but she lingered over every detail of the meal, telling me how much went into its preparation, and then she talked a lot about the wine and how it was the best vintage from the vineyards of somewhere or other. Then she talked me through all her paintings, her butterfly collection, her husband's medals, it was a long time before we got round to talking about the baboons.

'I know they have moved in, I don't care what anyone says,' she said. 'They were very noisy earlier this evening. I heard something breaking, I'm quite sure of it. They dropped a glass, or threw one at the wall. And do you know what – I heard the lavatory flush. What do you think of that?'

I shrugged. 'At least we can be thankful they are using the toilet,' I said.

'Well, they weren't using the toilet for their private business. They were playing with the handles. They have probably turned the taps on and will make the place flood. I can never look at a baboon without noticing the tartar on their teeth. It reminds me of my mother, I'm afraid, she always had a problem with tartar. Would you like some more spinach?' I said no. Mrs Bredell went on fussing with the meal, spending much more time over the arrangements than was necessary, getting bowls to put things in, looking for clean tumblers and matches to light the candles, more than she spent eating anything.

She had made something that looked like schnitzel, something that had been pounded flat with a rolling pin and coated in breadcrumbs. Once seated she would be up again, having forgotten something important, floating off to the kitchen to find salad tongs, or whatever. When she finally sat down to eat, she paused, knife and fork in hand, looked at me with a curious wrinkle in her nose, and said, 'Oh this is nice.'

She was just about to take a bite of something when she remembered her wine, and picked up the glass. This seemed to set her off thinking about things. 'Have you noticed something strange about this room?' she said. I looked around me. There were so many things strange about it that I didn't know where to begin, so I said, no, I hadn't. 'Well, there's nothing purple in it,' she said. 'When I was little, I was in love with purple, as a colour. I asked my father to decorate my room in purple, and to have purple furniture in there, and I wanted purple clothes, purple everything, and I got it, mostly. When I was fully dressed in my room you couldn't see me, just purple on purple. Then the other day I realized there wasn't a single purple thing in this room, or in the whole flat, in fact. Not a single purple thing. This is not from any conscious choice, it just seems to have happened. How do you explain it?'

'I think it's a silly idea, having a favourite colour,' I

said. 'How can you favour one colour over another? It's as silly as having a favourite musical note.'

'Oh, mine's B-flat,' she said adamantly, 'never been in any doubt about that. B-flat, ever since I heard the B-Flat Major symphony of Beethoven when I was a teenager. In fact, if I think back on it, I'd have to say that I've led a B-flat sort of life.'

We fell into silence for a little while. She still hadn't taken a mouthful of food, but preferred instead to prod it with her fork, then take a sip of wine. I wondered for a moment if I was being poisoned. But I couldn't think why she would do such a thing.

'My mother would have been heartbroken to see me living like this in my old age. Sitting all on my own in a shabby little apartment. She had held me in her arms as a baby and must have dreamt of such a splendid future for me, full of beautiful things. It might have happened if we hadn't had everything taken from us. It killed my husband to have to give up the house, just so those clowns who'd taken over the offices of state could claim they were making a new dispensation. He'd fought for this country. His best friends had given their lives for it.' She had put something in her mouth but was having trouble chewing it, and used a napkin to spit it out. 'Well, I've been leading the conversation all evening – why don't you start something?'

I struggled to think of anything to say, then something came to mind and I opened my mouth to speak, but a most horrible scream came out, or so it seemed.

The sound was the unmistakable call of a baboon a few feet away from us through the party wall. Mrs Bredell slammed down her cutlery and said, 'There, what did I tell you!' She was pointing a knuckly index finger at me. 'You tell me now that there aren't any baboons in Mr Caro's flat. You heard it plainly, a baboon just the other side of this wall.' She gave the wall a slap with the same hand that had pointed at me, then picked up her silver pepper pot and cracked it several times against the wall. 'You get out of there now, you tartared devils, I'll have you shot I will . . .' Pepper had been ejected from the pot in dark clouds, and suddenly Mrs Bredell was sneezing fiercely. I had not thought before about how difficult and punishing it can be for a frail elderly person to sneeze, but I could see that every convulsion seemed to jolt and tear at her body, as she frantically held a napkin over her face, the tears streaming from her eyes. She stood up. 'Oh, I can't stand it any more. We must do something now, do something immediately. You must go round there, please. I'm begging you. Go round and do something.'

I was at a loss for what I would be able to do, but eventually, seeing there was no other way of dealing with Mrs Bredell's distress, I went round to Mr Caro's flat, and banged on the door. Of course, there was no answer. Mrs Bredell goaded me on to knock again. She was standing a few feet behind me, sheltering against the wall by her own front door. To my horror she was holding what at first I took to be a broom, but which on a second glance turned out to be a double-barrelled shotgun. She had shown it to me before. It had been decommissioned, and couldn't be fired even if it was loaded.

'Say something,' she called to me, 'don't just knock, tell them to clear off.'

But how does one talk to a baboon? Mrs Bredell seemed to think that the beasts had become so clever they could flush toilets, play cards, close windows, so why not understand basic human language? Urged on again, I made a show for Mrs Bredell.

'We know you're in there,' I called, by now other neighbours were peering from their doorways down the hall, 'and you know you've no right to be in there. This is private property. If you don't leave immediately I will call the police.' How could a baboon understand anything of what I was saying? It was all for Mrs Bredell's sake that I spoke the words. Had she gone completely mad? I wondered if it might be an idea to play to her madness, and pretend that the baboons had replied. 'Wait,' I said, 'I can hear something.' I put my ear to the door.

'What is it?' said Mrs Bredell. 'Are they speaking?'

I nodded.

'What are they saying?'

'I can't make out the words – it sounds like they are saying they will leave soon.'

'Tell them to leave now.'

I did so.

'They are saying they will leave tonight.'

Mrs Bredell came fully out onto the landing, still wielding the gun. The expression on her face suddenly changed. 'Are you making a fool of me? Do you think I don't know baboons can't talk?'

I shook my head.

'Because if you did, and this was a real gun, I would shoot you.'

I remembered something my old girlfriend had said. She loved dogs, and once said wasn't it an amazing thing, how humans could manipulate the wild dog by selective breeding so that we have chihuahuas and Great Danes, and dachshunds and bulldogs. Yet no one had thought to select for intelligence in their breeding programmes. They had selected for bulldogs with the biggest heads so that now they couldn't be born naturally, their heads were too big to pass through the mother's birth canal. If they had measured the intelligence of bulldogs, say, and had only bred the brightest with each other, then surely we could have ended up, by now, with dogs that can think like people, with huge brains in those huge heads. Dogs that could talk, and read, and have religion. Even stranger that someone hasn't tried it with baboons. Or perhaps they had.

Mrs Bredell was standing behind me, still with the shotgun in her hands.

'There, you see?' she said in a voice of satisfied vindication, as she gestured towards the door. 'What did I tell you?'

She had noticed, before I had, that there was something working the handles on the other side of the door. Locks were being thrown back, bolts drawn. I took a step back as the door suddenly swung open, and couldn't quite comprehend, for a moment, that what stood before me in the doorway was a man, fully evolved, young, healthy, beautiful. He was wearing jeans with the belt undone, and a white T-shirt. His feet were bare. He conveyed the sense of hastily covered-up nakedness.

'What you want?' he said.

'Nothing,' I replied. 'I'm sorry, I didn't mean to trouble you.'

'Sounded pretty urgent, the way you were shouting. Thought you were the police or something.'

'No, I'm sorry, we thought the flat was empty.'

The man noticed Mrs Bredell for the first time. 'Hey, tell your old lady to put the firearm away.'

'It's OK, it's not a real gun.'

'It looks pretty real to me. What are you, crazy? You're pointing a gun at people?'

'Don't come any closer,' Mrs Bredell said through clenched teeth, pointing the gun directly at the man's chest. By now a young woman had appeared at the doorway. She had the rumpled, fluffy, loose appearance of the recently fucked. She screamed. 'Paul, be careful.'

'It's just some crazy Mother Hubbard with a shot-gun.'

'Get her out of here.'

'You've got a damn nerve,' Mrs Bredell said, 'moving

in when the owner's away, making my life a misery with your noise and your damn antics.'

'We've got every right to be here, Clive's my brother, if it's any business of yours.' He turned to me. 'Are you going to make her put her gun down? I don't care if it's real or not, you don't point guns at people. I'm a peace-loving man.'

I tried guiding Mrs Bredell away, steering her with a gentle arm back towards her own apartment, but she suddenly flinched from me, her frail little body suddenly rigid with energy. 'Get your hand off me. You're protect-ing this scum? What sort of man are you!' The gun was now loosely swinging in my direction. 'You should be protecting and looking out for your neighbours, not letting them be taken over by filth that's just come down from the hills. This is my husband's shotgun, and he killed more wild buffalo than could fill a football stadium. Hey . . .' The man from next door had been slowly moving forward during Mrs Bredell's speech, and he made a sudden lunge for the shotgun, grabbing hold of the barrels. But Mrs Bredell had a ferocious grip and she held onto the stock, and indeed she pulled the trig-gers uselessly several times, so the hammers tapped at the chambers, sounding like nothing more dangerous than teaspoons on an enamel plate. But they struggled, the young man and the old lady, while I tried to separate them as they swivelled round the length of the gun, until suddenly Mrs Bredell was over on her back in a most undignified way, her skirt suddenly up to her waist and her undergarments exposed. She screamed, then moaned, gave pathetic cries, making the most, I could see, of being the victim of this assault. I was pretty sure she wasn't badly hurt.

'Look what he's done to me,' she said, feeling the back of her head, then looking disappointed when she couldn't see blood on her fingers. The man, Paul, was clench-faced, his whole attention turned exclusively to the shotgun, inspecting it to make sure it was harmless.

'Piece of junk,' he said, and threw it on the floor. He looked up and down the landing at the various faces watching him. 'I don't expect to be disturbed again this evening,' and he withdrew into the flat, closing the door behind him. Aware that any display of infirmity was now useless, Mr Bredell picked herself up. She was shaking with anger. I retrieved her gun and guided her back into her own flat.

'We have to call the police,' she said.

'If he's who he says he is, what's it to do with us?'

'He assaulted me.'

'He thought you had a gun on him. I don't think there's anything we can do.'

In the flat, the remains of our meal were still on the table.

'I had a dessert prepared. I don't feel hungry now. Would you like some?'

I suggested she sit down in the armchair while I cleared the dinner things away. She accepted my suggestion without argument, while I cleared the table. I was relieved to see she had a dishwasher. I put everything in there, and some stuff back in the fridge. Inside the fridge I saw what she had planned for dessert – a fruit salad sitting in a bowl, looking colourful and expectant, like a guest who's been shut out of a party. I closed the door on it.

'Don't leave,' said Mrs Bredell, as I returned to the living room, 'not yet.'

'Sure,' I said.

'Not for a while. I'm all shaken up. If my husband was still alive he'd have given that young man a hell of a time. He wouldn't have stood a chance, the little fool. Who does he think he is, pushing old ladies over?'

'I know, it was disgraceful behaviour . . .'

'And I have to live next door to him, have to listen to him and that woman of his doing what they do.'

'We'll lodge a complaint with Mr Anderbolt on Monday,' I said, 'and if necessary raise it at a block meeting. Don't worry, it'll be sorted.'

Mrs Bredell was sitting back in her chair, her eyes closed. She seemed so suddenly calm and serene I thought she might be asleep, and stood there for a while wondering if I should leave. Then suddenly she spoke, opening her eyes. 'Hold my hand,' she said, 'just for a little while, before you go.'

I obeyed immediately, just as I would have done almost anything Mrs Bredell asked, because she had that manner about her that couldn't be refused, though at the same time I felt a little shocked at the request, at the prospect of such physical intimacy. It wasn't as though we were mother and son, this old lady and me, we were just neighbours, we hardly knew each other. But I drew up one of the dining chairs alongside Mrs Bredell's armchair, and sat obediently. She held out a hand and I took it. It felt rough and cold, and it was trembling very slightly. She didn't say anything, and so I didn't say anything either. I thought it best to keep silent. I kept silent for what seemed like hours, of us just sitting there. I didn't say anything even when I saw the face appear at the window behind her, the small, intensely alert face that suddenly looked in on us, without seeing us, eleven floors up. The bright yellow eyes, the bluish fringe of fur, the gourd-like muzzle. Like something mechanical yet alive, its head made short sharp turns as it took in everything in the room, everything but us, and then, hauled by powerful arms and fingers, was gone in a second.